Some Rather Antiquities

William Ardin

HEADLINE

Copyright © 1994 William Ardin

The right of William Ardin to be identified as the Author of
the Work has been asserted by him in accordance with the
Copyright, Designs and Patents Act 1988.

First published in 1994
by HEADLINE BOOK PUBLISHING

First published in paperback in 1995
by HEADLINE BOOK PUBLISHING

10 9 8 7 6 5 4 3 2 1

All rights reserved. No part of this publication may be
reproduced, stored in a retrieval system, or transmitted,
in any form or by any means without the prior written
permission of the publisher, nor be otherwise circulated
in any form of binding or cover other than that in which
it is published and without a similar condition being
imposed on the subsequent purchaser.

All characters in this publication are fictitious
and any resemblance to real persons, living or dead,
is purely coincidental.

ISBN 0 7472 4481 2

Typeset by CBS, Felixstowe, Suffolk

Printed and bound in Great Britain by
Cox & Wyman Ltd, Reading, Berks

HEADLINE BOOK PUBLISHING
A division of Hodder Headline PLC
338 Euston Road
London NW1 3BH

Some Dark Antiquities

Chapter One

'Don't look down, whatever you do,' said Charles Ramsay, keeping his voice under tight control. Like a fool the other man did, of course – and it was then that he started to scream. His harsh cry tore at the ears, stopped as he gulped in a breath, and then resumed on a higher, yet more stringent note. The white face with its yelling mouth, smelling of whisky, stared with disbelief from the other side of the grey stone parapet, face to face. It was almost as though Ramsay was looking at a reflection of himself, except that underneath his own shoes there lay the wide reassuring roof of the church tower, while there was scarcely anything beneath the feet of the man opposite. A little further down on the outer face of the parapet a fragile ledge of stone offered the unfortunate a sort of toehold, but apart from that there was nothing – nothing under him, under his straining heels, except empty air. Emptiness.

It was just like Johnson to get himself into such a calamitous fix – clinging on to the outside of the church tower by his fingers and thinly-shod toes like some kind of rowdy insect ready to be brushed off there by nothing more than the wind. An insect. Easy enough to call him that, Ramsay allowed, from where he himself was standing – safely inboard. A couple of feet of mediaeval roof made a notable difference to one's view of others.

All at once Johnson stopped the noise as abruptly as he had started it – as though he was running out of energy, or hope. His whole body began to tremble with effort. The ache burning in his thigh and calf muscles must be growing by the second. Support – if he didn't get support he was going to end up as a sack of dead meat at the foot of the tower in no time at all.

Ramsay glanced down over the edge. Down was a long, long way. Far below him he could see the roof of a small grey car over by the vicarage – so the Reverend Stanfield had to be around somewhere. From up here the dark yews in the churchyard looked like toy trees set among the irregular rows of gravestones. Tiny and remote. Yes, a long way.

In the unexpected silence he thought he heard something down there, a cry, something like that, but the wind blowing across the roof carried it away. A voice? Or was it the cawing of one of those rooks swirling round overhead? Perhaps it was just the protest of some discontented beast in the farm building on the other side of the road.

Johnson's hands, knuckles white, gripped the coping stone. It had shifted, slid very slightly out of true, which wasn't encouraging. The vicar was right for once. He'd always said that the masonry at the top of the tower needed repointing. But whatever the state of the stonework, the important thing was not to distract this man in distress from his number one task – holding on for dear life. With great care Ramsay began to ease his right hand towards him – slowly, extremely slowly.

'That's better, Johnson. Ian. Just hold on. You're quite safe as you are.'

His voice was a lot steadier than he felt. The tense face peered at him, desperate for any kind of reassurance. He must have climbed out, intending to do away with himself, and then changed his mind when he saw exactly what that involved. It was strange, because when Ramsay had visited him only a couple of days earlier he had seemed all right. Not in the grip of a depression – not as far as he could see – just his usual awkward self, offhand with all and sundry – even his wife Margaret.

'You're looking good,' commented Ramsay. Maybe that was a bit of an exaggeration, but the chap needed encouragement.

High up on the flagstaff in the centre hung the white banner with the red cross of St George, agitated by the breeze. To celebrate some festival or other, Ramsay supposed. His hand inched further towards Johnson, who was clasping the ridge of stone with considerable determination. Whatever happened, he mustn't startle him. He guessed, or hoped, rather, that enough of the man's weight would be supported by the ledge to allow him to unclamp one of his hands when the time came, and reach out to . . . that was one solution. Another possibility would be . . .

Without warning Johnson grabbed his hand, grasping fiercely, and almost had him over. Instinctively Ramsay knelt down to lower his centre of gravity; his knees slid along the roof for a few inches and rammed into the base of the parapet.

Hell and damnation!

Through the cloth of his trousers he could feel its roughness biting into his kneecaps. A fraction of a second later his arm was almost wrenched from its socket as the full weight of the other man tore down at it. What the . . .? He couldn't see over the top. Obviously, Johnson had lost his footing, the fool. He could hear the toes of his shoes scrabbling against the further side of the parapet as he struggled to recover, groping for that narrow ledge which, apart from Ramsay's overstretched resources, was all that lay between him and eternity. It seemed like twenty-four hours – twenty-four hours as a minimum – before he found it and the pressure eased. The bloody man was hopelessly drunk.

At least he hadn't started yelling again, though he was gasping quite a bit. Slowly Ramsay raised himself. They had reached a rough and ready sort of stalemate, but how long was that going to last?

Silence now, except that every so often the flag at the top of its pole flapped against its staff – snapped in the breeze.

Ramsay looked down at the coping stone and thought he saw it shift another couple of millimetres. Suddenly he felt himself overcome by a sensation that he had experienced only once before in his life, as a schoolboy at the first stage of the Eiffel Tower. Leaning over the rail, he had been overcome suddenly by a need to let himself fall gently, and with imagined safety, into that desirable space in front of him. That time he had been saved by a fellow schoolboy who, coming up behind him and pinioning his arms, had pretended to push him – just as a joke. At that instant he had awoken to reality.

This time he had to deal with it on his own. He felt helpless, in the grip of an urge to let go of Johnson, allow him to tumble easily backwards into the huge emptiness which lay beneath him and then follow after. He imagined them both floating effortlessly down in space towards the ground by the most direct route, swinging a little as though each was on the end of a parachute. The simple idea mesmerised him.

Then one of those odd, out-of-the-way, things happened. A beetle, about as long as his little finger, crawled into view on the stonework in front of him. Perhaps it had been blown up there by the wind. With its black body gleaming with a shiny blue iridescence it was both irrelevant and beautiful. Doubtfully it stopped as if it found itself intruding on a scene it didn't quite understand. The important thing was that it broke into his trance, and he continued to hang on.

'It hurts. I can't . . . manage . . . much . . .' Johnson's voice was jabbing at him. His desperate hand dragged at Ramsay's in a new spasm, and it slipped a little. He clenched his own, which felt as though all the blood had been driven out of it by the pressure.

'Keep it up. You must!'

Somewhere below, beneath the noise of the wind in his ears, Ramsay heard an intermittent sound which grew louder by the second. The rising thunder of a pair of feet hurrying up the wooden steps to the roof – there must have been over a hundred of them – there had scarcely been time to count them on his way up.

'Tell Margaret I . . . Tell Margaret . . .'

'Help's coming. Hang on.'

The trapdoor slammed open. Turning his head as far as he dared, to look behind him, Ramsay could just see a pair of well-worn shoes and above them the edge of a black cassock.

'I heard him scream. What do I do?' asked the vicar.

What did he think? Idiot!

'Grab hold of him. Get the weight off my bloody arm.'

In three steps the parson was at Ramsay's side and, grabbing a generous handful of Johnson's denim jacket, he gave a heave. Luckily the material was not as old as it was meant to look. In a disorganised and frantic second or two they dragged the drunken man inwards over the parapet to safety, anyhow, thump and scrape, arse over tip. For a moment he lay twitching on the grey roof like a landed fish and then started to retch. Ramsay looked the other way – out of embarrassment as much as anything.

Rubbing his shoulder, he thanked the vicar. 'Better late than never.' He himself felt like throwing up.

Together they half-carried Johnson down the stairs and into the vestry – pitch-pine benches and Victorian cast-iron hooks where rows of red cassocks and white surplices had hung in palmier days; it had been a kind of choristers' changing room which smelt ecclesiastical, of mothballs, dust and incense. The previous incumbent had been very High Church, a closet Roman. Ramsay sat down still panting on a bench, and felt something poke him in the back as he did so: a hook which had a torn label below it with the name 'Wilson' crossed out and 'Shepherd' substituted in red ink. Somehow that flicked the world back into focus and brought it home to him that it was over.

'A mug of tea, that's what we all need. Would you lend a hand while I run over to the vicarage to telephone Margaret?'

There were those who complained that the vicar's manner was overbearing, that he asked too much of his handful of parishioners. However, this particular thing was no problem; Ramsay did as he was told.

While he filled the electric kettle and threw spoonfuls of tea into the battered aluminium teapot – no teabags of course – he reflected on the vicar. He was youngish, celibate and with no apparent weaknesses – unless one counted moral certitude as one such. He was one of those difficult people who have to practise what they preach, insisting on pushing the tenets of Christianity to the ultimate with a fierce rigour when it would have been much more comfortable all round if he had eased up a bit. Sometimes Ramsay caught a breath of something unconventional about him, something not normally associated with clergymen and which he might have difficulty in explaining to his bishop if he was ambushed with it. Perhaps that was the cause of his tightly strung manner. For all his virtue, the man was a considerable pain.

Once, the year before, the vicar had decided to sell one of his few possessions on behalf of some pet charity and had asked Ramsay to find a buyer for it. A Crown Derby tea service, or what was left of it – an heirloom which had to be valuable because his mother had told him so.

It wasn't, that was the trouble. Two cups and three saucers short and cracks and chips here and there on the survivors – way below Ramsay's usual run of business – and who needed a tea service these days, anyway? However, he'd done his best with it as a favour, eventually finding it a home with a dealer who was certainly in need of redemption, twisting his arm to part with two hundred and fifty pounds for it in a good cause, rounding the figure up to three hundred out of his own pocket to make it more respectable. That had turned out to be a considerable waste of money. Three hundred... 'Is that the very best you can do?' the vicar had asked, his eyes affronted as though that figure was an insult to him and to his departed mother.

Why, after that episode, had Ramsay agreed to handle the sale of the reliquary? Being an honest young man, he had to admit that it was much more his line of country than a knackered tea set. The thing was grand and enormously valuable, having been created by a master gold-smith centuries ago to hold the fingerbone of a very early and upmarket saint. The bone had disappeared, probably stolen by an over-zealous believer in the days when the relic was worth even more than the casket. It was an odd kind of thing to find in an Anglican church in Suffolk.

That was because it wasn't a home-grown treasure but had been imported, a mediaeval work of art which had been bought specially and donated to the church of St Nicholas back in the Fifties by Sir Simon Burnill, the washing-machine millionaire, the man who claimed to have liberated the British housewife from the drudgery of the wash boiler and the scrubbing board. According to some of his – no doubt envious – contemporaries, the Burnill Twin Tub, and the gift of the casket, were the only items on the credit side in what one obituary described as a 'thrusting and colourful business career, in which the ends, alas, were called in all too often to justify the means – and didn't.'

When the Reverend Oscar Stanfield had arrived in the parish, which was one of a clutch of duds the bishop had told him to resurrect, almost the first thing they had shown him was the precious reliquary, standing behind toughened glass and iron bars a half-inch thick in its niche in the empty nave. One glance at it, and he was convinced that it had no business to be there. There was no way he could justify it to his conscience and it would have to be sold.

The parish council would have agreed like a shot if he had suggested that the proceeds should be used to restore the fabric of the church, but what was the point of that, he asked with devastating logic – the building was scarcely used at all. The congregation in the tiny village of Chaffield never amounted to more than a couple of pewsful even at Easter.

Restoring the church wasn't what he had in mind. No, he wanted the money to be given to an organisation set up to succour the street children of Brazil. He saw this as an act of disinterested Christian charity, but the parish council had objected strongly at first. They hadn't given in until he had

SOME DARK ANTIQUITIES

bullied them from his position of advantage on the moral high ground for fully six months and they had been given a stern talking-to by Ramsay's father, Ernest, who was chairman of the trustees and thought the world of the new vicar for some reason.

His father's enthusiasm for the project was the real reason why Ramsay had agreed to handle the sale of the reliquary for them. No commission had been mentioned, of course, and he couldn't bring himself to ask them for one, although now that he was a serious London dealer he had every right to. Still, there was an element of kudos in the job, he wouldn't dispute that. The only stipulation he had made was that part of the money should be used to pay for a replica which could be displayed in the church in place of the original casket. After all, there was a need for something to remind visitors of Sir Simon Burnill, if not of the parish council.

The person whom Charles Ramsay had chosen to undertake this healing task was the man hunched opposite him in the vestry, looking silently at the scrubbed pine floor – Ian Johnson, the best craftsman in gold and silver in the area by a long chalk, proprietor of a thriving jeweller's business in Wickingham the local market town – with an odd wife though. She had to be, to put up with him.

Johnson was one of those men who seem to have unresolved skirmishes going on in their heads, part of a civil war of the soul which they won't allow to go to arbitration. He wouldn't even acknowledge that inner battle but hid it as far as he was able. Only now and then did it break the surface in an overt spasm of self pity. He was a driven man, that much was clear. Driven by what? And where was it taking him? He had seemed to Ramsay until an hour ago to be well on the right side of sanity. Just a touchy and unpredictable kind of chap who was an artist in his way, not simply a craftsman. One had to make allowances for people as talented as he was – they were thin on the ground.

This outing on the church tower was a disturbing thing, though, wasn't it? It was scarcely the action of a man at peace with himself, and the worrying thought was that Johnson still had the Burnill reliquary in his possession, under his control. In the safe in his workroom – that was where it was, or at least where it was supposed to be. Get it out of harm's way, Ramsay warned himself, needing no reminder that it was his responsibility since the parish in the person of the vicar had given it into his charge.

He looked down at Johnson, who had started to shiver, his hands nursing his mug of tea.

'Drink it up. Go on.'

Obediently the man lifted the mug to his lips without speaking. It was no time to start cross-questioning him about the casket, but Ramsay felt a need to say something to fill in the silence. He went on, 'Lucky I was passing the church at that precise moment, and saw you up there. Five minutes earlier or later and there might have been an altogether more difficult problem to cope with.'

Not the most cheering thing to say perhaps and Johnson ignored the remark. He deserved it though for the trouble he had caused.

Banging the door, the vicar returned at that moment. Concussion seemed to be a habit of his. He strode in as though he was ten minutes late for the cleansing of the temple.

'Margaret's coming directly.' Turning towards Johnson, he said more softly, displaying a sympathy which was unexpected, coming from him, 'She's on her way. I said merely that there had been an accident – that you were all right. She won't be long.'

Johnson offered no acknowledgement but still sat silent and ashamed of himself, lost in his own private thicket of anxieties.

'You are all right, aren't you?'

All at once the tears tumbled down the jeweller's face, which had become patchily red and white. There was no explanation for them either; he just sipped his tea without a word. A loose tear plopped into it. Ramsay repressed an urge to offer him the clean handkerchief he always kept concealed in his top pocket.

Stanfield looked disappointed in a way, as though his priestly office entitled him to a confession, an explanation at least. Nevertheless he had more sense than to demand one from the little jeweller now.

He turned towards Ramsay. 'We must speak. And soon.' His grey eyes looked meaningfully at Johnson and then away.

'I am sure there is nothing to worry about,' said Ramsay, who had a feeling that there was.

The vicar looked resolutely at him. 'I am glad you think so.'

The 'you' was emphasised just enough to push his message at Ramsay without it reaching the self-absorbed man sitting on the bench.

'I had already decided to make an investigation,' replied Ramsay, nettled, wishing he'd never set eyes on the bloody casket. Too late now; he was landed with it. He glanced at his wristwatch unobtrusively. How long would it take Margaret Johnson to get over from Wickingham? A quarter of an hour, twenty minutes? It was going to seem a lot longer in the company of these two. Neither of them was a bundle of laughs. He settled down to wait.

At last there was a noise outside as somebody turned the wrought-iron handle on the outer door of the church, and it was pushed inwards. Footsteps approached across the tiles of the church floor.

As soon as Margaret Johnson entered, the vicar opened his mouth to start a painful inquest into what had happened.

Ramsay leapt in. 'Ian got into difficulties on the tower. He'll tell you about it himself. He's in a state of . . .'

She put up her hand, palm outwards to shut him up; she was wound up, nervy. 'I'll see to it.' She looked across with troubled eyes at the man she had drawn in the lottery, her man. What she had seen and heard didn't seem to surprise her in the least. It was as though she had been anticipating some undefined disaster and was thankful it wasn't worse. At least her husband was still in one piece.

Johnson woke up and noticed his wife.

'You took your time – and you look a fright. Small wonder I can't honour you as a husband should.' An unpleasant thing to say and an odd time to say it. He screwed up his face in a petty agony. 'How can I be expected to . . .' Suddenly conscious of the others, he shut his mouth.

She walked with decisive steps across the room and, instead of slapping his face, merely bent down and pressed her palm gently against his cheek as though to console him for yet another thing he couldn't manage.

'I didn't even have time to brush my hair,' she said in a voice which seemed to carry like the sound of a string of a viola, no more than stroked, into every corner of the room.

She did have something of the look of a traveller about her with a magenta cardigan which clashed in a lamentable way with the vibrant colour of her skirt. Ramsay couldn't imagine why she dressed like that and found himself wishing he could see her in some decent clothes, properly coiffed and cared for.

At eighteen her beauty must have caught the breath of any man who was lucky enough to have sight of her, and it was still there to a discerning eye like his, he told himself. No doubt she put up with that kind of vulgarity from her husband simply because he was too vulnerable; he needed propping up, not knocking down. She turned her head, caught Ramsay's glance, and a look of annoyance clouded her face. Those in trouble are always at the mercy of those who are not, that look seemed to say. Leave me alone.

Ramsay's uneasiness returned. This business of the reliquary had a whiff of the plague about it and he would be glad to see it sold. Then the thought of those street kids came to him – half of them stupid from sniffing glue – gunned down by off-duty policemen. They were in trouble, too, and he was not. It wasn't his fault.

Margaret Johnson took a firm hold on both her husband's hands to pull him up to his feet.

'Home, James.'

With the other two following, she led him out of the church and down the path through the lych-gate to her car. It was eight years old, with rust nibbling at the bottom edge of the doors. Ramsay couldn't think how it had passed its MOT. Wasn't it odd that their prosperous jewellery business couldn't support a better car than that? As he accelerated away noisily, it struck him that it had taken her no more than two minutes to whisk her husband out of harm's way. It had been a deft operation.

The reliquary – the sooner he had it safely back where he could see it, the better.

'May we have a word?' murmured the Reverend Oscar Stanfield in a voice which cut through the air like a steel wire.

* * *

It was already six when Ramsay turned off the coast road, down the long tree-lined avenue to Bressemer. Behind him was the sea, its troubled little waves crested in white. The sunlight flashing off it hit the car mirror now and then, and dazzled him. He brought the car to a halt for a moment so that he could take a look at the house. It had a cared-for look now, freshly painted, the stonework scrubbed, spruced up like an elderly actor in trendy clothes brought out of retirement to appear in a television sitcom. Its rejuvenation had been worth every penny of the hefty price they had paid for it.

Now that the outside had been renewed, something should be done about the interior. There were rooms on the upper floors which his father, Ernest, probably didn't visit more than twice a year if that. Sealed quiet rooms containing furniture that was never disturbed, with tall curtains half-drawn to protect the watercolours and the rugs from undue sunlight. It was an enormous place, most of it Elizabethan, some of it earlier – a broad frontage embellished with an extravagance of windows, surmounted by majestic, carved brick chimneys. There weren't many mansions as grand as this left in the eastern counties – the two World Wars, estate duties, and inflation had seen to that. Bressemer was one of the few survivors, and it had been his future inheritance – future obligation was nearer the mark – ever since his elder brother, Rodney, had been blown to pieces by a landmine on a country road in Northern Ireland.

A nasty death, but Rodney hadn't been much of a loss and the upside was that his father had never had to face the truth about him – that for all his candid manner and military good looks he was a hollow and selfish bastard who couldn't wait to get his hands on the estate, sell it up, and run through the proceeds. He had often said as much to his friends, boasting in the boozy small hours after a dining-in night in the mess.

The downside for Charles was that he had been forced to compete with a sibling who was a dead hero in the eyes of his father – to be dutiful, above reproach, far more so than his brother would ever have been. Perhaps that experience had made him, at thirty-three, something of a young fogey. Maybe there were those who thought so, but he didn't give a damn if they did.

To be dutiful – that wasn't a fate he could have escaped in any case. He and his father were all that was left of the immediate family, and he had to come down to Bressemer from London, whenever he could get away, because the old man now lived on his own. His wife had left him many years ago – abandoned him, the life he represented, and her sons as well. They had been brought up by Jane, her replacement; who had also departed a few years later for some closely-kept reason known only to his father. Fortunate in many other respects, Ernest Ramsay hadn't been lucky with the women in his life.

Charles wondered sometimes if he was any better off himself. He knew plenty of women; girls he had been brought up with in the neighbourhood, and people he met in London. There was nobody in sight at the moment though. His last experience, with Elizabeth, a would-be actress, had made him chary. Actress was what she had chosen to call herself, and he allowed that she had some flimsy kind of claim to the title; she had been convincing enough to take him in at any rate. Graceful and disgraceful. Simple rejection he could cope with – he was an adult – but fraud and betrayal were another matter altogether. Elizabeth! He shut the name out of his mind and, restarting the engine, let the car carry him slowly the rest of the way to the house.

His father came to the door with Wellington, the elderly

Labrador, swaying behind him. Charles regarded them both with an amiable but dispassionate eye. Like the house they too were in need of a bit of sprucing up. Although the dog was stone blind now, his nose was still in good order and it sniffed as a matter of course at Charles's newly-arrived ankles. Satisfied, its owner slouched back down the passage, a law unto himself.

'I was just about to put the steak under the grill.' Following his father into the kitchen, he took over while the old man pulled the cork out of a bottle of burgundy with an upward jerk of his elbow, concentrating on his task but listening as his son off-loaded his report on the events of the afternoon. He grunted now and then, seemingly unimpressed by his heir's lifesaving effort. That was because he had something else on his mind and, as soon as Charles paused, he got it off his chest.

'While you were out at St Nicholas's doing your errand of mercy thing, I had an unwelcome shock. That bloody man Maxton rang – the freelance. He'd got hold of the story about the reliquary and of course he's coming on after it like a lurcher after a rabbit. Thinks he'll sell it to one of the quality dailies, but I beg to doubt. At any rate he's imposing himself on us this evening, I'm afraid.'

'Did you have to?'

This wasn't a case where all publicity was necessarily good publicity. The sale of the reliquary was a sensitive matter, the market was narrow, no more than two or three very rich individuals, and it wasn't going to be improved much by a paragraph in a liberal broadsheet. After all, they were looking for a couple of hundred thousand for it, rock bottom. All this journalist's article was going to do was to inflame the local pressure group which had sprung up out of nowhere to demand that the casket shouldn't be sold at all. Sir Simon had given it to the community, said they, and the community should keep it. Full stop.

'It never does to antagonise the press,' his father said, inspecting his supper with satisfaction.

The bell at the front door rang with a generous clangour.

Charles rose. 'I'll go.'

It was Maxton, who else? An hour too early, with his young photographer in tow, both wearing suits, for goodness' sake. Walking down the passage towards the study, the journalist's little black eyes flickered here and there, taking in the worn Caucasian runner, the good longcase clock, an Adam side table with a Chinese charger on it.

'I haven't been here before.' He sounded resentful.

'We were just about to have our meal.' That wasn't going to stop him.

'This needn't take long.'

Thinking of his steak getting cold, he showed them into the study. Again Maxton's eyes did a quick survey for clues to the background of his subject, a survey which ended on the wall close to the desk where the family tree was kept hanging on the wall. It was a full-scale effort done in Victorian times showing all the Ramsay's and their connections complete with coats of arms, going back for centuries. Suddenly Ramsay wished it wasn't there for the journalist to ridicule; these days it did look a touch pretentious, as though he and his father needed to keep it hung up there to bolster their self-esteem.

Maxton walked over and stared at the crest which surmounted it – beneath that the family motto. A single word: PROBITAS.

'I didn't go to the sort of school where they taught you Latin,' said Maxton, 'but it's not difficult to guess, is it? *Probitas*. It must mean honesty, rectitude, probity?'

'That's right.' Ramsay wasn't going to discuss it – the man could take it or leave it. Even if the word was out of date now, most of the people whose names were on that family tree had chosen to live by it. Not all of them, of course, that would be too much to expect – but the majority had, and they had never had cause to regret it, leaving behind them a name in the county which was synonymous with integrity. It wasn't a dead letter to him either. He felt as though the word had been worked like a pigment right into the clay he was made of so that he didn't have to force himself to conform to it; for him it was a positive discomfort to do anything else.

'Nice to be able to afford it,' commented the journalist, and Ramsay knew that he had a point. The young photographer standing by the door, his paraphernalia lying beside him, smiled a sycophantic smile.

'You're an antique dealer, I understand, Mr Ramsay. Do you really live by that motto? Be honest now. You're with friends.'

Friends? He wasn't going to explain to this stranger that the absolute need for honesty in all his dealings, commercial or otherwise, had been dinned into him by his father ever since he had been able to read the word *Probitas* – that it was a matter of pride to him that he could succeed in his chosen vocation, if that was the right word for it, without using any of those stratagems which other dealers sometimes had to employ in order to survive. He joined no clubs or rings, neither did he have to con the uninitiated out of their heirlooms. If he tried to tell this Maxton that, he would sound impossibly quaint and self-righteous. Perhaps he deserved to be laughed at.

'Yes,' he replied to the question. He would have done better to have ignored it.

SOME DARK ANTIQUITIES

The journalist whipped out a tiny cassette recorder and put it on the desk after intoning the details of the interview into it as though they were important. He cocked an eye at his host.

'You don't mind? It saves lots of misunderstandings.'

Charles shook his head.

'First off, could Ben have a couple of shots of the article? . . . The reliquary, I mean. You holding it, perhaps?'

'I can't, I'm afraid. It isn't here. Why didn't you ask?'

The photographer looked down at his gear with discontent in his eyes.

'We did,' cut in Maxton. 'I dare say your father forgot. He *is* getting on, isn't he?' He looked round him idly. 'Where is this famous reliquary, then?'

Ramsay knew he mustn't lose his temper. It would be fatal. 'Ian Johnson . . . You know, the local jeweller? He's been commissioned to make a facsimile of it and carry out some scale drawings for a display which is going to be placed in St Nicholas's church after the original is sold. A nice idea, don't you think? He has it – in his shop, I expect.' He spoke as languidly as he could.

Maxton pounced. 'Do you mean to say you aren't sure where it is?'

'Of course I'm sure. I handed it over to him a month ago.'

His interrogator looked pleased.

'But you aren't one hundred per cent certain that it's in his shop now?'

'I can't be absolutely certain. One can't be certain of anything. For all I know it may be in a safe-deposit box now that he's finished the job.'

'You, Mr Ramsay, are responsible for it? Yes?'

'Yes,' Ramsay agreed.

'*Thank* you.' Maxton switched off his recorder with a decisive forefinger.

Of course nothing is amiss, Ramsay promised himself as he went back to his supper. Still he ought to check up on the casket's whereabouts, and then put Maxton straight before he got his piece into print. He couldn't impose on Margaret Johnson now, not while she was coping with that walking crisis of a husband – couldn't crash into their shop demanding to see for himself that the thing was still there. She had to be given time. As long as he had the answer before Maxton's article appeared, that would be good enough.

For a moment he had allowed a doubt to slip into his mind, a doubt which gave him a twinge as it returned. Drunk as he was at the time, sane as he seemed to be afterwards, there must have been a compelling reason for Johnson's suicidal behaviour on the tower.

Chapter Two

'Do try and do your duty straight after breakfast, Mr Becket, won't you?' chattered the nurse, dragging the curtains aside with relish to expose the rain-soaked traffic held up by the lights in the street below. Jean she was called, and he detested the arch phrase she used.

Still, it made a change from the brutalist approach of Dorothy, his other jailer.

'You must move your bowels once a day, you know, Mr Becket. Constipation is the besetting sin of the elderly,' she would hoot, like one of those factories he remembered from the early mornings of his boyhood, only adding the words 'Isn't it, dear?' if the sun was out and the hypocritical mood was upon her.

Frank Becket was a sensitive soul who deplored public discussion of his private functions. Besides, she was wrong as usual. Old age, that was the besetting sin of the elderly and he had an acute attack of it. Still warmly half asleep, he turned his face to the wall.

'Up you get.'

He cringed as the command hit him in the small of his back.

She had broken into his dream and he could still remember it: how he had revisited the home he had possessed once upon a time, during his real life, his flat overlooking the sea in Laver, one of the few unspoilt towns on the Suffolk coast. On the first floor it was, which gave him a choice view and spared his legs. Once upon a time, when he had been a human being.

Bracing himself against the cold outside the bed he put his feet on the floor. Eyes still closed, he called it to mind as he did so often – its delicate Regency furniture, the antique rugs glowing here and there, one or two understated and exquisite oils. It had been his kingdom, a kingdom which his work and dedication had earned him and which he had owned outright. Every time he had opened the white crisply painted front door and entered into it his spirits had lifted. Every time ... until one autumn in that other life when he found himself returning to the flat from his evening walk and the usual magic had failed to work. Life had suddenly ceased to be worthwhile.

It was frightening; he had found himself in the grip of a grey and persistent unease which he did not understand and could not remedy. To begin with, it simply angered him, making him tetchy at the newsagents, irritated with the woman upstairs despite her amiable cocker spaniel. It was simply age – age which was beginning to rob his life of pleasure – something he had to get used to, he told himself resentfully. Sometimes there seemed to be a kind of remission for a day or two and then, just when he was congratulating himself that he had recovered, he found that he had slipped again. All he wanted to do was to hide from it, whatever it was, and that was possible only when he slept. It worsened by the day. Before long he felt himself moving fearfully into a dark space of despair, his mind becoming blank and forgetful. His life which, until then, win or lose, had always been vivid with colour became a monochrome tunnel which led nowhere. He lost the will to get out of bed in the morning, even ceased cleaning the flat, and that wasn't like him at all; let it go, let himself go, let everything go. When for a whole week nothing had been seen of him, his upstairs neighbour, alerted by her eager dog sniffing at his door, called the police. They broke in and discovered him speechless and dehydrated, crumpled on the kitchen floor. Alzheimer's disease was his GP's routine diagnosis before he was consigned tidily to the Sayonara Rest Home for the Elderly.

The rules, explained the Department of Social Security in a formal letter to the Director, were quite clear. The Sayonara's fees were Frank's responsibility until his own means were quite exhausted. Only then, they conceded, would the state take over his upkeep. So, while he was out of action, his solicitor sold his beloved flat and its contents down to the last ornament to pay the fees. His kingdom was despoiled.

Too late, a new and competent doctor took him in hand and came up with the discovery that it was not senile dementia which had laid Frank low, but clinical depression which should have been dealt with in a hospital, free of charge on the NHS. It wouldn't be a difficult condition to deal with, the young man promised – so he dealt with it. Before long Frank was as right as rain and properly grateful for his rescue from the destructive wilderness of melancholia. Right, he was cured and ready to leave. Where to? That was the question, for by then he had nowhere else to go. His abode had shrunk to a single bed with a locker beside it.

However. However, he was determined to get out of the Sayonara. To get away from sly Jean and fierce Dorothy, and old Smythe who made such a variety of noises in the night. His lawyer had been dim and the DSS evasive, but one of these days, never fear, this intelligent bag of bones which once had been Frank Becket was going to rise up and smite them like a bolt of lightning, get even with the people who had stripped him of every penny. He would appear on investigative TV programmes demanding restitution, write a hundred letters, enlist the support of his MP . . .

As he groped for his slippers head downward with the blood pounding in his ears, he caught sight of a familiar oblong shape under the bed. A smart cowhide attaché case initialled STB in gold, which was his passport to the outside world. STB – Simon Timothy Burnill, latterly Sir Simon Burnill, his employer of thirty years' standing who, having forced all his business rivals into submission, had himself succumbed in the arms of his third and most buxom wife . . . succumbed to death, to her surprise.

By the Fifties it was unusual for a financier to have a male secretary. It was one of the earlier wives who, after a difficult discussion with a honey-blonde girl stenographer, had forced one on Sir Simon. So Frank had been taken on as shorthand writer, later to become factotum, confidant and manager of Sir Simon's famous collection of pictures, antiques and objets.

It had been a congenial time. Given the freedom of the tycoon's Personal Number Two bank account, Frank had ranged up and down the country, bidding on his behalf for masses of rare and beautiful items, saving him a small fortune in agents' fees.

Although alongside his collection of art Sir Simon had a comprehensive collection of vices, no one would have included ingratitude among them. His will had left Frank an index-linked annuity and a large enough sum as well to pay off the mortgage on the flat. His beautiful flat.

At the memory, Frank's eyes flashed with indignation as he

pulled on his dressing-gown and made for the bathroom.

Coming late from breakfast to the Quiet Room, he found that the old sinner Smythe had grabbed the only quality newspaper the Sayonara thought it worth buying for its residents. Contemptuous of the tabloids, he made do with the *Eastern Courant* (founded 1739), and walked over to the corner furthest from his bête noire. When he caught sight of the second feature on the front page it took him a moment to bring the tremor in his hands sufficiently under his control to be able to read it:

> FAMOUS CASKET'S WHEREABOUTS A MYSTERY
> Charles Ramsay the well-known London dealer confessed today that although its safekeeping was his responsibility he was nevertheless uncertain of the whereabouts of the Burnill reliquary, the mediaeval casket . . . subject of some controversy . . . to be sold and the proceeds donated to a foreign charity . . .

Frank waded through the *Courant*'s prose again, line by line. He was acquainted with the name Ramsay because it went with an Elizabethan house along the coast which he and the walking wounded from the home had been invited to visit one Sunday the previous summer. He searched his memory for the name, and it took a moment or two . . . Bressemer. When he had realised that Frank was knowledgeable, Ramsay had detached him efficiently from the main party and taken him off to show him one or two of the less public treasures of the house. It had been a change to be treated like a person instead of a wrinkly. Remembering his host, his father, the house, Frank had a flash of insight which highlighted two things. First, that Ramsay was a man you could trust, an honest antique dealer, which in his jaundiced view was as rare as a set of Chinese Chippendale chairs; flowing from that came the second – the conviction that Ramsay could help him answer a question which never seemed to go away these days. It wasn't his field, that was the problem. He needed advice.

But he had to get in touch with him. He went to the writing table and sat down with his back to Smythe – fortunately there was still some paper left.

The letter took Frank a while to write, but eventually it was done and an envelope found. No stamp, though, and in order to lay his hands on one he would have to venture out of the Sayonara, to the sub post office in Queen Street. He never liked having to go out and now, having used up so much energy writing the letter he was more reluctant than usual.

Jean. He knew that she passed it on her way home from work. Did he dare to ask her to buy the stamp and post his letter for him? To give him that small service? What would she say? He quickly calculated the worst outcome for him in terms of damaged pride and dignity foregone. It was worth it, he decided.

He sought her out in the sluice room, peering round the door, to see her leaning against the big stainless-steel sink, coffee cup in one hand, taking a minute or two before she went off duty to gossip with the others – the big red-haired woman Evie, the auxiliary, and the one whose name he had forgotten, one of the cleaners. Hovering outside in the corridor he waited obediently, not wanting to expose himself to comment but at the same time anxious not to miss Jean and waste a whole day.

Since, apart from being the most highly qualified member of the staff, she was also the youngest and most presentable – the only one with any pretension to a love life, any future in the romantic line – she was at the top of the Sayonara's pecking order: the queen of the walk.

She set down her cup. 'Must be going, you people. Garry's such an impatient hunk. Impatient!'

The look she threw at the ceiling suggested anything they chose. Evie giggled; the cleaner tried not to look envious.

Catching sight of him, Jean opened her eyes wide, graciously inviting him to speak.

'I have this letter.'

She looked down at it.

'So you have.' Evie's busy eyes watched, alert to pick up any reaction from him.

He pressed on. 'I wondered if you could post it for me – on your way? I haven't got a stamp, you see, but I have the exact money. Twenty-five pence.'

He held out the envelope towards her, placing the coins precariously on top of it. Forcing it on her.

Jean took it from him, catching the coins and sliding them into the pocket of her starched white dress; she had to put them somewhere.

'Thank you,' he said, trying not to sound humble.

When she did not reply, he turned back awkwardly to the door. In silence they watched him leave, closing it behind him.

The gaze of the two underlings shifted to Jean. How was she going to handle this intriguing act of lese-majesty? A fully trained nurse invited to run errands?

Disdainfully she held the envelope up by one corner, conscious of the need to make some assertive gesture that would stamp itself on their memories. Evie began to chuckle, then the sound died as Jean, grasping the letter in both hands, tore it across and dropped the two halves in the plastic pedal-bin standing next to her. There!

On the instant she knew that she had gone too far, that the gesture, though impressive, had its dangerous side, had violated a code which all three of them subscribed to, or felt they ought to. She was vulnerable now.

'I didn't say that I would post it,' she protested with bravado, careful not to sound as though she was excusing herself.

Neither of the others spoke.

Unable to undo what she had done, Jean hesitated, then made for the door. 'Must be going,' she said. 'Bye.'

As she went quickly down the corridor, the thoughts clicked through her head. It couldn't have been so important. Who did old Becket have to write to? Nobody had ever visited him at the home. He had no family that she could see, and his friends must be dead, most of them.

Anyway who needed a letter from him?

Chapter Three

In the telephone kiosk Ramsay propped the folded newspaper up at his elbow and forced himself to read through Maxton's piece again. Why hadn't he handled that interview with greater care? With such a talent for making bricks without straw, Maxton had a great future as one of those legless things in the tabloids. The slithering Thing from the *Sunday* . . . He had to put this right straight away.

In his ear the ringing tone stopped.

'Hullo.'

'Is that Margaret Johnson?'

'It is.' He could hear how musical her voice was even with its harmonics and overtones constricted by the telephone line.

'Charles Ramsay here. Look, I rang to apol—' But she cut him off.

Doggedly he dialled the number again. If he didn't jump to it this time he would be in the phone box all morning. Then that option disappeared. A woman weighed down with plastic bags parked them outside the kiosk and then her bulky self beside them. She blinked her small eyes at him with hostility before turning her back on him.

When Margaret Johnson answered his second call he threw the words at her and hoped for the best.

'Just listen, if you would be good enough. Maxton published that nonsense about the casket without my authority.'

'What if he did? We still have every reason to sue you, him, and the *Courant* for libel. The implication was quite clear . . .'

'What implication? What do you mean?'

'That my husband and I had stolen it.'

Suppose she was in the right, could the Johnsons afford a libel suit? No – that was the answer to that, not by the look of them.

'Let me come round and put things right.'

'Certainly not. What you really mean is that you want to check up on the reliquary . . .'

That had been in his mind, yes, but . . . how could he put it?

'. . . because you don't trust us.'

Feeling shabby, he deployed the sincerest voice he could manage. 'Mrs Johnson, you deserve an explanation . . .'

Seeing the opening, she went for it. 'Precisely – but at another time. Now, Mr Ramsay, you saved my husband's life and I shall always be grateful' – she didn't bother to sound as though she meant it, the word was dry and cold. 'However, that doesn't give you the right to play fast and loose with our good name, does it?'

He tried to think of a reply.

'What you have done to us is inexcusable.'

She put down the phone again, bang, on the word 'inexcusable' and that was that. He had been left not an inch nearer to establishing that the object was where it should be, safe and unharmed in the safe in her husband's workroom.

Turning his head, he found his face six inches away from that of the woman waiting outside, the rounded tip of her nose, a white and bloodless blob, pressed against the pane of the kiosk door. Breaking into an angry sweat he shouted at her through the sound-deafening glass, 'Madam, take your nose away, if you please.' Startled, the end of it sprang back to normal.

Forcing his way past her, he glanced at his watch. He had to get to the saleroom before it closed for lunch. He ought to have insisted on seeing that casket straight away. Lack of moral fibre – that's my problem, he thought, and immediately contradicted himself. She was having a difficult time and he was a considerate young man. Cowardice didn't come into it.

Harry Oakes, the auctioneer, was one of the permanent fixtures of Wickingham. He clamped his hand around Ramsay's and shook it; his voice was the same as usual, like the crunch of loose gravel because he smoked too much.

'That carpet I mentioned, it's over there. Quite a tasty item and I think you'll be interested.' He nodded at it, folded over and tied with twine, bundled up in a corner along with other pieces of carpeting ripped up by his weary men from somebody's floor in a house clearing.

'The owner says it has a history attached to it; made to order, she says. According to her, a royal duke went up to Norwich to be given the freedom of the city years ago, before Hitler's war, and that carpet was woven especially for the occasion.'

Ramsay raised two sceptical eyebrows and put him on the defensive.

'Anyway, that's the story I was told,' he coughed, 'for what it's worth.'

What was the carpet worth – that was the question.

It measured about five metres by four. The pile seemed all right, but on one side it had been slit by some philistine so that a flap could be folded back to fit round a fireplace – easy enough to repair . . . expensive, though.

The colour of the field had been ivory originally, but it was dirty. Overall there were small medallions with vines radiating from them and palmettes, mostly in dark red, the colour of burgundy; those were also woven into the wide border. Ramsay cogitated. What on earth was it? It wasn't a village or tribal effort; it looked more like something produced in one of the large factories in Persia employing many pairs of hands – the Ziegler workshops at Arak, somewhere of that kind. That would figure if indeed it had been commissioned specially. Obviously it hadn't been woven in the Caucasus or Central Asia, and it wasn't Turkish either – of course it wasn't, the design and colours ruled that out. No, he'd never seen another like it. It was a puzzle – the kind of puzzle which he always felt driven to solve.

Perhaps Molyneux, at Crowther's, could give him a clue. Immediately he went to the phone to see if he could squeeze a provisional opinion out of him. But their expert on oriental rugs wasn't having any – he wanted a chance to look at some photographs first, including a close-up of the back so that he could see the weave – often the best clue to where a rug had been made.

Photographs? There wasn't time for all that. The sale was the following morning.

'I see . . .' Wanting to be helpful, Molyneux got thoughtful and let his guard down just a little. 'The tale you were told about the royal duke. We've heard that sort of thing so often before, haven't we, Charles, you and I? People do like to wrap a web of romance around their offerings. However, if it were true . . .'

'Yes?'

'... it's possible that it was made in India. Those colours suggest an Agra carpet. Have you thought of that as a possibility?'

No, was the answer, he hadn't.

'Tell me more.'

'The story goes like this. Back in 1851 some fine-quality hand-knotted Indian carpets were shown at the Great Exhibition. They made such an impression on the gentry that a workshop to make them was set up in Agra jail where labour was nice and cheap – a bowl of rice a day and not much else.

'So?'

'The workshop was patronised by the upper classes in a big way, including members of the royal family. Agra carpets are much sought after these days.'

'How much sought after?'

Molyneux mentioned one of two figures realised at recent Crowther's auction sales in London, all of them considerable. 'Any royal connection would be a bonus, of course.'

Perhaps the burghers of Norwich had indeed ordered a carpet from that particular workshop to make HRH feel more at home when he came on his brief visit. It was a possibility, but he only had two or three hours to check it out. Where was the nearest public library?

To begin with, the girl in charge of the reference section was anxious to help, although, she warned him, 'We close at four today because it's Thursday.'

It was already twenty past three and the sale was first thing in the morning.

Yes, on the computer they had a comprehensive index of the *Eastern Courant* going back to 1895. Fine. Next question: had a royal duke been given the freedom of Norwich in the Twenties or Thirties?

Her fingers flickered over the keyboard and were still. 'Afraid not.' She looked up at him expectantly.

Had any spare royal dukes simply visited the city? That set off another flurry of tapping.

'No. Nothing at all on file.'

He had reached an impasse, and the second hand on the clock above her head was ticking onwards.

Wait . . .

'What about the Prince of Wales?' he asked.

'The Prince of Wales? Oh, *that* Prince of Wales. The Mrs Simpson one. Why didn't you say?'

'I'm saying now, and I'm in a hurry.' That was a mistake.

Bridling, she turned back to her keyboard and immediately struck oil. That Prince of Wales had come to Norwich twice, she reported grudgingly, first for an investiture in 1919 and again just before he succeeded to the throne. She shook her head. No, she didn't have the exact dates.

It was three thirty-one.

'There must have been a press report,' he said.

'The *Eastern Courant*? The back numbers are all there.' She flipped an unhelpful hand at the large volumes bound in blue cloth ranged on the shelves behind her.

'I need all the volumes for 1919 and 1935,' he said.

'Feel free,' she answered, staying firmly in her chair and watching him collect them all and carry them over to the polished oak table. Thump. The six volumes hit the top. Get a move on, Ramsay. The yellowing pages of Volume I for 1935 were getting brittle and had to be treated with respect. He turned them as fast as he dared, page after fragile page, then stopped.

SOME DARK ANTIQUITIES

Why not use his brain instead? The odds were that the carpet had been ordered for the investiture and it would have taken the convict weavers inching forward day by day at their wide loom at least six months to complete it, so it couldn't have been delivered until well into the second half of 1919.

It was three forty-eight by the library clock.

He grabbed the last of the heavy books for 1919 and started to work backwards from the end of the year. Page followed page again until the headline hit him: 'ROYAL INVESTITURE – HIS ROYAL HIGHNESS HONOURS OUR HEROES' and underneath a close-up of Prince Charming in uniform pinning medals on loyal East Anglian veterans of the Great War. Rapidly he read the account underneath. The citations. More photographs on page eleven, it said.

'Afraid I shall have to lock up soon,' the librarian announced with pleasure.

He turned to page eleven and there was a full-length photograph of the Prince and his ADC, both wearing service dress tunics, riding breeches, boots and spurs. And underneath those polished boots and spurs, beneath the royal feet, lay the carpet. There was no mistaking it, the strongly marked pattern of the border.

'I'm closing now,' she called out triumphantly.

'Yes, yes. Just a moment.' He raced through the text.

'A particular feature of the ceremony was the superb carpet in ivory and deep crimson which covered the dais. Ordered specially from the workshops at Agra in India some months ago by the city authorities it brought a touch of Eastern splendour to compensate for the dull weather and reminded us of the incredible range of skills and craftsmanship to be found within the broad confines of the British Empire.'

Not least in its jails.

He went early to the saleroom the next day to make sure of a good seat well behind the old ladies for whom the whole thing was a weekly event. They brought their own coffee and sandwiches and made an indoor picnic of it.

The bidding for the carpet was half-hearted because it was dirty and cut and nobody else had any idea what it was, except him. It was knocked down to him for one hundred and thirty pounds. Harry Oakes could have run it up a bit if he'd wanted to, but he didn't take bids off the wall as a matter of principle. Not as a rule and, besides, Mr Ramsay was a friend.

After the sale was over, Charles took some instant photographs to send down to Molyneux. It was while he was rolling the carpet up that he heard that voice again, the voice of Margaret Johnson talking to the girl at the desk who had finished taking money from the successful bidders.

It had to be then that Harry, sitting in an elbow chair recuperating from his auctioneering with a cup of dark brown tea in one hand and a cigarette in the other, called across to him, 'Pleased with your carpet, then? Reckon you must be if you're taking all those pictures of it.'

Ramsay didn't notice Margaret's back stiffen, and anyway he was too pleased with himself to resist calling back, 'It's going straight down to Crowther's, I should think.' He was conscious the moment afterwards that he should have kept quiet. Public gloating did nothing except lose one friends.

The silence that followed expanded into the four corners of

the saleroom while Margaret slowly turned to face him with the auctioneer observing her over the rim of his mug of tea. Then the enchanting voice spoke, simply seeking information.

'Mr Ramsay, did you buy my carpet?'

Bent low over it, wrestling with it, he froze. Her carpet? So it had been hers? That was just what he needed.

Standing to face her, he owned up.

'And you are sending it down to Crowther's. Is that what I heard you say?'

'Yes, that's what I shall do, I think.'

That was his privilege, since it was his carpet now, bought fair and square.

'How much will it make?'

'No idea.' He wouldn't know for sure until Molyneux had seen the photographs and given him a valuation, but a great deal more than a hundred and thirty pounds. Since he was sending it down to London, that much was obvious. Did she have any right to ask? Of course she didn't. Since she and her husband were dealers with a prosperous business in Wickingham, they had to take their chances like everybody else. She really ought to have known better than to put an interesting carpet like that into the local saleroom.

Anxious to keep it peaceful, Harry interposed, 'There's always the risk of being wrong, you know, and there's their commission to pay and I don't know what.' Being an auctioneer, he did know what, of course. Fifteen per cent buyer's premium, photographs, VAT. Even so . . .

Charles Ramsay heard himself saying, 'Let me give you a lift home and we can talk about it.' He had at the back of his mind the vague idea that he might, just possibly, offer her something extra on the carpet. A share of the profit, perhaps? If he could wrap it up in some way as a commission or whatever, she might not be too proud to accept. He was too scrupulous – it sometimes surprised him that he was able to make any kind of profit in his business.

'A lift?'

'No, thanks. I'll walk.'

He didn't say it.

As his father pushed the slices of bread under the roaring gas grill Charles could sense that he was searching for a tactful form of words. He could have tried harder.

'This article of Maxton's makes you look a complete ass,' he announced. Crouching forward and peering into the heat to check that the toast was browning, he went on, 'Can't you get them to print a retraction? Talk to the editor or whatever? Collins, isn't it?'

He still lived in a long-ago world, one in which you simply wandered round for a quiet word with the chap and fixed it up. He wasn't conscious at all that these days editors weren't for squaring, even the editor of the *Eastern Courant*.

Because it was too late in the day for an argument, Charles merely replied, 'Maxton's little effort will be forgotten in a week. The safety of the reliquary is what matters.' He was letting down his father more lightly than the old so-and-so deserved.

An orange flame erupted from the grill.

'Damn the bloody thing!' growled his father, snatching his hand away.

'You ought to get yourself a toaster. They're not expensive.'

The old man didn't choose to hear that – just dropped the charred pieces of toast into the bin and doggedly went back to square one. He never compromised.

'Johnson's wife would have shown it to you if you'd asked her properly.'

Not a hope now. How could he be so obtuse?

'Didn't want to worry her. She's had a hard time . . .' There was no point in elaborating – that would merely give him something more to grunt about.

Suddenly he seemed to cheer up. 'I'll wager you offered her a share of the profit from that carpet.' Ernest cocked a confident eye at his son. Probity was the word . . . and fair dealing. In his book all this sharp practice was a contagious disease. Ever since Charles had gone into antiques he'd made a point of giving him a check-up from time to time to make sure that his standards hadn't dropped; as though that was still his business. It was an irritation.

'No, I didn't, as a matter of fact. There wasn't time.'

'Not even to ask her about the whereabouts of the reliquary?' the old man persisted, straightening up with a tiny groan from his watching-the-toast position.

'Not even for that. Keep an eye on that toast.'

But his father's open gaze had swung round to focus on him.

'That was bloody slack of you! Being chairman of the trustees for my sins, ultimately it's on my charge. What are we both going to look like if you've lost it?'

What he meant was, if the Johnsons had stolen it, but as usual he was too pussyfoot to say so. Stolen it? They couldn't have done. Since they'd had it last, there was no way they could get away with it.

'What evidence do you have that you handed it over to them?'

Evidence, what did he mean? Evidence? He'd got to that

point unnervingly fast. Ramsay felt an empty space open up in his inside. There was no receipt. You didn't ask people like that, people you knew, for a receipt every time. He said nothing.

'So there isn't any?'

'Calm down. There's no problem. I've got to go and see Johnson anyway tomorrow. I'll check up on it then. Right?'

Although that seemed to satisfy Ernest there was a sediment of doubt left in his own mind. Suppose for a moment that they couldn't produce the casket – where would that leave him? . . . There, exactly.

For the second time a tongue of flame licked greedily from the grill, rolling up and over the top of the stove, flamboyantly blue and orange and gold.

'You really ought to get a toaster, you know,' Charles said.

Perhaps they both lived in a long-ago world.

Chapter Four

The eyes reflected in the mirror were looking intently at him, or rather at his image in it – the mirror with the crisply carved Italianate frame. They were a pair of pale blue eyes from the Baltic. German eyes, Chalon decided. A Boche, that was what he was. You could always tell by the . . . He stopped himself. These days Germans were people just like everybody else – he and this visitor were fellow Europeans now, under the busybody sway of the Commissioners in Brussels. Besides, the man hadn't even been born then – you couldn't visit the sins of the fathers on the children. For some reason the word 'children' made him shiver.

Was this the courier he had been told to expect? That was the question. This Kr . . . German person . . . in his expensive cotton net shirt, sandals and well-pressed shorts?

It was already Monday morning – six whole days since the telephone call. So why had nothing odd happened yet? That was what he wanted to know. Perhaps, after all, now that he looked at him again, the person wasn't sufficiently out of the ordinary to qualify as the courier.

Not that there weren't plenty of people to choose from. There had been a positive stream of browsers, chic weekenders in judiciously casual clothes coming in from their second homes in this or that outlying village in the hills, mingling with tourists taking a cheap refuge from the sun's heat in the tranquil cave of his antique shop in the ancient city of Vauban in the Haute Garonne. Things were slackening off now a little only because it was lunchtime. In the main square the restaurants were filling up; the waiters would be rushed off their feet, leaning across the tables to distribute carafes of wine and baskets of crisp rolls to keep the customers occupied until the *plat du jour* was ready.

No, life wasn't bad, Chalon admitted, you couldn't say that. It was just the same as usual when it ought to be different. That was what was wrong with it. Unless that Boche over there... He sat at his bureau and made a pretence of writing out some new price tickets, scarcely daring to be expectant. His scalp prickling, he glanced sidelong at the fellow now and then.

A man and girl wandered arm in arm along the aisle, muttering the occasional comment to each other, their voices pitched low to prevent him from hearing quite what it was they were saying about the Charles X table – the possibly Charles X table – or the smiling Art Nouveau lady in gilded bronze holding a lamp above her head with a smile on her face and an elegant hand trying to hide her breasts with a fold of drapery and somehow managing to fail. No, they wouldn't be discussing her because she was out of their league, being signed 'A. Léonard' on her base. The genuine article. Fortunately, she was as heavy as she was valuable. There wasn't much in the shop which was small enough to be spirited away easily by shop-lifters. Thieves weren't his preoccupation today. It was the non-appearance of another sort of visitor that frustrated him – like a cadence left unfinished, a postponed lawsuit or an unpaid invoice hanging over from day to day...

He was getting fanciful. He took off his glasses and stared after the middle-aged German who was into his second systematic tour of inspection, and rubbed his eyes. The man's walkabout ended once again at the handsome boulle clock standing on its wall-bracket at the dealer's shoulder. The man towered above him, seeming to be waiting for the young couple to leave. Don't let it be him, Chalon thought. Still, you never knew, perhaps he would be fool enough to buy that curse of a clock which had been standing there for three solid years eating its head off, looking important, but quite unsaleable at the price he was forced to ask for it because somebody had jogged his elbow while he was bidding at the auction of the old marquise's effects and he had been left high and dry.

The young lovers went out into the street, which left the dealer alone in the afternoon silence with the German looming over him. For a split second a scene from Chalon's childhood came into his mind . . . A corporal dressed in field grey standing over him like that . . . demanding to know where his father was.

The man spoke. In French too, which made a change. 'The clock. How much is it?'

'Forty thousand francs, monsieur,' Chalon replied quickly, doing his best to make it sound an inconsiderable sum for such a timepiece as that. But the visitor knew his clocks; a series of sharp questions followed:

The movement? Vincenti.

Did it strike? Assuredly, monsieur.

The provenance? A local aristocratic family, the old Marquise de Rovanne.

Chalon felt hope blossoming inside him. Even if he wasn't the courier, the German might at least take the clock off his hands. There was a silence. Then, without explanation, the man turned on his heel and walked away down the aisle to the door. The doorbell clinked as he closed it with care, looking down at the lever handle to see that it was properly secured.

Just like a Hun! That was a bit of a let-down. Not only wasn't he the courier but he'd had the sheer gall not to buy the clock. Very well, you could say it was a shade over-priced, perhaps . . .

Who was it going to be, then? If he didn't have the delivery by tomorrow evening that bloody man Volet would have scored yet again and, worse, his own plan, his brainchild, would probably be jettisoned even though they were already halfway through the operation. It would be a defeat, and in the ensuing shambles he would only be able to count on Grimaud, rich and shrewd, the owner of the casino, to stand by him. The rest of them would go over to Volet and heaven knew where he would lead them. Like lemmings, straight over the cliff probably. Volet, with his oft-repeated stories of 'his' harkas in the war in Algeria and what they had done to the local women, was his pet hate in the Brotherhood, but apart from Grimaud, he didn't think much of the rest of them either. Wasn't it all a bit ridiculous? A group of grown men calling themselves the Brotherhood, dedicated singlemindedly to this one objective, which held them together despite all the friction and in-fighting which they got up to. They were a funny bunch to be Knights of the Round Table, but not one of them had ever missed a meeting. No, they weren't ridiculous, he decided, though once they had achieved the quest no doubt everything would change. After they had put away their helmets and bannerets they probably wouldn't even recognise one another in the street.

SOME DARK ANTIQUITIES

* * *

It was next morning after Chalon's breakfast of a bowl of hot chocolate and half a fresh brioche that the courier arrived. It was astonishing. He couldn't believe it. A commercial courier as large as you like, pretending to be a riot policeman with a blue plastic helmet and a baton swinging at his wrist – and behind him a large snub-nosed van with FRANCE-SECURITAY printed in bloody great letters on its corrugated side. How subtle! What finesse! Why hadn't they rented a motor-cycle escort and the Republican Guard? FRANCE-SECURITAY, for heaven's sake! The widow Orval on the opposite side of the cobbled street would be on the telephone to her friends already.

'Sign here,' invited the guard as his companion backed the van. Chalon did as he was told and took possession of the parcel with steady hands.

'*Au'voir, monsieur,*' the thick-set guard added automatically, swinging back into his seat, nodding to the driver. A blind instrument, ignorant of the significance of what he had just delivered.

Chalon shut the shop door after himself, checked that the sign said 'Closed' and went right back to the rear where he had a safe, made of the hardest available steel. With the utmost delicacy he peeled away all the layers from the package to expose what it contained under the strong light. For a long time he sat there looking as though he were a collector secretly enjoying some miracle of erotic art. Reluctantly he re-wrapped the package, put it away in the safe and closed the door – then turned back to open it again, pushing the crumpled and intrusive packaging to one side in order to prolong his pleasure over its arrival. Finally he closed the door on it for good and spun the combination lock with a twist of his thumb and forefinger. A faint click, and another.

At five to seven that night he found himself in the stone courtyard of the Palais (dating from 1632, restored 1977), which they were allowed to use for their meetings because one of the members of the Brotherhood had some pull in the Mairie. It was pretty well his only contribution to their activities.

The lights were on in the hall on the first floor. Once he was into the building, behind the noble façade, he mounted the corkscrew of stone steps with the help of the thick rope attached to the wall which served as a handrail. Heads turned as he entered, they were all there as usual. Volet was just reminiscing, explaining how he had finally induced a couple of conscripts to inflict the *baignoir* on some FLN prisoners. It was his horror story number three – a favourite of his, but by no means of theirs.

'They soon got the hang of it,' concluded Volet, the bourgeois, in his beautifully enunciated French . . . who nevertheless consorted with those curious types at the Café du Centre in town. Café du Centre? Café of the Extreme Right was nearer the mark. These days those young men of Volet's persuasion wore blue suits and had their hair cut short, trying to look like business consultants. They were thugs all the same and scared the waiters so much they scarcely dared even to give them a bill. The story went on as Chalon seated himself at the table.

'The harkas on the other hand didn't need to be taught anything like that. They were born interrogators.' He gave a hard bark of laughter. 'Good fighters, too. They just went for it – which is what we ought to be doing. Isn't it, Chalon?'

Volet searched the newcomer's face for a sign of success

while hoping for an admission of failure. Seeing no clue in it to either, he shrugged and looked away.

By way of reply, Chalon picked up the case beside his chair and placed it on the polished refectory table smelling of beeswax.

'No, Volet,' he jeered, 'that does not contain my sandwiches.'

He exchanged a glance with Grimaud, who raised his eyebrows in a question. Chalon responded with the ghost of a nod before continuing, unable to keep his excitement out of his voice. 'Gentlemen, the courier arrived this morning and this is what he brought us.'

Around the table there was a rustle of interest as the members of the Brotherhood prepared to change their minds again. Pressing open the locks of the case with his thumbs, Chalon raised the lid and reverently lifted out the opened package.

'Fantastic! My congratulations,' cried Volet with unnecessary emphasis, turning on a sixpence like the politician he was. Consoling himself no doubt with the thought that there was still plenty of rope left for this *brocanteur* to hang himself with.

'Thank you,' Chalon murmured, accepting the praise at its face value, handing Volet the package across the table. 'Would you care to open it and show us all what it contains?'

As he did so, someone drew in his breath and Grimaud smiled a broad smile, looking like a circus owner whose best trapeze artist has just brought off a seemingly impossible feat. Ironically, he put his palms softly together to invite a round of applause from the Doubting Thomases ranged round him.

When the meeting broke up just after ten, Volet made his way to the Café du Centre and found a table in an inconspicuous corner well away from the too public plateglass window. After giving his order briskly to the waiter, a mere fetcher and carrier, he grunted, 'Has Raquin been in?'

The waiter shrugged – his duties didn't include being helpful.

'Raquin?' insisted Volet, looking up to find himself offered a view of the man's receding backside clad in black. In a moment the waiter returned with his cognac, set it swiftly down in front of him, uttered the single word '*M'sieur*' as a pretence of a concession, and withdrew.

Volet sipped his brandy obsessively as though he was in need of it for once. It didn't always work, but this time the liquor helped him concentrate as he became oblivious of the sounds around him, the over-merry wedding party two tables away and the occasional mournful cry of a seller of hot *crêpes* in the street outside. If the splinter group to which he belonged was to flourish and extend its power it needed money – that was the most basic fact of political life. If at the same time Chalon could be upskittled, that would be a juicy bonus. By the time he had put his empty glass on the table he had pushed his thinking all the way to the end of his rival's plan and had sketched out a counterploy or two of his own. It was then that he caught sight of Raquin threading his way between the chairs left haphazard by departing customers. The dark, crop-haired young man came and stood at his right hand. Volet had his people well trained.

'You never seem to be here when I need to talk to you. Sit down,' he grumbled.

Catching the note of promise in his voice, Raquin did as he was told. In that dull town, the desire for physical action sometimes seemed stronger inside him than the need for a woman, but what Volet told him only excited his lust without satisfying it.

SOME DARK ANTIQUITIES

He was to hold himself in readiness. Be prepared, Volet told him. Like a boy scout, thought Raquin, but he kept his lip buttoned. Volet's scorn could cut like a whip.

Chapter Five

To feel gratitude towards someone who has saved your life is no easy thing and Ramsay hadn't expected Johnson to be an exception to the rule. It is even worse when the circumstances do you no credit. That was why, when he let Ramsay into his sun-filled shop, he didn't mention the church tower episode at all; instead he displayed a sort of off-hand amnesia.

A pair of Regency elbow chairs nicely embellished with brassware and a muted Fereghan rug gave the showroom the right atmosphere for the kind of clientele the Johnsons aimed for, although it didn't fit somehow with the clues to the couple's lifestyle that Ramsay had picked up elsewhere. Their elderly car for a start, those unusual clothes of hers, the hurried sale of that troublesome carpet; somehow, none of those went with the interior of this shop, with its admirably reticent classical wallpaper and precisely moulded cornices.

Fussily, Johnson lowered the metal grille which protected the shop window and double-locked the door before speaking.

'The job's ready,' he said, meaning the replica the committee had commissioned from him.

'Fine. Let's have a look at it.'

Having switched on a tape of background music for his visitor's benefit – The Art of Fugue, which was a touch pretentious – Johnson retreated to his workroom and stayed there for much longer than he needed, as though he were trying to reassert himself after his shaming adventure on the church tower. Ramsay was kept waiting under the insistent sound from the tiny black loudspeakers to do what? The obvious thing was to inspect the stuff on display.

A selection of modest jewellery was laid out in the showcase which served as a counter; no doubt the valuable things were locked away in the safe. He didn't deal in jewellery himself; one couldn't cover everything. However, silver was another matter, how about that? In the centre of the shop some bits and pieces – a couple of caddy spoons, a vinaigrette, the odd snuff and vesta box – were displayed in a glass-topped table along with a pair of oval Georgian salts with blue glass liners. Decent bread-and-butter items – nothing to get him reaching for his chequebook there. Where did the Johnsons show their more important silver? There must be some. In the window, obviously – he leaned forward to look into it – no, there was nothing to get fussed about there either. Only when he turned back to survey the shop again did he register the glazed display case which rose behind the counter, and saw half hidden in the shadows inside a set of four Georgian silver candlesticks ranged on the top shelf – nice and simple ... and absolutely right, which made a change.

They *were* interesting, because they would suit a client of his. These days there weren't so many of them around with real money to spend but this one, a metal broker, seemed to have cheated the recession; at any rate he'd bought a huge D-ended dining table from Ramsay three weeks back, and that hadn't been cheap. Now the man was after just the right kind of silver to dress it up with, and, as they always did, he wanted it yesterday.

SOME DARK ANTIQUITIES

As the decisive conclusion of another fugue came hammering out from overhead Johnson came back from his inner sanctum with a tray in his hands and on it an oblong object covered with a piece of dusty velvet. Having put it down on the glass-topped table, he was about to lift away this covering like a conjuror when Ramsay interrupted him. Those candlesticks, there on the top shelf, they were rather attractive.

Johnson received the message and sidestepped it. 'Candlesticks? Yes, they are good. Not for sale, I'm afraid.'

It was time to get down to business and he was keen to show off his handiwork.

'There,' he breathed. 'What do you think of it?' His manner had changed. Now he was the craftsman, modest but confident because he was on his own ground and he knew that in its own way this copy of the reliquary which he had fashioned was a masterpiece. It was Ramsay who had insisted that it should be made of solid silver, gilded like the original, with no expense spared, and he was glad he had done so.

As they admired it together Ramsay wondered, not for the first time, why such a talented silversmith, who obviously got such an enormous buzz from his work, had been trying to put a full stop to himself two days earlier. He had been stoned, of course, and alcohol was said to be a depressant, but not to that extent, surely? Whisky on its own was never as lowering as that.

After a moment's hesitation, Johnson ventured, 'I hoped you would be pleased with it . . . because I was wondering if you could put in a word with the committee about payment.'

Uh? Nothing more was due yet.

He drew in a shallow breath. 'After all, the job is finished now, to your satisfaction, and it would be helpful if they could settle up.'

'But that isn't what we agreed. Not at all.'

'I know, I know.' He put up a defensive palm as Ramsay laid it out.

'The agreement was that sixty per cent of your price for the job should be paid in advance, as indeed it was . . .'

His eyes on the silver model in front of him, the craftsman listened without enthusiasm.

'. . . and the balance as soon as the sale of the original was successfully put through by Golver's. We both have that in black and white – you have, and so have I.'

Johnson's voice sharpened. 'The committee ought to make an exception here. I've put a lot of work in on this and I've done them proud.'

'That's not in dispute, but it isn't the point.' Ramsay had to raise his voice to compete with the intrusive counterpoint of J. S. Bach which was still filling the shop.

Johnson, tight-lipped, went and switched it off, demanding over his shoulder, 'Very well. What is the point, then?'

'The committee couldn't settle with you earlier, even if they wanted to. They haven't got the money, nor will they have until the reliquary is sold. They had enough trouble raising the advance payment, as it was.'

'I was never told that.'

'No reason why you should have been. It was their business. You knew the terms and you accepted them.'

A muscle working on the edge of his jaw, Johnson said nothing, but made as if to walk out of the street door, then stopped as though that offered him no escape from his problem and turned back abruptly towards the table. For a moment Ramsay was afraid that he might decide to take out his frustration on the replica. Instead he flipped the piece of velvet back over it, picked up the tray and strode back with it into his workroom. The door slammed.

Relaxing, Ramsay inspected the candlesticks again. Not bad at all. Now that it was clear what Johnson's difficulty was, perhaps he could offer a solution. He followed him into the workroom and found him putting his handiwork away in the large safe which was concreted into the whitewashed wall. That was the precise moment, he chided himself afterwards, when he should have asked to see the reliquary, the original one – but the trouble was that he was too preoccupied just then with the size of the inducement needed to get Johnson to part with those candlesticks, having rubbed him up the wrong way rather. It took a hard half-hour and several thousand pounds to prise them out of him – and when it looked as though the job was done, he still held back.

Now what was the problem? Running true to form, the awkward sod wouldn't take a cheque – that was the problem. He'd been acquainted with Ramsay for years, knew where he lived, that he was good for the money. A cheque? No, thanks.

'I'd prefer cash,' he repeated, standing behind the candlesticks ranged now on the counter and looking round discontentedly for an appropriate wrapping for them.

Any more argument, and he might go back on the deal. There was a branch of Ramsay's bank on the other side of the square; he'd better get over there.

When he returned with the money, the candlesticks had been parcelled up for him. He took them out to his car and locked them in the boot while Johnson checked the cash, head bent over the table, breaking open the neat packs of fifty-pound notes and counting through each one.

'Right, but only just.' He spoke the cliché with a grin. It was miraculous, the therapeutic effect of a fair-sized quantity of sterling.

It was only then that Ramsay remembered the other burning question. As though the thought had just occurred to him, he said, 'That facsimile really is magnificent, you know. It would be a great treat to compare it with the original. Do you have the time?'

'No, he doesn't.'

It wasn't Johnson's voice but that of his wife, standing framed in the inner doorway, which hit him. She must have come in through the rear door.

'He hasn't the time and neither have I.' Take it or leave it.

Her husband glanced at his wristwatch. 'I do have something urgent to do, as a matter of fact. Perhaps I could leave you with Margaret? She has a set of keys to the safe.' Before either of them could say yea, nay, or wait a moment he had unlocked the street door, ducked out and gone.

'He said he had a certainty for the two o'clock at Kempton.' She spoke as though it was the most ordinary thing in the world for her husband to break off like that and rush across the square to the betting shop. She moved over to the window and watched him through its steel grille as he hurried away with his legs moving busily.

'He'll be worrying about the state of the going, I expect, or the odds. You know what punters are.' She spoke as if she had managed to fit this interest into her world, her scheme of things. Her look defied Ramsay to pull aside the curtains and let bleak daylight into it.

Perhaps I'm reading too much into what I saw, Ramsay mused. On the other hand, if Johnson were in fact a compulsive gambler he wouldn't be the first one to consider throwing himself off the nearest available church tower. He was neurotic and unstable, for sure, and on top of that she'd just declined to produce the reliquary – which wasn't promising. Where was it? For the first time that question sent anxiety pumping through him. Calm down, he told himself. All he had to do was to deploy his charm. He would pretend that he simply hadn't heard her point-blank refusal a few moments earlier.

'I had just been saying to your husband before he left how nice it would be to compare the facsimile with the original, just to see how . . .'

He was interrupted by a young man and his girl knocking on the shop door wanting to see some engagement rings. In a nervy rush of words, Margaret Johnson explained that a meeting was taking place in the shop at the moment. Could they possibly come back in half an hour? While she asked the question as tactfully as she could, it was clear that they felt she had snubbed them. Robbed of their moment, they retreated in the direction of the cheap retail jeweller in the main street.

'You've probably lost a sale. Why didn't you show them something?'

'And have you hanging around in the shop for another half-hour?'

'Thank you.'

'Look, I want to be left alone. Would you please . . .'

The time had come to lay it on the line. 'I'm not leaving, I'm afraid, until I have seen the reliquary with my two eyes.'

Where the hell was it? And, incidentally, where was her husband? Ramsay glanced at his watch. Surely it didn't take this long to place a couple of bets?

'In any case,' he added, 'I want to take it up to London

tomorrow and hand it over to Golver's, now that the copy's finished.'

'Golver's?' Surely she knew the name?

'Golver PLC are handling the sale,' he explained. A new offshoot of the leading refiner of precious and noble metals in the country, an aggressive firm with contacts everywhere, well placed to know which museums and collectors world-wide would be both interested in the reliquary and rich enough to pay for it.

'So . . . may I have the reliquary, please?' he concluded.

She considered for a moment, looking at him without much relish. 'No, not until we have a written apology at the very least.'

So she was determined to make him sweat because of the *Eastern Courant* nonsense although she didn't look the kind of person to be as small-minded as that. Perhaps when Johnson got back he would make her see sense. *If* he got back. Where had he got to? Suppose he'd been bluffing and the thing wasn't in the safe in the workroom at all but on its way to some bent private collector on the Continent? As his father had been good enough to point out, it would be his word against theirs that they'd had it last, a thought which made him feel a heap less secure. Do something, Ramsay. Try to embarrass her into yielding it up.

'I am not leaving this shop until it's in my hands.'

Margaret shrugged elaborately, sat herself down on one of the Regency chairs and waited while he stood with his back against the counter and did the same. Neither of them spoke.

In the silent and almost motionless battle that ensued, the tiniest event became vivid and meaningful. About six minutes after it had started she coughed, covering her mouth with her right hand, and laid it decorously back in her lap.

After what seemed like an hour, he looked at his watch and found the time to be almost eleven twenty-six. How exciting – and still no sign of Johnson. Perhaps they were both behaving like children. All right, if that's what it took. He tried a new ploy.

'The sooner you hand it over, the sooner your husband will be paid.' As soon as he had said it he wasn't really surprised that the remark was ignored. You couldn't call it diplomatic. Gazing at her face, trying to will her to concede defeat, he realised that she was in tears and immediately found himself in retreat, outgunned and outmanoeuvred.

Standing up, he said, 'I shall see you in the morning and collect the reliquary then. Shall we say eight, so that we get an early start? Here in the shop?'

As he passed her on his way to the door, he thought she nodded assent, but he wasn't sure and didn't ask, even though it meant that she would have him on the hook until the morning.

However, later on that day, he was surprised to see her again.

He was in the study showing off the candlesticks to his father, who, as soon as he had seen what they were, had gone to the tall bookcase and taken out his copy of Jackson's *English Goldsmiths and Their Marks*; now he had it open on the desk and was busily looking up the maker's mark. Charles knew the maker's name already but he wasn't going to wreck the old man's evident wish to help him in his chosen métier. Perhaps at last he was managing to swallow the indigestible idea that his only son was an antique dealer.

When the doorbell rang, he was too engrossed in the lists of names of London goldsmiths to be aware of it. Slipping out of the room, Charles walked through the panelled hall, pulled open the front door and found Margaret standing there in the brazen light of the overhead lamp.

'Have you seen Ian? Is he with you?' This time it was her defences which were down and that voice of hers was agitated, tinged with accusation.

'No. Should he be? Come in.'

For once she had taken some trouble over her appearance, he thought without taking much of it in. A sort of linen suit, adventurous plum-coloured stockings and patent leather shoes. Her hair had been brushed till it shone like a golden helmet. Why had she bothered? Obscurely, he felt flattered.

'He hasn't been back since he left the shop.' The words came rattling out. 'I've been everywhere. Then I thought he might have come over here, with some message for you about the reliquary.'

What might that have been? What were telephones for? Did she really mean that she hadn't seen her husband since he had made off towards the betting shop about an hour before noon? Yes, she did.

She was overreacting; what a twitchy couple the Johnsons were. Her husband might simply have remembered an appointment out in the country somewhere and not had time to phone to tell her he would be late home, but . . . he glanced at his watch . . . it was nearly ten, which was stretching it a bit . . . Then a picture came back to him, the picture he had seen when he had first leant over the parapet of the church tower – Johnson's ineffective face looking up at him, saying, 'Get me out of this, can't you?' Ramsay had come across pleasanter images in his time – and pleasanter people, come to that. Margaret Johnson, standing next to him, was one of them – you didn't have to look far – and now the boring man was putting everybody out again.

She was wearing a light perfume, he noticed, one of the sweet and flowery sort. Perhaps it was just the soap she used. Alluring, he thought, before putting the word out of his mind.

'Phone the police.'

It was what they were there for.

'It's too early,' she said. 'They won't take me seriously.'

'Given the circumstances, they will. Anyway, the local lot are not a frantically busy body of men.'

Refusing to allow her to argue with him, he led her to the telephone in the study, where his father looked up with a smile of recognition, then, marking his place, he closed his heavy book, put it under his arm and withdrew with the dog at his heels.

She scarcely seemed to notice, because she was gazing fixedly at the candlesticks gleaming with a subdued brilliance on the desk.

'Where did those come from?' she demanded, as though they both didn't know perfectly well.

He shrugged an apology. 'From your shop.'

'Did you buy them from Ian?'

What did she think? This petty inquisition was getting up his nose.

'No, I helped myself to them while he was in his workroom.'

That made her try to be more diplomatic. 'Do you mind telling me how much you paid for them?'

He did, but presumably she had the right to know, so he told her.

'In cash?'

'Yes, as a matter of fact.'

'Then there's no point at all in phoning the police.' Her voice now sounded as though she were blaming him for something else, which was irritating because he didn't know what it was. She went on, 'He's gone to London. That's where he'll be. He has a friend who lives in Wandsworth – they were students at the Bermondsey School of Crafts together. He'll have gone to his flat or . . . there are other people we both knew; they may have put him up. I must go and find him.'

'It's too late tonight.' Perhaps. 'I have to take the reliquary up to town and hand it over to Golver's soon, so I might as well do it tomorrow. I could pick it up from the shop and give you a lift, if you like.' That car of hers was scarcely up to the journey.

'Thanks, but I think I'd better not, you know.' As though her sensors had touched something they had not expected, she had withdrawn them and curled up into a convoluted mother-of-pearl world of her own.

'Why on earth not?'

The unwelcome telephone rang. It was Molyneux, and there was no escaping him. Yes, the photographs and the description had reached him in the post overnight.

'I hope you don't mind me calling this late. I wanted to catch you before you came down here. Your carpet . . .' He spoke like a solicitor about to break unwelcome news about a will, searching for the words that would cause the least distress.

So, what was wrong with the carpet? Come on, Molyneux.

'Your carpet . . .' He hesitated as if he were looking for something on his desk, the letter, the photographs, to support the verdict that was coming next '. . . was indeed made in the Agra workshops, and it is rather intriguing. You're sure the pile is in good condition?' A hint of suspicion clouded the public school voice.

SOME DARK ANTIQUITIES

'Looks fine to me, although it does need a good clean. I said that in my letter.'

He looked at her face – no, it said, she wasn't going to come with him – he could see the decision hardening in her eyes. He rocked his head in mock impatience as Molyneux went on, 'You did . . . Yes.'

Then the expert came out with it. 'Well, it's a find, a real find, particularly with that royal connection. I liked that. Any link with the Windsors is still good news, you know, even these days. The market's quite bouncy at the moment by the way despite the slump. We did rather nicely with our last sale of fine rugs and carpets.'

'How much ought it to make?'

'Oh, five or six thousand, I should think. In that region.' The voice was careless but that was a pretence. Molyneux was on solid ground now – Agra carpets were all the go.

Ramsay looked uneasily towards her as she affected not to be listening.

'Excellent,' he said uncomfortably.

There was a small silence at the other end of the line. 'I should've thought you would be pleased.'

'Yes, of course. Delighted.'

How much exactly had she realised from the sale of that carpet in Harry's saleroom? He did a quick sum in his head – about a hundred and ten pounds net of commission, and it wasn't a lot. His gaze shifted guiltily towards the candlesticks. In a way he had got them for nothing – that's what it amounted to. The trouble with me is that I'm too scrupulous, he thought as he caught her eye and tried out a smile on her.

When he replaced the receiver, she agreed to let him give her a lift to London, much to his surprise. Needs must where the devil drove. Something like that, he guessed. She would take the train back.

He had fixed an early time for their meeting so that he would be able to find a parking space close to the shop. She was standing out in the street, fresh from overnight rain, as still as a statue beside the white-painted Georgian front with wide-paned windows. The prosperity of that façade might be deceptive but she was genuine enough – there was no sign of her husband.

Welcoming Ramsay with the merest wave of hand, she bent down to unlock the door, beckoning him to follow her. Once inside, the first thing she did was to find a card and a felt pen and write out a neat notice to say that the shop was closed until the end of the week because of unforeseen circumstances. With deliberation she fixed it to the window, while he allowed her to keep him waiting, observing how her straight back tapered elegantly to the waist. Why the delay? Was she simply aiming to punish him a little more or was she steeling herself to make an inevitable confession about the casket and the safe? How, inexplicably, the former was no longer inside the latter because her husband had filched it. That would account for her odd behaviour at Bressemer the night before. Johnson had taken it weeks ago and hidden it somewhere in London. That was why he had disappeared.

She turned round to face him with a challenge in her face. 'Now, I think you asked to see the Burnill reliquary, didn't you?'

Yes. She'd got it in one.

She looked down at the bunch of keys in her hand with a deliberation which might have been meant to tease him or might equally well have been part of a comedy she was playing out to its final moment, before its credibility collapsed and the whole scene slipped out of her control. Looking at him sidelong, she selected a key between her finger and thumb and pointed its business end at him like a blunt little weapon. Then she went briskly off, hips swinging, to the workroom and reappeared in slow time holding the Burnill reliquary reverently in front of her, as though she were a newly ordained woman priest in prudent charge of the Host.

It was an oblong silver-gilt coffer raised on legs resembling those of a lion; the long sides were divided into panels each surrounded by a border decorated in bright enamels and encrusted with cabochon gems. Its most important and astonishing feature was the presence in the centre of the panel on each of its long sides of a huge polished but irregular sapphire. The naivety of the mediaeval workmanship, the way the ornament was moulded and its lack of symmetry gave the casket a force and authority which it was impossible to deny.

Putting it down on the top of the showcase, she became suddenly matter of fact. 'There you are.'

There indeed he was. Without question it was the authentic article. Feeling released from anxiety and at the same time slightly foolish, he made a show of inspecting it for damage. There was none.

Well, that was all right. Nothing the matter with that, he acknowledged, and was grateful that she had the grace not to rub salt into the wound.

She sat next to him in his unfamiliar car, puzzling over its perfectly normal seatbelt.

'How does this thing work?' She put out a hand to fend off

his attempt at assistance, murmuring, 'No, I can manage, thank you.'

He persisted, however, and then, absolutely without meaning to, found that he had pressed the palm of his hand against her waist, feeling warmth and a frontier of silky underclothing, marked by thin elastic, beneath it. That small accident aroused him – which was not appropriate so soon after breakfast – and at the same time transformed her in his eyes. It brought it home to him that she was not really a remote votaress in a golden casque but a woman of flesh and blood who smelt faintly of morning toothpaste and put up with a bad time once a month, who enjoyed the feminine routines – long baths, reorganising cupboards in her kitchen, leafing through magazines at night beside that odd man Johnson in bed. Sure, those details were all supposition, but that was the general idea.

Taking the pierced tongue of stainless steel, he drove it down into its socket, thus: *click*.

'Thank you so much.'

That voice of hers transmuted the banal words into a song. Safely a priestess again, she sat back as he let in the clutch and stalled the big car's engine. Once he had dealt with that, he dared to ask, 'Why on earth did you give that carpet to Harry Oakes to sell? How much did you think he'd get for it?'

She shrugged. 'I needed the money. Spot cash, quickly.'

A hundred and ten pounds? She was pushed for a sum like that? The Johnson finances must have been precarious. When they came to a red light, he took the opportunity to look across and offer her a smile of encouragement; certainly she had his vote. Hidden under what was left of her early hopes and shared, childless, life which had succeeded them there must have been – beneath all that – a sense that life had not kept its promise to her. While her husband was undoubtedly a talented man, she must have learnt by now that talent was not all that it took. By no means all.

'Would you do something for me?' he essayed.

'It depends.'

'Let me have a new start. Clear your mind of everything against me, all the complaints that have been cluttering it up since you first read Maxton's article. Go back to the status quo before then.'

After a moment's consideration she agreed to put him on parole, which was an advance. The next step forward was to decide what should be done about the Agra carpet.

His upbringing, his scruples, the motto on the emblazoned family tree hanging dustily on the wall of the study at Bressemer forbade him to take advantage of those private citizens who didn't have his experience and expertise. The sort of people who queued with their paper bags for the *Antiques Roadshow*. On the other hand not only was she a dealer but he had bought the carpet at auction, at arm's length. According to his code, that meant he was relieved of all further moral obligation. One had to draw a line somewhere, and that was where he drew it.

Except that the carpet was worth what it was worth, and all that the troubled woman sitting next to him had got for it was a hundred and thirty pounds less fifteen per cent.

Except that she had an inadequate husband and had just been through a hard time with him. This case was different, an obvious exception to his normal rules of engagement. So?

So, would she accept half the net proceeds of the sale of the carpet when it was auctioned by Crowther's in London? Having put the offer into words, he felt better.

'Why ought I to?'

'Why not?'

'That doesn't answer my question,' she said.

Which meant that he ought to be honest with her, up to a point. 'To salve my conscience and relieve the frustration that you understandably feel.'

Staring at the windscreen, she thought for a moment.

'No. It's a generous thought, but I can't.'

He glanced at her irritably. Was she trying to prove herself as awkward as her husband? Why couldn't she just accept the offer gracefully and get on with her life?

Because it would compromise her, because she was too much in his debt already, because . . . And she still hadn't fully answered his question.

Unwilling to give up, he all but pleaded with her and found her adamant.

'Mr Ramsay.'

'Charles,' he suggested.

'Mr Ramsay, how would I explain the transaction to my husband?'

How old-fashioned could one get? Very well, he resolved, he would try again later on.

She gave him a fastidious smile.

'Thanks for the thought, but I'd better not. In any case, it won't make any difference to things.'

The sombre note in her voice prompted him to put a hand out towards her, but he changed his mind halfway through and put it back on the driving wheel where it belonged.

Looking away from him, pretending to study the yellow fields on her left she began to speak in a newly intimate tone, as if she were a relative who was confiding in him – a sister, say – instead of a recent adversary. Although she was inhibited at first, her story soon flowed out, gathering momentum because it had been held back for so long.

Her husband had been an occasional punter, the sort who liked a ten-pound flutter on the National, nothing more disturbing than that, until a weekend about three years earlier when a Newmarket trainer, after a successful day, had bought an extravagant piece of jewellery in the shop and then, feeling expansive afterwards, had given Johnson a tip on a little fancied horse which he said would not be allowed to lose. On an impulse, Johnson had backed it much more heavily than usual and to his delight the animal had come in, as predicted, well ahead of the rest of the field, winning him thirteen hundred pounds in the process. Much encouraged, he had pestered the man for another tip. When eventually it came, he had put all his winnings on it and a great deal more besides, in the hope of making a real coup, something which would give them a worthwhile nest-egg, shift them into a higher league financially. He had lost.

Some commentators thought it was the going, some a change of jockey, but he'd lost just the same – all that money. There had been recriminations, of course; she had blamed him and he had blamed the trainer. Having antagonised him, he was on his own now; driven by the guilt he felt towards her and a manic faith in himself, he had been determined to get that money back.

'It was then that he started to go up to London more often. He said it was to buy stock for the shop, but that wasn't true. He'd joined a gaming club . . . . several. He was into roulette and baccarat. Once he lost a month's profit in an hour. That was what he told me when he had to own up because he couldn't hide the losses any longer. He swore to me that he could recoup them.'

'How?'

'By counting cards at blackjack.'

Ramsay pulled a face. 'And . . .?'

'He had no self-discipline. It needs a great deal of practice, and he didn't make the effort. The dealers were too fast for him – that's what he said.'

'Couldn't you have done something to stop him?'

'There wasn't a hope. He went back to roulette. By that time he was addicted, completely, quite unable to pull out while he was ahead, whatever I said or did. He just went on playing until he'd lost all his available cash. Then, somehow, somewhere, he laid his hands on some more.'

Because he had plundered their savings and the business's overdraft at the bank to its limit, they were operating now from hand to mouth, she said, at the very edge, with the bank ready to pounce and their suppliers badgering them continuously for payment. Having given up trying to talk her husband out of his obsession long ago, she was waiting fatalistically for the bank to put in a receiver.

She pushed away the sympathy he offered, becoming distant again. She had a lot going for her, charm and intelligence, plenty of that, but where was her common sense? Since Johnson wouldn't cut his losses, she should have cut hers and left him. That was the only way for her to survive – didn't she see that?

What was she thinking of as she watched the traffic in the other lane rushing towards them? Nemesis?

'There's one thing you must understand.'

'Yes? What's that?'

'I'm not available,' she said.

He concentrated his gaze on the road. No, she conceded presently, she didn't mind if he put the radio on.

SOME DARK ANTIQUITIES

The late rush-hour traffic slowed down their progress into London. The saving grace of Golver's set-up not far from Shaftesbury Avenue was that it had its own underground car park. Lowering the window on his side, he handed their letter to the sedentary security guard, who gave it back to him like a robot before punching the button which activated the sliding door of blue-painted sheet steel to let them through into the echoing space below.

A gentleman to his finger-ends – no doubt in his own mind about that – Sir Anthony Andover stood up instantly when he saw her enter his spacious room and was careful to show no surprise. Because Golver's building was situated where it was, he didn't have much of a view from its large sound-proof windows, which was why he had brought up from the country a pair of eighteenth-century landscapes, unsigned but very decently painted, to hang on the wall opposite his outsize partner's desk – outsize like Sir Anthony, although in his case superb tailoring had diminished his apparent volume. A man who took good care of himself, he was blessed with a pink complexion, a well-barbered head embellished with tight iron-grey curls and all the self-esteem which an easy progression through life had given him.

His fellow directors didn't share his confidence in his abilities, but the problem facing them was that he had inherited a large block of Golver's shares and they couldn't ease him off the board. His enthusiasm for dealing in precious objects had been a godsend. It kept him quiet while they got on with making money out of the company's real business – the international trade in precious and noble metals.

'Ramsay, do come in. Have you brought it with you?' he

asked in a voice which was used to issuing orders.

Nodding, Ramsay set down the steel-lined box containing the reliquary, and introduced Margaret – the wife of the talented craftsman who had made the replica of it for them, he explained. With a worldly look in his pale blue eyes Sir Anthony took all that in, flattered her a little, fussed over her, ordered coffee.

Lifting the reliquary out of its case, Ramsay unwrapped its covering and set it down on the gilded darkened leather top of Andover's desk. After he had expatiated enough on it, Sir Anthony rang for underlings to deal with the formalities involved in handing it into his company's safe-keeping.

Meanwhile, he made silky conversation. As a specialist, he said, Mrs Johnson could not fail to be interested in an exhibition of early jewellery which he had put together to send out on tour to the provinces – part of a PR exercise for Golver's. As a kind of dress-rehearsal it had been set up in the reception area on the ground floor.

'Very exciting. You must see it before you go.'

She was anxious to break away and start the search for her husband. She ventured an excuse and had it bulldozed by Sir Anthony.

'No, my dear,' he said archly. 'You are not allowed to leave the premises until you have seen my little show. Unique pieces every one, borrowed from all over the place. My powers of persuasion are legendary.'

His laugh boomed implacably around the room; in his experience most women needed a bit of jollying along. He led the way to the lift.

When she reached the ground floor and saw what was on offer, her professional instincts swamped her annoyance and she allowed the display to take her over. Being a man who liked to be proved right, Sir Anthony watched her succumb with an indulgent smile.

'A word with you,' he muttered to Ramsay, grasping him alarmingly by the elbow and steering him out of earshot to a low-slung stainless steel and brown hide seat beside the massive glass window engraved with Golver's logo – a stylised design of crowns and sceptres.

Leaning forward, he confided, 'There is a candidate . . . I think it's not too early to tell you that we have wind of a potential buyer.'

That was a relief.

'Fine. Anyone I know?'

Andover made a serious face. 'I'm not at liberty to say. They insist that their identity is not revealed, and of course we have to respect that.'

He made it sound as though such discretion was a unique feature of Golver's service.

Ramsay drove straight through that. 'However that may be, I'm sure my trustees will want to know whom they are dealing with. What am I to tell them?'

Sir Anthony pretended he hadn't heard that. 'I'm meeting their man shortly,' he said. 'We're having a shooting party at the company's place north of the border and I've asked him up for the weekend.'

'And I suppose you can't tell me who he is, either?'

'I'd rather not,' said Sir Anthony, suppressing a frisson of displeasure. Wild horses wouldn't have dragged the name out of him, he assured himself.

'Shall we join your lady friend?'

She was standing motionless in front of a glass case that contained an exquisitely wrought silver myrtle wreath laid on a wide block of transparent plastic which glowed with light. A small card said:

> GREECE
> Silver myrtle wreath taken from a tomb. 5th or 4th century BC.
> A wreath of myrtle was said to dispel the fumes of wine, while a wreath of roses had a cooling effect and was a remedy against headaches.
> Lent by the National Museum of Antiquities

Andover's fine baritone voice bore down on her. 'Isn't it a splendid piece? They asked me to authenticate it, you know, and I was only too pleased to be able to do so. Now,' he said, suddenly conspiratorial, 'shall I give you a treat? Would you like to hold it for a moment?'

When she nodded, he summoned a minion with a great fuss and had the case unlocked. Holding his breath, he removed the wreath from its perch and placed it on her outstretched palms.

'You are holding twenty-five centuries in your hands,' he said portentously, when another mischievous idea struck him.

'Put it on,' he said.

'I daren't! Anyway, I might look silly.'

'Go on,' he urged. 'We won't tell the owner.'

Standing upright, she lifted it and placed it on her head, and then without daring to look down she groped in her handbag for a mirror so that she could see herself with her golden helmet of hair surmounted by it, looking more like a priestess than ever, more unapproachable.

* * *

SOME DARK ANTIQUITIES

It was a surprise when she agreed to go back to his flat, but probably it was merely because she needed a London base for this search operation of hers and had no alternative. Refusing to let Ramsay buy her lunch, she did accept a sandwich and a glass of fruit juice when they got back.

Now, seated at his desk in the captain's chair which he was so fond of, she glanced at the small address book in front of her and punched out another number on the handset. 'Hullo, is that Walter? Margaret Johnson here . . . Yes, Johnson . . . You know . . . Is Ian with you?'

He won't be, he decided, as deftly he cleared her used plate and glass and made for the kitchen.

After she had run through all the possibilities, she still hadn't had any luck. Only then did she look to him, sitting patiently behind her for advice.

'Time to try the casinos,' he said, reaching for the directory, finding the page, and handing the list of gaming clubs to her. 'Which of them does he belong to?'

Her finger ran down the column, her lips speaking the glitzy come-on names silently. No . . . no . . . not that . . . But – the finger stopped – possibly that one.

She phoned the place. They wouldn't confirm, nor would they deny, that her husband was a member, let alone whether he was inside at the tables.

When she rang the next one, she was put through to a floor manager whose tone suggested that the idea that he would betray any husband patronising his gaming room was richly comic. Gentlemen's privacy should be respected, it insinuated in her ear. They should be allowed to pursue their pleasures in their own masculine way.

Taking the receiver from her, Ramsay searched the pages for

the name of the PLC that controlled the club. There had to be a better way than this – a way of giving this guy a grievous time if nothing else.

Chapter Six

'There,' exclaimed Ethelred Lewis, making a slow-motion pirouette in the centre of the floor of the shop, the multicoloured stones of the ring which he wore on his little finger flashing in the overhead light. 'What do you think of *that*?'

'Stunning,' responded Julia, since that was what he wanted to hear. Ethelred gave himself another pat on the back; self-congratulation was always an enjoyable thing. It had been a financial coup, getting the girl's aristocratic mother to pay a premium so that she could learn the antiques business – at least the respectable end of it. On top of that, the mother *knew* people. A portion of the cheque had been spent on this outfit, business being less than brisk in Brighton just now what with this dreary recession and so forth. All that was going to change, he decided, after the weekend in front of him.

Head on one side, he studied his reflection in the conveniently placed cheval mirror – 1830, more or less. That was one of the joys of running an antique shop: you never knew when items of stock would come in useful. There was that time . . . He dragged himself back to the present. The trousers now. No, not trousers, nor plus fours, really. Knickerbockers, his tailor called them. Umm. And the jacket with those *huge* pleated pockets for dead rabbits and so on, and the cloth belt. He supposed it was right, but he did look rather as if he had stepped out of the *Tailor and Cutter* for 1905 – he giggled inside. Should he have chosen a quieter colour? Mustard was so ruthless . . . Still, there was no turning back now; all the money was spent and that was that.

'You'll need a gun,' Julia pointed out, being a country person. He could scarcely go on a shooting weekend without one – or perhaps he could.

A gun? What an unhelpful girl she was. On the other hand she was a sort of paying guest, something like that, and her mother really was truly formidable. In his mind he pronounced the last word in the French manner, which made him feel quite gay and cosmopolitan.

'I can't run to a shotgun, dear. I don't suppose they hire them out?' he asked – Julia knew all about such things. Smothering a grimace, she shook her head. He made his considering face. 'Very well, I shall borrow one from somebody.'

As soon as she opened her mouth to speak again she knew it was no good, that he wasn't going to listen, so she closed it.

'The hat,' he demanded, and put it on. Half a size larger, and it would have been perfection.

Three days later, having left her in charge with a long list of things to do, he was transported by the railway to a world of forests and moors and white-painted farmhouses, which wasn't like Brighton at all – altogether less populated, and it hadn't stopped raining since he had stepped off that tedious little train into the kingdom of Scotland. Yes. Still, it was all in a good cause, wasn't it? – and this country house hotel, The Cock Pheasant, was very *sympathique* and quaint. Warm, too, thank goodness. He raised his eyebrows at the young barman, noting the breadth of his shoulders, and pushed his empty glass towards him with a nod. The barman picked it up to refill it, semaphoring with those same shoulders in reply. Yes, it was all right here.

There was more to it than that because of Ethelred's background, or lack of one. He came from what, he confessed to his intimates, had been a no-parent family and had spent most of his early years in terrible children's homes ending up with foster parents who had taken him in only for the money and had turfed him out as soon as his sexual preferences had become clear. At the age of fifteen he had found himself in London at last, where he had started out with a stall in the Portobello Road selling – oh, bits and pieces – and gone on from there. He'd had his ups and downs, of course, and he was no more finicky in his business methods than the next man, but he'd survived and still managed to keep his nose out of the water, breathing, even these days. So for him this shooting weekend was a kind of fulfilment. This was where he belonged, rubbing shoulders with the landed interest, those for whom a children's home was unimaginable, like Limbo.

Looking round him at the room full of shooters, all Golver people and their guests in their hunting gear with wet dogs wandering about searching for titbits, he felt even better. The smell of the place was so very *right*, he thought: damp tweed, whisky and expensive tobacco. It was a good room, eighteenth century certainly, and it hadn't been ruined by an over-enthusiastic landlord – it was spacious, and the windows were original; he approved of that. Pushing away the large head of an inquisitive dog which was nosing at the thick woollen stockings he had bought on Julia's say-so, he took a generous bite out of his sandwich, munched, and ruminated.

Sir Anthony had proposed they meet for a chat over a dram

after the shoot. That was a promising thought, a moving forward. For a moment the crowd in front of him parted and he saw his host standing by the chimneypiece on the opposite side of the room. They exchanged glances, and with a sudden sense of power Ethelred felt sure that he knew exactly what the other man was thinking.

Sir Anthony Andover looked down at his well-cut plus fours with contentment; he always enjoyed the shooting weekend, having taken part in every single one since he had become a director of Golver's – an enviable record. They did wonders for the company's commercial relations all round but particularly within the Community, because there was nothing much left to shoot in Germany and those Latins shot everything, of course; starlings and I don't know what – he shuddered inwardly – and they all dressed like Lewis over there. The sight of Ethelred brought him back to earth, reminding him that he had a rather tricky interview with him later on. No point in anticipating that; he would deal with the thing when he got to it. Didn't want to let it spoil the afternoon's shooting.

I trust he's taking care of that gun I lent him, he thought, as though it mattered. It was only a mass-produced Continental affair he kept for his guests, nothing like the equal of his own pair of Holland and Hollands, sidelock ejectors – beautifully balanced guns.

Sir Anthony plucked his gold half-hunter from his waistcoat pocket and glanced down at its elegant dial, then out of the window. The vehicles were back – standing in a tidy row on the expanse of gravel, each driver in his seat under cover because it was raining.

He clapped his hands with a flat bang like a gunshot, and

expectant faces turned towards him.

'Well, gentlemen, I see the transport's back, so drink up. I suggest we make a start in five minutes.' He cast a knowing eye up at the foliage of the big oak trees outside. 'The good news is that the wind has dropped; the bad news is that it's still raining. That's Scotland for you!'

One or two members of his staff laughed as if this time he actually had made a joke. Ethelred went out into the stone-flagged passage to look for his hat.

'Stand next to me in the line this time,' said Sir Anthony generously. 'I might be able to give you a hint or two.'

For the next few minutes he bustled about organising the guns; each of them was allocated his position in the line, his dog beside him. Then he turned his attention to the men whose dogs would pick up the 'runners' – the winged birds – and those which fell behind the line of guns, making sure that the helpers stood well back from them. He had always been a stickler for safety – it did his image no harm.

His gaze swept down the waiting line of guns and to either side of the killing ground, then, satisfied, he gave the signal to the beaters and the drive began. For a moment they waited expectantly. The black Labrador at his heels gave an eager whimper . . .

And his first bird was a beauty, a cock pheasant flying high and fast straight towards and above him: this will make up for all the frustrations of the day, he promised himself. Feeling all-powerful, master of life and death, he swung his gun first up to his shoulder, the walnut stock nestling into his cheek, the engraved steel shining dully in the grey afternoon light; then he brought the barrels skywards, sighting along them. The movement had all the grace and flow of a classic cricket stroke – a leg glance or a cover drive.

His finger tightened on the trigger, but a microsecond before he could fire, bang! The pheasant crumpled in the air and slid down to fall fifteen yards from his feet. He hadn't fired. What had happened? The sound had come from his right. That bloody dealer had shot his bird!

He turned, the back of his neck flushing, red rage boiling up inside him, as powerfully as steam behind the pistons of a pre-war locomotive.

Lewis was standing there holding his gun in one hand. It wobbled as he poked it in the direction of the dead pheasant. 'Not bad, eh?' he said with modest pride. 'Just like falling off a log, shooting, once you've got the hang of it.' He grinned with relief and satisfaction. Julia would be proud of him.

A small vein throbbed in Sir Anthony's temple. It was touch and go for a moment, then with an effort he remembered what he had to do after the day's shooting was over. The fellow represented a client, and later on he had to break a certain piece of news to him.

'Good shot, sir. You can teach us experienced guns a thing or two,' he called into the wind, his well-known laugh resounding down the line of damp shooters; that was as much restraint as he could manage. The brim of his hat flung icy raindrops across his face as he turned quickly to look to his front. In the next sixty seconds he was bloody well going to shoot something, even if it was only a beater.

By the time the shoot was over and they were back in the hotel bar, Sir Anthony had recovered his sang-froid. After they had each collected a generous measure of single malt from the nubile barman who with a grin contrived to give Ethelred a little extra, he led his guest to a secluded corner in the smoking-room.

Ethelred declined a cigar and watched his host thoughtfully piercing his. Now was the time to get him on the defensive.

'You brought the reliquary with you, of course?'

Having lit the Havana, Sir Anthony checked that the business end was glowing to his satisfaction.

'No,' he said.

'No?' Ethelred did not raise his voice, but did raise an eyebrow which said: How am I expected to make an offer for this object if I'm not given a chance to look it over?

Sir Anthony looked moodily out of the window at the heavy clouds moving across the darkening sky. The rain hadn't stopped; it thrashed against the window panes.

'No, I haven't brought it with me. Fact is, there's been a slight cock-up.' Own up and get it over – always the best thing.

As if he had all the time in the world, Ethelred waited to hear more.

His host went off at a tangent. 'When we are given something to sell at Golver's, we carry out certain checks as a matter of routine, you understand.'

So I should hope, thought Ethelred, but he replied with gravity, 'I would expect nothing less.'

Sir Anthony took a sip of his whisky and set it down. He shifted slightly in his chair.

'The thing is, there's something rather odd about the reliquary that we can't explain. A puzzle. Something which your principal will have to be told.'

Ethelred offered an understanding smile. The world of antiquities was such a minefield, wasn't it? Then he pounced. 'What's wrong with it?' he demanded.

Sir Anthony winced. 'The sapphires. You remember the big sapphires, one on each side of it?'

'Yes.'

'Well . . . Fact is . . . They're synthetic.'

'That's impossible!'

'I can assure you that that is the case,' answered Sir Anthony with dignity. 'The man we use is adamant, and he's got over twenty years of experience. There can be no mistake. The distribution of the colour within the stones is much too regular, he says, for them to be the real thing. The other giveaway is the shape. The original stones would have been, you know, rough and ready, not cut but just polished *en cabochon* with a sandstone wheel or something of the kind. The ones in the casket now are clearly symmetrical stones which have just been ground down to make them look like that.'

No, he had no idea when the substitution had been made. It could have been done anytime, years before, and the original stones could be anywhere. What was he going to do? Advise the vendor's agent. Whose name was? Charles Ramsay. That was a name Ethelred knew very well.

Sir Anthony's hand rested on the table beside him, his forefinger tapping the polished surface unconsciously in the pause that followed.

'What view do you think your people will take of this?' he asked at last.

'What do you think? I'll speak to them, of course, but would you be much interested in a mediaeval reliquary with a couple of synthetic sapphires attached to it? Perhaps they'd be prepared to take it – perhaps – at some kind of a price . . .' He pursed his lips, betraying his disappointment and avoiding any kind of commitment. He undertook to ask them. After that, he kept his feelings to himself and to Sir Anthony's relief there were no reproaches. Obviously the fellow wasn't going to allow this setback to get in the way of his relationship with Golver PLC. For a few minutes the two of them batted possible solutions to the problem listlessly across the table until Ethelred dreamed up an excuse to leave. He would be in touch, he said.

Watching him go, Sir Anthony relaxed – that hadn't gone too badly, had it? Take the bull by the horns – always the best thing in the end.

Chapter Seven

There was rarely any mail for Frank Becket on the big black table in the hallway in any case, and now that he had a reason for actually expecting something it made the waiting more difficult to take. As he walked along the scarlet and dark blue Turkey carpet towards the table, he kept his eyes averted from it as though he were a child following a ritual meant somehow to increase the chance of discovering a letter there for him. His gaze swept up and focused on the glossy surface. It was empty.

Nothing, again nothing. Why was there no reply yet? These days the Post Office delivered letters overnight; that was what they said they did, wasn't it? He had handed that letter of his to Jean, the nurse, to post on a Thursday, so at the latest it should have reached Ramsay by the weekend. The man hadn't struck Frank Becket as the sort who neglected his correspondence. Now it was more than two Thursdays later and still there was no word from him. He sighed inwardly because he would have to tackle Jean again – he went off in search of her.

She wasn't in the Quiet Room or the office. In the Television Room, on his own, watching a long-ago musical starring Betty Grable at ten-thirty in the morning sat Smythe, who looked up with guilt in his face, guilt which had nothing to do with the TV or the image on its screen. No, there was a smell of tobacco smoke in the air, and smoking was forbidden in there, everybody knew that. Frank was about to tease him by pretending that Dorothy was on the warpath when he noticed that the other man's eyes looked wetter, more rheumy than usual.

'Even Winston Churchill gave way to tears sometimes,' Frank wanted to say, or 'I remember the war, too, old son. I was in uniform, too.' But the words wouldn't get as far as his lips even though he and the man sitting there with the stub of a glowing cigarette hidden in his palm had much in common. The wartime song 'The White Cliffs of Dover' slipped into Frank's mind, but the bluebirds had come and gone an age ago and had left both of them lying stranded on the beach like abandoned weapons of war – which was just about what they had been. The difficulty with Smythe was that you couldn't merely sympathise with him for a few minutes and pass on – you could tell from the look in those eyes that it would be all or nothing with him.

'. . . Tomorrow, just you wait and see.'

These days, Frank Becket was running short of tomorrows and had none to waste on Smythe, couldn't afford to let him into his life – so all he said was, 'Have you seen Jean at all?'

Smythe shook his head impatiently and went back to watching the technicolour fragment of his past unrolling in front of him on the small screen, anxious not to miss another frame of it. For these few moments he had escaped.

Frank found the nurse coming up the stairs with a medical-looking tray in her hands – some unfortunate was due for a jab. He stood in front of her on the landing.

'I wonder, can you remember where you posted that letter of mine?'

The hypodermic tinkled tetchily in the bowl on her tray as she made to move past him.

'Mr Becket, please, not just now. I'm busy, you can see.'

The voice was not meant to humour him, and he saw her gaze darting here and there, trying to sidestep his. It ended ceilingwards to give her face an expression of saintly patience overtried.

'You did post it, though, didn't you?'

She exhaled a single lengthy sigh and nodded emphatically, her eyes looking past his shoulder.

'I said yes. Right? Now may I get on?' She gave him a smile that was no smile as he stepped aside to allow this barefaced liar in her starchy white uniform to pass him by. At least she had made up his mind for him.

'I'm going out for a bit,' he called after her. 'I may be late back.'

'Sign the book,' she said, 'and don't forget this time, Mr Becket will you?' Once it had slipped his memory and there had been a hue and cry which they never allowed him to forget. At the Sayonara they didn't like their inmates getting out.

Putting on his raincoat, he carried out his customary check to make sure nothing essential had been left behind. The key word he used was SWAMP – Spectacles, Wallet, Attaché case, Money, Pen. Leaving out the C of attaché case was cheating, really, but who could get his lips round SWACMP?

He wasn't in the habit of venturing out much because he found it a strain. Probably he lacked the energy – a little more seemed to drain out of him each day. It was difficult to believe that when he was a boy there had been a surplus bubbling up inside him like a spring, forcing him to sprint, hop or play football for hours, keeping him at it. Now it was like having a weight shackled to your feet. No, not that exactly, more like a lassitude. You could do it if you really set your mind to it, but it took a hell of a lot longer. That was why he didn't go out much.

'Out' used him up, 'out' was dusty and noisy, so generally he simply made for Festubert Park where there were trees and seats and he could read his paper paragraph by paragraph in peace and quiet in the open air. Perhaps it meant that he had become whatever they called it . . . institutionalised. It was partly this bloody weariness that had done it to him. Today, though, whether he liked it or not, he had to go further afield, out into Queen Street where all the frenzy was, uncaring mothers pushing baby buggies at him as though he wasn't there, young men with aggressive eyes . . .

He moved along the pavement until he came to the traffic lights – which were in his favour – and looked about him like a cat checking for enemies before making a jump. Then, too late, he began to cross the road in front of a heavy lorry, the pine green cover along its huge side neatly buckled down, its diesel engine thundering as if with pent-up rage. Although when he was halfway across the road the lights changed, he didn't realise it until prankishly the driver revved his engine with a roar which sent Frank into a fluster; he scuttled across to the pedestrian refuge in the middle of the road, releasing the torrent of traffic as though he had lifted a sluice-gate. Having amused himself, his tormentor swept past him as though Frank no longer existed.

Safely across, he made himself calm down, rest for a moment and think: the first thing he had to do was to find a photocopier.

In the printing shop, the pert girl behind the counter watched him taking the bundle of manuscript pages out of his briefcase. The handwriting was clear, easy to read.

'Looks interesting. Did you write it, dear?' Without thinking, she had raised her voice.

'Me? Oh no . . . and I only need copies of the first three

SOME DARK ANTIQUITIES

pages,' Frank instructed her anxiously.

'Right you are. One copy of each A4 double-sided?' Whatever did that mean? Hoping for the best, he grunted, and watched the machine blink its green light and slide out his copies one after the other. Carefully he counted out the forty-five pence into her ready little palm.

One or two shops in Queen Street had closed down since he had last been there. He wandered along, enjoying the window displays of the survivors, which to him, an expatriate, were both novel and exotic. If only he had the money, he could own a camcorder? a palmcorder? a mini hi-fi with compact disc? a compact midi hi-fi? The windowful of baffling options still there to be grasped in the Final Week of Sale belonged to a different civilisation far ahead of the Sayonara.

That name reminded him that he was hungry and it made him look guiltily at his watch. He was too late for lunch, served at one o'clock sharp, which meant that he would have to eat out, here in this shopping precinct. A strange territory – this outing of his was turning into an expedition.

He searched about with purposeful eyes – the first place was far too noisy, the second had hard plastic bucket chairs. Then Frank Becket, the explorer, an old man with a leather attaché case sporting the golden initials STB, found the sort of café he had been used to when he had been truly alive, one with waitresses who didn't hurry you, who stood patiently by while you made up your mind.

It was after the meal, when he realised that he had to find somewhere to write his letter, that it came home to him that the decision couldn't be postponed any longer. Was it to be the Quiet Room, or was there another solution? He stood there, halfway down Queen Street, feeling force of habit, a fear of isolation perhaps pulling him back towards the Sayonara, while at the back of his mind there lay an elusive idea, more attractive somehow, which he didn't quite dare to formulate yet.

He allowed himself to drift down the street as though on the tide, scarcely conscious of where he was, allowing chance to carry him, feeling the power of the Sayonara diminishing as he went, the new idea becoming more coherent and brighter. As he wandered along, the fascias bearing important retail names gradually gave way to humbler shops where they sold petfoods or cast-offs for charity. Then he reached a terrace of dwelling houses, the one in the centre bearing under its eaves the date AD 1906 deeply carved in brick.

He looked up at it. The black and white painted sign beside the front door said B & B, and beneath that hung the temporary invitation: VACANCIES. The words were everyday enough, but to him they were a revelation – their message intoxicating. His idea was clear at last. Simple. He rang the bell.

The woman who answered it scrutinised him as he told her that his name was Becket. Could she give him a room for a couple of days?

An elderly man who looked honest and harmless – she decided not to demand a deposit,

'I'll show you.'

Time enough to get himself a toothbrush, pyjamas, later that afternoon. He wanted to deal with his letter first – it had priority.

There was a double bed with a green candlewick bedspread, very restful, and his own television set – no Smythe to dispute which channel they should watch. A bathroom of his own. I'll need to go and see the bank manager tomorrow and fix up a financial accommodation, he thought. When his landlady had gone, he sat down at the table and took out the writing pad and packet of ballpoints he had bought. Lastly, he extracted the photocopies and checked them, front and back. The silly girl had got it wrong; she had copied both sides.

Lifting his spectacles up to his forehead and bringing his face close to get a better view, he saw that on the back of the first of them, in old-fashioned print, with not every letter properly registered, was typed: 'On the other hand, an examination of Crusading castles in Syria itself, and a comparison of them with contemporary castles in France, appears to lead to conclusions wholly different. It is obvious that in the early state of the Latin Kingdom, the period of the private feudatories . . .' Feudatories?

Beside the first sentence someone had written faintly 'my words', probably in pencil, on the original, and a little further down the page, 'A little too abrupt a way of putting it'. The handwriting was the same as that of the manuscript on the other side of the sheet, but less mature, almost the writing of a schoolboy.

It looked like an extract from an academic article or thesis of some kind. Since it might be a clue to the identity of the author, he might as well let Ramsay have the photocopies just as they were. His hand trembled as a wave of impatience swept over him – to know what he would make of them. It was important.

He didn't pluck up the courage to ring them at the Sayonara until much later that evening. When he did, he got the duty housekeeper, who at least made an effort to keep the exasperation out of her voice.

'Where are you, Mr Becket? We'll send a car for you.'

A car. They were indeed anxious to recapture him.

For a moment he fantasised. A low-slung black car would

scream to a halt outside the boarding house. He would be bundled into it by men in long dark leather coats and the door slammed shut on him. It would scream away from the pavement to rush him back to the Sayonara, where he would never be allowed out again as long as he lived, however long or short that might be.

Pushing that thought from him, he interrupted her. 'Don't bother. I'm perfectly all right. I'll ring tomorrow.' As he put the receiver down, he came to accept that things had changed for good.

When he had finished his letter to Charles Ramsay, he lay on the bed with a cup of strong tea beside him watching TV, control in hand, luxuriously switching from channel to channel and back again just as the fancy took him. Freedom of choice – that was what it was all about. No, not that alone. This was utter freedom, the apple that had been waiting so long for him to pluck up the courage to pick it, and it tasted sweet – as sweet as honey.

'. . . But you were in charge of it at the time. That cannot be gainsaid,' the Reverend Oscar Stanfield concluded, his glance drifting round the chilly splendour of Ernest Ramsay's drawing-room at Bressemer, censuring everything it saw and ending up fixed resentfully on a large Chinese Imari vase and cover, all cobalt scarlet and gold, standing on a low table beside the carved fireplace of white marble. The price of that vase today at auction in London would have fed an African family for a year.

Charles imagined that his father had deliberately brought his visitor to this room in the hope that its sheer formality would stop their meeting from getting out of hand. No doubt he wanted to keep the proceedings short as well; that was why there was no fire in the basket grate. There was nothing like a coolish room for getting people to stick to the point.

On one side of it Charles sat in one broad Georgian armchair, with the uptight parson in the other. On the floor between them lay a spreadsheet newspaper with its folded Art and Collecting page lying uppermost. Abstractedly, Charles reread the opening words of the sly paragraph in the gossip column.

AN UNRELIABLE RELIQUARY?

The whisper around Bond Street is that the famed Burnill reliquary which was to have been sold by Golver PLC . . . may not be all that it appears to be . . . Doubts about the authenticity of the pair of large sapphires which are the mediaeval casket's crowning glory have now arisen, it appears . . . When approached, Sir Anthony Andover, a director of the firm, was unwilling to be precise . . .

Nettled at being ignored, Stanfield raised his voice a decibel or two. 'If you were not in charge of it, who was?'

Charles pulled his stare away from the newspaper and fixed it on the tedious man.

'Come on! You've no more idea than I have when it was interfered with. They've been making synthetic sapphires since the beginning of the century. All you have to do is to melt aluminium oxide and add traces of iron and titanium.'

That's fixed him, thought Charles, but it hadn't. The parson trundled on regardless.

'As soon as Sir Simon gave it into the church's keeping, it was locked in a secure niche in the nave . . .'

'That's beside the point!'

Their voices were crossing over one another as Stanfield

forced his way through the interruption. '. . . and until I handed it over to you, it remained there, as you know very well.'

'Since you do not seem to have taken what I said on board, I shall say it again. The sapphires could have been switched at any time in the last ninety – repeat ninety – years, long before the reliquary came into Burnill's possession. Years before that. Do you understand? *If* you understand, nod your head or something,' Charles concluded.

His opponent sat rigid with anger, his head thrusting hard against the scuffed leather of the chairback.

With an effort, he managed to keep his voice coherent. 'That's for the police to decide,' he said, standing up as though the decision to call them in was a foregone conclusion. The man was deaf, blind and stupid.

At the mention of the word 'police', Charles saw doubt pass across his father's face – a cloud. Then it was gone. There hadn't been distrust there, surely? It wasn't the kind of thing one could ask, certainly not with Stanfield glowering there. His ten commandments hadn't changed, or his commitment to them – even if his business was scarcely more than ticking over these days with the country in the grip of the most persistent recession since the war, the South-East devastated and property sales down to a trickle. On top of that the massive slump on the Japanese stock exchange had ruined the trade in oriental works of art. However, he wasn't a fool. Seeing it coming, he'd done all the right things – reduced his inventory, cut down his overdraft, all that – and while customers were few and far between at the upmarket end where he operated, times weren't so disastrous that he had been forced to sell his principles short.

Suspecting that his father was veering over to Stanfield's camp, he felt less than cheerful. They didn't imagine, surely, that he had entered into some kind of conspiracy with Johnson to downgrade their precious casket? With the jeweller still missing, it looked as though those two had at the very least made up their minds that it was he who was guilty of the substitution – in the bright white glare of hindsight. Admittedly, he had a reason, the necessary knowledge . . . the opportunity . . .

'The police must be approached immediately,' repeated Stanfield, who was a solid, twenty-four-carat bore.

Happily it was then that his father managed to rise to the occasion. In his view, Ernest said firmly, it would be premature to contact the police. Whatever they privately thought, what evidence could they offer that there was in fact a crime to be investigated? None whatsoever.

'Much better to focus our effort on putting this matter straight ourselves,' he concluded.

It was odd, thought Charles, how a crisis seemed to bring the best out in the old chap. Usually he played like just another landowner slipping into dotty old age.

Not at the moment, though – at the moment he was being positively brisk.

'However, as chairman of the trustees it's my responsibility, and I want the answers to some questions.'

He turned to his son. 'First, what's the thing worth as it stands?'

Charles was at a loss. When the idea of selling it had been mooted in the first place, Sir Anthony Andover had identified only a handful of museums and collectors who would be willing and able to buy it. Nothing similar had come on the market for years, so that any estimate of its value was no more than an expression of faith, a target really. Now that it had been rubbished so effectively, who could say? He did his best to think, but his mind was obstinately blank. They couldn't expect him to be an expert on everything.

'I simply don't know whether anybody would seriously want it now. Maxton's contribution . . .' Charles pushed a foot at the newspaper lying on the floor, '. . . won't bring any buyers hurrying out of the woodwork.'

'Don't you *know*?' Stanfield burst out. 'It's ridiculous. The casket isn't visibly changed. If it takes an expert half a day to tell whether the stones are synthetic what does it matter if they are or not?'

How could he be made to understand that of the host of factors which affected the price of an object – beauty, craftsmanship, age, condition – it was authenticity that took precedence. The reality of the thing had to correspond exactly to its image. Imitation, restoration and substitution were ideas which undermined the self-esteem of the owner and removed the confidence of the buyer. While it might seem irrational to somebody as hopelessly logical as Stanfield, the truth was that what an object looked like was far less important than what it actually was. Could Charles get that across to the parson in the time he had at his disposal? Not a chance.

'It has to be authentic, that's all.'

Stanfield seemed to think it was his fault. He shook his head. 'The reliquary has been despoiled and those abused children will be the poorer. Your son . . .' he intoned with a gesture that accused and at the same time forgave. The bloody man! He didn't have a monopoly of concern for the world's woes.

Instead of leaping to Charles's defence, his father turned a guileless eye on him, merely seeking information.

'Suppose the sapphires, the original ones, I mean, could be

recovered and put back where they belong, how would that be? Would that restore the value of the casket?'

'I guess so.' Charles ventured. 'As good as. If the job were done by an expert.' He knew as he spoke what was coming next. No, no, no! He had a business to run, profits to earn, and they were difficult enough to find these days. The reliquary had already absorbed much more of his energy than should have been allowed. Now he was going to be asked to take off on a hopeless expedition to get its sapphires back, and they could be anywhere. Of course, the field would be narrowed down enormously if Johnson had in fact stolen them. Find the man, and you had a fighting chance of finding those stones... and the other person looking for him was his wife. The thought of joining forces with her in the search was the only cheerful aspect of the whole thing. It did make a difference.

His father put the question, 'Would you be prepared to help us?'

How could he refuse? He'd had an easy life – not like those poor bloody kids in Brazil.

'I'll do what I can.'

Stanfield, his breath smoking slightly in the cold, looking holier-than-everybody-else in his frayed black cassock, insisted that if they had made no progress in, say, three weeks, the police should be brought in. To shut him up, they agreed. Having won that point, he went on to stipulate that Golver's should cease offering the casket for sale and return it to them for safe-keeping.

'Fair enough. I'll organise a safety-deposit box in London,' Charles suggested.

'There is no need to go to that expense. Not at all,' came the harsh reply. 'I intend to take charge of the casket from now on.

It can go back into its proper place in the nave.'

The vicar was off his trolley. After all the publicity the thing had received, it simply wouldn't be secure there in the church. Before he could protest, Charles caught a look in his father's eye that said, 'For goodness' sake, humour the stupid man.' Very well, he washed his hands of it. He had other jobs to do, like explaining to Margaret Johnson that her husband might be a thief, like locating that husband in order to get the sapphires out of him – assuming that he still had them in his possession and hadn't bet them on a busted flush or a horse that felt off-colour as soon as it found itself lined up at the starting gate.

On the shop door, the sign said: 'Sorry, but we are closed until further notice. We deeply regret any inconvenience.' He recognised the neat script readily enough. Now what was up? Getting back into the car, he took off for Margaret's home on the outskirts of town.

He had always thought it a pleasant house, timber-framed with a skin of lath and plaster – it always amazed him that such fragile materials could withstand a few centuries of wind and rain. The walls were painted pale blue, but that was probably authentic. He seemed to remember that in mediaeval times the local people had cheered themselves up by painting their houses any colour that they fancied, to take their minds off grievous taxes, plague, rapine, scutage and so on.

When she came to the door, he saw that he had interrupted her chores – the vacuum cleaner stood on the carpet in the wide part-timbered hall behind her. Dressed in slacks and a jade green sweater which had seen better days, with an old silk scarf at her throat, she didn't seem very pleased to see him. What was she doing cleaning the house in the middle of the morning? If

SOME DARK ANTIQUITIES

she had any sense she would be in the shop earning a living, he thought, because he was feeling like that – puritanical – today.

'Come in, then.' There wasn't much enthusiasm in that special voice of hers.

Entering, he glanced round and approved the absence of horsebrasses, copper hunting horns or similar. No fussiness, just one or two decent pieces of country oak, and there a Cromwellian refectory table running the length of the hall set off by a simple bowl of flowers, not bought but taken from the garden. That table was worth a few thousand, so perhaps they weren't so badly off, after all.

'Yes, Mr Ramsay?' she challenged him, hands in pockets, her questioning head slightly aslant as if to say: thus far and no further.

'The shop was closed. I thought I'd better come over and see how you were getting on. In case . . .' His voice petered out. In case what? In case she needed his help – which sounded pushy somehow. Thinking better of it, he kept quiet, which left both of them at a loss, caught in irresolution.

For a moment he thought she was going to invite him to go elsewhere. No, she seemed to have changed her mind.

'So you haven't heard? You must be the only one in the district who hasn't.'

'Heard what?' Her husband? Had something happened to him? He hadn't climbed up some other church tower in the neighbourhood and succeeded in falling off this time, had he?

For a moment she didn't say a word, looking ill at ease, as though she knew it was going to be painful to speak but, at the same time, that it was a relief which she simply had to have.

Then she blurted out, 'The bank put in a receiver three days ago. We're bankrupt.'

Holding absolutely still in her humiliation, she watched his face to gauge his reaction.

'An ordinary man in a very ordinary blue suit came and made me close the shop, hand over the keys . . . and the keys to the car. Credit cards, accounts, chequebooks . . .' She shuddered. 'It was like being strip-searched. There was I scrabbling about in the showroom trying to find everything while he kept asking me where Ian was. "I've no idea" – those were the only words I could utter. I could feel him behind me, not believing me. I had to come home afterwards and give myself a hot bath. Do you know I only just had enough money for the taxi?' she concluded with indignation. For her, a feminine victim, it had been the last straw, and she had to confide in somebody. That she had chosen him to unload on didn't mean a thing; he just happened to be standing there, that was all, like a lay figure. A thing, a convenient thing.

'How much cash do you need?' That was something practical he could do.

'I can cope,' she replied.

'Let me . . .'

'I told you, I'll manage,' she repeated fiercely, then, seeming to repent, she added, 'Anyhow, how could I repay you?'

'Out of the proceeds from that Agra carpet. You remember?'

In fact there had been no agreement about that, as he knew very well.

She hesitated, and made a half-hearted gesture. 'Surely that money would have to go to the receiver?'

'Nothing to do with him,' Ramsay said promptly. 'Would five hundred keep you going until you can get things straightened out?'

Scarcely, but at least it would resolve one of her immediate problems while she got to grips with all the others she had been landed with by that husband of hers. Of course he knew that to be put under an obligation to him, or anybody else for that matter, was the last thing she wanted but there was no way he could spare her that.

To his surprise, she accepted, absently. 'If you could ... Yes ... Thank you.' Then she roused herself. 'Look,' she said, 'I must get on. Their surveyor is coming this afternoon and I've got to have this place ready for him.'

It was going to take time for her to comprehend the cataclysm which had hit her, and until she did so her everyday routine was her only lifeline. As if it was the one thing that would save her from drowning, she clutched at the upright handle of the vacuum cleaner and was about to switch the thing on again and put a barrier of noise between them, when he stopped her.

'Wait a moment. There's something else.'

Feeling as though he was twisting the knife, he told her about the reliquary and the false sapphires. There was no way of side-stepping the issue – she had to be made aware of the facts without delay otherwise she might find herself compromised. No, they were wrong, without question, he insisted. As yet nobody knew how, when or where the substitution had been made. He didn't mention her husband nor even hint at his possible involvement because he knew he didn't need to. She heard him out, and when he had finished simply stared ahead without saying a word. Then she started up the machine and began to push it over the carpet obsessively to and fro as if her life depended on getting it spotless for her creditors.

'Wait a moment,' he shouted above the roar, but she couldn't hear him. What she needed was a drink. He went past her into the kitchen and searched the unfamiliar cupboards. Ian Johnson must have been keeping some liquor there somewhere. By the time he had run to earth a bottle of whisky two-thirds empty at the bottom of the tall broom cupboard and found a suitable glass, she had switched the cleaner off and brought a benign silence back to the ancient house. When he went into the hall, she had disappeared.

'Margaret?' he called, using her Christian name for the first time, experimentally.

No reply. He went into what he supposed was the sitting-room and there she was sitting on a button-backed chesterfield which badly needed re-covering; a piece of vivid patchwork had been thrown over it to cheer it up. Face turned away, her body thrust into the huge corner of its arm for protection she was crying uncontrollably like a child, sobs wrenching at her, ample tears streaming down her face.

He put the tumbler down on the floor in front of her as a kind of offering. 'You need the release. It'll get better,' he promised.

'Get lost,' she shot back. 'Leave me in peace.' But still she reached down for the glass, holding it in both white-knuckled hands to bring it to her lips.

'Why did you have to tell me about the sapphires – piling on the agony?'

Beating aside her recriminations took him several minutes, sitting beside her but not too close, to convince her otherwise. While he admitted that he might have been clumsy she had to be told, surely?

The only reason he stayed was that she ought to have somebody there. The last thing he wanted was to appear to be taking advantage of her. On the other hand . . . on the other hand she was in trouble. She was busy with a handkerchief, trying to dab away the damage from her tears. Drawing in his breath he held it for a fraught moment – then, without going too far in analysing his motives, he laid a tentative hand, palm uppermost, on the sofa beside him for her to take or leave alone as she chose. It was a kind of test, that was what it was. He waited, then felt something solid and unyielding.

'Thanks,' she murmured. He looked down at his hand. She had put the empty whisky glass into it.

Chapter Eight

Ian Johnson looked into the hooded slot of the cash dispenser and considered the fluorescent numbers which told him how much money was left in the current account he had opened in the name of Ian Cunningham. Their debt collectors were implacable, and there was his hotel bill outstanding. Whatever others said, he wasn't the kind of man who would walk out without paying it; mentally he subtracted it from the total together with the money he would need for meals, drinks and all the other onerous little costs which accumulated so fast in London. The sums told him that he had enough cash left for about two and a half days' play if he took it really slowly – two and a half days before he went over the cliff – and that was strictly on the understanding that he stayed among the modest risks, with red or black, even or odd, and didn't have a brainstorm and gamble on single numbers as he had done at two o'clock that morning. How much of his store of cash had he lost in those few tired and emotional minutes? How much . . . ? His brain refused to remind him of the figure.

He could ration himself, couldn't he? Impose an iron limit. Pushing his cashcard back into the machine he withdrew three hundred pounds and counted it pedantically, face and body hunched towards the granite wall of the bank, husbanding it from prying eyes as he slid it, there, into his wallet.

From the outside he could have been a sales manager on a visit to the capital – dark suit, pink candy-striped shirt and a richly embossed tie – with a lightweight overcoat, since he had slept poorly and the cold early air was getting to him. As a gentleman member, he was expected by his gaming club to dress the part even in the morning when only the idle or the addicted were to be seen around the tables – when the stakes were low, the action sporadic and the big gaming-room continued to function only out of habit, or that was how it felt.

As a sign of special favour the doorkeeper at the club, in his frock coat and cockaded top hat, helped Johnson off with his coat and handed it with a kind of flourish to the cloakroom attendant, his hand covertly cupped to receive the banknote he expected for this service. There was a superstition among the members of the club that a generous tip on arrival brought good luck, a superstition which the doorkeeper hadn't gone out of his way to discourage. He watched his guest with sympathy as he squared his shoulders before going through into the gaming room.

'All ready for action, sir?'

'I feel lucky today,' said Johnson; that was an essential part of the ritual as well.

'We'd better watch out then,' replied the doorman, using the jocular tone of a staff sergeant anxious to please, and went back to viewing the ever-changing traffic outside. Most of them said something like that – about feeling lucky. They came regularly for a bit, then after a while they dropped out of circulation and you never saw them again. All his temporary gentlemen.

Sitting over a cup of coffee provided by the management, taking a break, Johnson exchanged an automatic smile with the waitress in a calf-length dress who leant in front of him to empty one of the heavy green ashtrays, wiping it round with a damp cloth afterwards. She was wearing one of the mass-produced fragrances of a French fashion house, and as she rose from her duties she didn't mind offering him a glimpse of her deep and creamy cleavage. She was probably called a hostess, Johnson reflected, and she wasn't what he needed. Even at a more fleshly time of day than eleven in the morning after the night before she wouldn't have aroused him; he had a much more tempting woman over there where the wheel was turning, and she was pulling him back towards her. He felt the bulk of the circular plastic chips worth ten pounds each in his jacket pockets, all eighteen of them. He was down to a hundred and eighty pounds, which wasn't much. A dose of panic at the fragility of that sum brought the sweat to his neck and armpits – no more than a hundred and eighty pounds, all ready to shrink away to nothing like ice in the sun.

He had been playing for almost two hours and still the gaming room was scarcely populated, hushed except for the murmur of dealers at chemin de fer and blackjack – those who weren't sitting with empty seats in front of them and nothing to do.

Without really taking it in, he heard the stolid voice of the croupier, 'No more bets,' followed by the tiny clatter and bounce of the ball flung against the spin of the wheel, and that set his appetite going. Ignoring the routine smile of the hostess, he rose and returned to the same table.

The only other player was a studious-looking Japanese who had in front of him a sheet of paper covered with columns of numbers and ideograms, the record of the recent performance of the wheel; he was trying to impose a pattern on it. When, on the next spin, the ball stopped at twenty-five he solemnly wrote down the result and looked into the distance, his fingertips tapping out on the green baize some arcane calculation of his own. Then, having consulted his paper again for reassurance, he placed two large oblong chips, each for a thousand pounds, decisively on the number nineteen.

How Johnson envied him that gesture, that macho affirmation of faith which he could not afford himself. From the mini pile of chips grouped in front of him he selected a skimpy single one and placed it on black. The wheel span. The ball rattled and tumbled into the section labelled with a green and unequivocal zero. As the bored croupier raked the oblong chips into the sump below the table, the Japanese jumped to his feet as if to protest and, realising that he couldn't, walked from the table like an automaton. Spinning round, he came stiffly back towards it, eyes reddened with rage, seemingly on the point of exploding into some physical release of the grievance boiling like steam inside him, his brain forcing him step by step to take on board the size of the sum he had just thrown away, betrayed by those calculations which he now held crumpled in his hand, which had gulled him into believing that the number nineteen was about to win him seventy-two thousand pounds. He had lost face, and there was nobody to blame but the wheel and himself.

It made Johnson feel better, though. Doggedly he put the Japanese out of his mind and another chip on black.

By four o'clock he was down to his last six chips and had to break off to go to the cashier, who changed a cheque for him against his banker's card. As she handed him the tubby cylinder of plastic chips held neatly together in her fingers she too flashed him a wide smile, using most of her teeth – back as far as her fillings.

'Enjoy yourself, sir,' she said.

Why were they all so bloody genial? Enjoy yourself? Enjoyment didn't come into it. That wasn't what it was about at all. They were all in the game, yet none of them seemed to appreciate how the urge niggled at you like unachieved lust.

Only when the evening crowd began to dribble in did he look down at the table in front of him and realise how much his pile of chips had grown. Actually grown. As he counted them, he was almost afraid to believe it. Black was in the ascendant at last; he was hungry – he could have murdered a whisky and a cheese sandwich – but he dared not leave the table now that the tide was running in his favour. Surely with this healthy-looking heap of chips he could afford to risk two on black each time the wheel was spun? Go on, why not? Before long it was five chips. Soon the pile in front of him had grown unwieldy and he had to change some of them for larger ones. He slipped a single fat oblong chip into his jacket pocket as a reserve. Before long, another one joined it.

The crowd round the table had grown and he felt people brushing against him, reaching over him to place their bets. There was a scent of unusual tobacco, a whiff of expensive aftershave on well-preserved skin; from the corner of his eye he caught the flash of a woman's white arm. None of those impressions distracted him from the rhythm of the wheel as he drove on, backing black, doubling up on black and backing black again.

Eventually a call of nature becoming more and more urgent forced him to break off. Emerging from the impeccable toilet, he made for the bar to grab that long-awaited sandwich, cramming it down dry in his mouth, chasing it with the drink so fast that he scarcely tasted it.

His seat had been taken, but he eased his way in behind the interloper, waiting before he started betting afresh in order to recapture the run of play. There were setbacks now and then – sometimes he felt fear grab at him – but overall he continued to pull ahead.

At about eleven the population of the gaming-room began to thin out and the electric atmosphere which had buoyed him up earlier in the evening began to seep away. He regained his former seat, sure, but it wasn't the same. The croupier had changed but not the message of the wheel which was still favouring him. Winning had become almost too easy and a yearning grew inside him to take a real risk, a man's risk like the Japanese whom he had envied that morning. As he thought about it more and more the desire became irresistible. If the Japanese had the fortitude to do it, so had he. Leaving a single oblong chip in his pocket, simply to keep himself in the game if he lost, he pushed the whole of his winnings on to the square labelled sixteen; sixteen, because his birthday was the sixteenth of March. He felt as if he was on a deserted beach somewhere, wading out square-shouldered into a grey sea – heroically accepting the outcome of his actions.

'May I, sir?' asked the croupier, fussily adjusting the chips so that they did not intrude on any other square on the green baize and risk giving rise to an unseemly argument later. Casinos are decorous places.

Now the bet was as clear and unambiguous as the odds of thirty-six to one against it. On the other hand . . . Johnson's eye surveyed his chips on the table and tried to count them . . . On the other hand, he might win what? Must be at least one hundred and fifty... one hundred and fifty thousand. Feeling lightheaded, he breathed slowly and deeply.

'No more bets,' intoned the croupier decisively as he set the big wheel spinning and delivered the ball obliquely into the whirling saucer of wood and metal. The white ball rattled quickly at first, bounced and ran, slowing down gradually until at last it was carried around in silence, cradled in one of the small compartments in the wheel. At length Johnson opened his eyes to make out the number.

Sixteen.

He had conquered Everest. He had wings. He was king of the universe.

It was a much more expensive hotel than the other one had been. Smoother. Johnson turned over in bed, lifted the telephone on the bedside table and punched the number for room service again. He was starving. The full English breakfast was indicated: cereal, bacon, egg and fried bread – toast and croissants to give it class – marmalade, jam. A binge of a breakfast with a great big pot of coffee. Where was it? And he wanted several newspapers. He had to think for a moment before he could specify one or two titles to the patient waiter at the other end of the line – he hadn't read a newspaper for ages and he had a lot on his mind.

After too long a delay, the splendid breakfast was brought and placed on the table beside the big plate glass window looking down on the hotel's spacious and peaceful courtyard shaded with exotic greenery – an oasis in the centre of London, as the brochure would have said if the management had felt it necessary to stoop so far as to issue one. He sat down at the table, poured himself coffee, and picked up the first of the newspapers that had been laid beside the tray. Feeling calmer, he glanced through the headlines, then opened it out, pulling and flicking it in an august way to straighten the folds. The story that caught his eye was on page three of the home news and low down the page. His eyes took in each line of print separately at first and he had to make a special effort to run them together and extract their meaning. He glanced at the byline – Jim Maxton. Putting down the paper, he turned and attacked his cereal hastily. Perhaps he would have to do without the croissants.

He didn't linger. Ten minutes later he was in a taxi on his way down Piccadilly, and ten minutes after that was in a travel agent making certain arrangements. By four o'clock in the afternoon he had checked out of the hotel and was on his way to Heathrow. While he was waiting for his flight to be called he did one other thing – he made a telephone call to Brighton.

Ernest Ramsay looked at the manilla envelope with irritation. Why did it have to arrive the day after Charles had gone back to London? Why couldn't he have stayed longer? Why didn't he come up to Bressemer more often?

The address was written in an unsteady hand, probably by one of those regrettable people he imagined his son knew in the antiques business in town. Suddenly, as a memory of Charles twenty years before came back to him he frowned. The boy had always seemed to be . . . The end of the sentence came adrift in his mind because he wasn't really anxious to complete it. He looked at the letter again and noticed that it had a second-class stamp on it, so it couldn't be monstrously important. Still, he would do his duty without any delay. He made for the study, sat down at the desk and carefully scoring out the address he neatly

SOME DARK ANTIQUITIES

re-directed the letter. Wellington the dog was sniffing at his ankles; he needed to go out so much more often these days, and his master, being elderly himself, felt it wasn't fair to keep the dog waiting. There was an impatient snuffle beneath the desk. Standing up, the old man left the envelope lying there and went to find the lead and his favourite walking-stick.

By the time they had both sauntered down the avenue and had returned to the great empty house with all its blank windows reflecting the sky, by the time he had encouraged the Labrador to waddle up the grandiose stone steps into the hall, the memory of the letter had slipped out of his mind altogether. It was several days before he noticed it again and, feeling guilty, sent it on its way.

'You are lucky to have a flat in London,' Margaret Johnson said.

It wasn't a brilliant remark, and, besides, what had luck to do with it? She might imagine otherwise but nobody had made him a present of the place, he would have her know. He had earned it by the sweat of his brow, by keeping his hands clean and behaving responsibly – ordinary virtues of that sort. The remark irritated him until he saw how ill at ease she was. It had been an attempt at small-talk, that was all, and, given her circumstances, she ought rather to be given credit for it.

She sat down, only halfway into the tub chair closely upholstered in dark leather – about 1820; it had been an adroit buy of his and he was proud of it. Sitting there, literally on edge, hands clasped in her lap, she was tense, aware that she had lost much of her freedom of action now. And she was unsure of herself, looking for guidance. If he said they ought to go out again to follow some other lead, she would do so. Or stay? She would do that, too. Stay overnight? That was a different matter.

The last time a woman had stayed in the flat, it had been Elizabeth. She had sat in that very same chair, but she had been so much more relaxed, leaning back negligently, knowing how well it suited her; she had never been less than elegant. He remembered how she had looked when he had last seen her, at the airport in Holland, turning away into the crowd, with her head held high, conscious of the burden of her treachery, but certainly not bowed down by it. Elegant and false.

That bleak parting had left his being frozen for a long while – unwilling to take any risks with his emotions, wary of any new relationship. It wasn't a comfortable state, but a safe one at least – that much you could say. Held in abeyance.

Glancing at Margaret Johnson, however, the possibility of a feminine presence in the place suddenly filled him with a rush of warmth, a thawing of the spirit.

Tentatively he said, 'Were you expecting to return home tonight?' He needed to know what she had in mind, in any case.

The question caught her unawares, leaving her nonplussed for a moment.

He went on, 'If not, where are you planning to stay? With one of your friends? There's a perfectly good spare bedroom here, or otherwise I could try the hotel down the road for you.'

He did his best to make the offer sound casual, and he saw in her eyes that he hadn't succeeded. The onus was on him to give her a let-out, but had he really done so when he would be paying for the room, as good as – putting pressure on her to refuse it? *She* couldn't pay for it, that was certain.

She burst out, 'I'm not an easy lay, you know, simply because I'm a bankrupt.'

'I didn't suppose you were,' he shot back, aggrieved. He'd

done nothing to deserve that. What cause did she have to doubt his sexual manners? None at all.

Reaching for the telephone he went on, '. . . Very well. I'll book you in.'

She put out her hand to stop him. 'Leave it . . . just leave it. For the moment. Please.'

She shuddered as though she was cold and stole a glance at her watch.

'Do you have an appointment?' he asked.

Her answering shrug said that was *her* business. If she didn't loosen up and relax, he told himself, she'd come apart – unable to cope with these disasters of hers. She needed to take them steadily, one at a time, but he wasn't going to press unasked-for advice on her.

He was about to offer her a drink, but thought better of it at the last minute because she was so touchy. She wasn't the type to accept that either – not so early in the day.

The morning they had just spent on the search for her husband had been altogether wasted. It was she who had insisted in the end that they should go to the police, and had given an edited account of the man's movements to a shirt-sleeved constable who had done his best to put up a show of interest.

Her husband had disappeared, and might be in London? Slow particulars were taken. Yes, he would be registered as a missing person. Yes, records of accident and suicides would be checked. Yes, yes, and sign here please.

Whatever happened it wasn't going to happen quickly. It had been their last port of call, and Ramsay could not see what else they could do to find the man.

She looked at the time again, and a minute or two later stood up, bringing herself close to where he was seated, looking down.

'I have to go off somewhere for a couple of hours,' she said. 'Could I take you up on your offer of a bed for the night?' She laid a forefinger lightly on his shoulder by way of apology; a touch merely. It was gracefully done and rather cheering. Obviously she thought he was human.

'Of course,' he replied, getting to his feet. 'Where are you going now, though? I'll take you, if you like.'

Quickly she turned her head away, her gaze resting blindly for a moment on an Italian bronze of Punchinello which he kept on his desk, then covertly she glanced down at her watch again.

'Look, I have to go now. I do have to go.'

'Come on. Let me take you.'

She refused; he insisted. A small tug of war, to and fro.

Laughing, she gave in. 'Oh, very well. As long as you don't jeer.'

Him? He wasn't that kind. Anyway, what was there going to be to jeer at?

'You mustn't knock it – what we are going to see. Promise me,' she demanded almost flirtatiously. That was a change.

He undertook not to scoff at it, whatever it was, and received another smile from her, looking back as she moved easily down the staircase, step by step ahead of him.

The façade of the building was grimy water-stained cement, its architectural style post-war utilitarian. That was confirmed by the legend WINSTON CHURCHILL HALL 1946 incised boldly above the double doors, which were open. A man who looked as though his white hair was the product not of age but of albinism relieved Ramsay of the hefty entrance fee for both of them and gave them a smile of saintly sweetness.

Most of the people sitting in the hall were middle-aged or elderly women, some with the menfolk they had brought sitting next to them. It was already fairly crowded, but the front row had been left empty. Presumably, because the light from the spotlights trained on the stage spilled over on to it, nobody wanted to sit there, on display to the rest of the audience. That didn't deter Margaret. She led him straight down the aisle and sat down proudly in the glare. Taking his place obediently beside her, he glanced around. What went on here? She was going to offer him no explanation. Obviously it was a prayer meeting of some kind because on one side of the stage was a neat little electronic synthesiser on a chrome stand and in the centre a single chair, an oak affair with magisterial arms and heavily carved back behind a rostrum covered in a pale blue material. In the bright light, Ramsay caught the gleam of one or two of the safety-pins that held it in place.

A young woman in a flowered dress, eyes too close together and a heavy jaw, came on from stage left, sat down at the synthesiser and began to sort through her music. Were they going to have to sing hymns? He looked warily round, but could see no sign of any people handing out hymn-sheets or anything of that kind.

The lights in the hall were switched off by an unseen hand, leaving him feeling even more exposed at the edge of the brilliant circle illuminating the empty chair on the stage. The ugly girl at the synthesiser began to play softly in the machine's piping organ mode – not music of an ecclesiastical kind but a Chopin nocturne, which was a tiny bonus, but what was going to happen next? Glancing again at Margaret for enlightenment, he was given none. As the hum of conversation in the hall began to tail off, the music shifted to a different key and became more urgent. Then, without warning, someone appeared in the glare of the spotlight. For a moment he thought it was a trick, but it wasn't, he had simply blinked at that precise moment.

When he saw the figure clearly, he blinked again. It was extremely odd, dressed in a dark brown suit with a chalk stripe whose style was about the same vintage as the building itself – a double-breasted demob suit, embellished with a beige shantung tie pierced with a stick pin, a matching handkerchief lolling out of the top pocket. The owner's hairstyle matched the outfit – short back and sides, razored regimentally on the neck.

'I am Robson,' this person said in a high alto voice. 'Welcome to our meeting, everyone.'

What is its gender, Ramsay wondered. He sifted the clues, and came to the conclusion that it must be a man. Margaret was oblivious, leaning forward in her seat with all her attention concentrated on the figure on the stage.

Without any kind of explanation, he pointed a forefinger at a man seated in the half-darkness two rows behind them, and said prosaically, 'I have your uncle here. He says you are in financial difficulties because you haven't been able to sell the business.' Ramsay looked behind him, and saw the man's eyes switch right and left with embarrassment. 'That's right, isn't it? Speak up if you would, because not everybody can see you.'

'Yes,' replied the man hoarsely, then he coughed to clear his throat.

'Your uncle gave you a kitten once, didn't he?' The medium sounded confident.

'Yes.'

'The kitten's name was Douglas.'

'No,' came the unexpectedly downright reply, but it didn't put Robson out.

From his inside pocket he drew a folded piece of plain paper and a ballpoint pen, which he held with its point in contact with its surface without looking at it. Instead, his pale blue eyes stared over the heads of the audience, seeming to focus their vision inwardly for a moment. All of a sudden, as quickly as a snake striking its prey, the pen skidded across the paper. Robson didn't look down but stood waiting, as though it hadn't finished yet, still staring towards the back of the hall. Again the pen made a flourish on the paper, the hand that held it acting independently of the rest of his body. Only when it was motionless again did he look down and examine what it had written.

'You're quite correct,' he announced. 'It was your dog's name that was Douglas. The kitten's name was Fancy.'

'That's right,' said the man with a kind of relief in his voice, and a murmur of excitement rippled through the audience. Automatic writing was an extra.

'Your uncle says not to worry, Ken, old son . . . those are his words . . . Just keep at it, try and try again. You'll find a solution to your difficulties soon.'

For the next half-hour Robson brought more messages of goodwill back from Beyond, each one enriched with supporting detail – the name of a street or a make of car, a description of a picture on the dining-room wall.

He turned to another grey-head. Just before her husband died she had gone to the kitchen to make him a cup of tea, and by the time it was ready, he had passed over. Robson went on, 'No milk. He never took milk in his tea, but always a single lump of sugar. Isn't that right?'

Dumbly she nodded her head.

Margaret spoke in an undertone. 'You've been very good. You haven't scoffed at all.'

Ramsay had lost the urge, and wasn't sceptical now so much as puzzled. There couldn't be collusion, not with Robson appearing week after week before so many people. It must be telepathy or something of that kind. While there was no applause, Ramsay could sense a build-up of satisfaction in the people who were sitting nearby – this was a good meeting. When the medium turned his gaze on Margaret and pointed to her, set apart from the rest of the audience by the rim of light which lay around her shoulders, he felt a mood of expectation growing in the hall.

After a long pause, Robson said, with no rancour in his high counter-tenor's voice, 'I have nothing for you. If you want to find your husband, go to a private detective. He has not passed over.' It seemed that he had read her mind efficiently enough.

Looking anxious, she stood up. 'Are you certain?'

'I have no message from him.' The reply was flat.

Margaret came back. 'I am in trouble. Can you offer me nothing more?'

Robson's tone softened as he explained, 'I can put you in touch only with those who have passed on.'

Which meant that if Johnson had indeed gone over to the other side, the medium hadn't got the wavelength yet. It was progress of a sort.

She still stood erect in the pool of white light, refusing to give way.

'That's not much help, is it?'

Because an argument would have spoilt the atmosphere, the medium decided to make an effort. Sitting down in his imposing oak chair, he stretched out his arms in front of him, palms downward on the table. For a while he stared ahead of him without moving, then he shuddered. There was a long silence in the hall except for a chairleg scraping the floor as somebody shifted their weight. The man with the unsaleable shop coughed again.

Someone behind Ramsay whispered reproachfully, 'It's not fair to him, really. He's exhausted. He shouldn't do so much.'

For a moment it struck Ramsay that perhaps the performance, if that was the right word, was over. Had his batteries run down?

It was then, just when uncertainty was beginning to take hold of the audience and the spell was about to be broken, that the voice, reduced to a thread of sound, said, 'I am inside a building made of grey stone. A square building, bigger than this, with pillars and rounded arches supporting the roof. It is dark here with a smell of candles burning. There is an altar and to one side a huge picture . . . a greybearded man . . . trees with broad dark green leaves, a couple leaving a garden. Behind them lies a snake with its head raised and its red tongue protruding between its open jaws. I can see quite clearly now. A powerful and primitive picture – the Expulsion of Adam and Eve from the Garden of Eden.'

Looking intently at her, Robson asked, 'Do you recognise this scene?'

Unwilling to disappoint him, she could only shake her head. 'No.'

'You are sure?' He was merely expressing surprise.

'I am certain.'

A rustle of dissatisfaction ran through the congregation as Robson shrugged off that particular failure to connect and went back to fielding bulletins from the other side for more rece clients. Those images had been uncanny, persuasive in their detail, Ramsay felt, but he couldn't recall ever having seen a church like that, nor that painting. It left him with a sense of frustration.

'Are you satisfied?'

Margaret looked at his face to see if he was ready after all to deride this private belief of hers, and saw that he was not. Not at all.

When they had left the hall and were walking back in the wet towards the car park, she betrayed no signs of discouragement.

'Come along. You're dawdling.' She thrust her arm through his; it was the second time they had touched one another, and he noted it.

Hurrying along in the rain, they were too busy trying to escape from it to discuss what they had seen in the Winston Churchill Hall, and then the rain was pelting down on their unprotected heads and they were forced to take refuge in a shop doorway. Panting, laughing, they shook themselves free from raindrops as well as they could. Searching in her bag, Margaret found a packet of tissues. Two of them she used to wipe her face, and handed the rest to him in a gesture made more intimate by the confined space. For a moment she stared at his face, her own still transfigured by laughter, then looked away, seeking some new topic that would steer him away from his obvious preoccupation with her.

A c' ough the glazed door behind them gave her what for.

ue shop!' she exclaimed, gratified to have seen 'ust our kind of thing.'

eir raincoats still dripping.

SOME DARK ANTIQUITIES

The only light in the place came from a low wattage standard lamp. It stood at the shoulder of a steel-haired woman whose face might have been large-eyed and elegant in the Sixties but now was merely pinched into angles – the lady proprietor lounging in a Victorian chaise-longue with one leg stretched carelessly along it, her thin superstructure, wrapped in an unusual cardigan, propped up against its back. She was leafing through a just serviceable copy of a country magazine.

Looking across at them through her enormous round-eyed spectacles, she blared all of a sudden, 'I do hope you're not coming in here just to get out of the rain. This is a business, you know, not a free exhibition.' Her cut-glass accent belonged in the Chelsea of her salad days – many miles of exile from where she found herself landed today.

Then, after the outbreak of spleen, her voice changed and became emollient, as sickly as warm honey and milk. 'It's not a dusty old exhibition, is it, Miriam?' she cooed.

Ramsay surveyed the shop, his gaze reaching into its shadows. No Miriam there; there was nobody else in the place. Did this woman also have contacts in the spirit world?

Then his eye was caught by a movement in the basket on the floor at her side – a fat cocker spaniel shaking its ears, sending a cloud of loose hairs swirling upwards. Sitting up, it observed him with interested eyes, hoping for a walk or any other antidote to boredom he might choose to offer.

It was ignored, as was its owner, who went back to her blemished magazine, looking up sharply now and then to check that every item of her stock was still where it belonged – the silver sugar-sifter (hallmarked *Chester, 1855*), the broken eighteenth-century fan (so prettily painted, don't you think?), the jade brushpot. None of them had disappeared into the pockets of these damp intruders. She looked disappointed.

Against the back wall of her shop was a rosewood chiffonier with a brass gallery, its doors embellished with brass trelliswork. Regency, and very nice. Ramsay peered at the price tag and raised an eyebrow; the woman was out of touch, she hadn't a hope of getting that figure round here.

However, on the chiffonier she had placed a Japanese cloisonné vase, the cloisons worked in silver wire, the design a pair of dragons fighting on a dark blue ground. It was about a hundred years old, a miracle of the patient craftsmanship of the Meiji period. Ramsay looked underneath the base. There was no seal and it wasn't signed; moreover, it hadn't been given a price ticket. Clearly she wasn't committing herself.

He ruminated. Two years earlier, the vase in his hand would have made a thousand pounds easily at a good London auction, and back in Japan would have retailed to a collector for treble that amount. These days, with the stock market in Japan flat on its back, it might be worth how much in London? Six hundred plus or minus, assuming it was undamaged. If not, if it had the slightest fault, no more than a fifth of that; Japanese collectors were sticklers for perfection. With care he picked it up and brought it over to the only available light, the dismal lamp close to the owner's thin shoulder; he had to thrust the vase close to her to examine it. While she pretended that he wasn't there, he turned it over in his hands to examine its polished surface minutely.

'How much is this?'

Her eyes assessed him with just the same kind of care, deciding how much he was good for. 'Two hundred and forty,' she said finally. 'Isn't it, Miriam?'

The spaniel wasn't feeling supportive – it had gone to sleep.

Two hundred and forty. Ramsay was about to slip into his bargaining mode when he saw the crack, scarcely visible, a tiny hair of light high up on the shoulder of the piece, and he grunted.

As he put the failed vase back where it belonged, her voice exploded bitterly behind him. 'You are simply a timewaster, I take it. Just here to gawp. You and your companion.' Having fired this salvo, she flicked over another page of her magazine, almost tearing it in the process. The dog shifted in her sleep, and kept her head down.

A novel marketing ploy, thought Ramsay – the Abusive Approach. It was time they went. Glancing round for Margaret, he saw her just behind him, lips pursed, then felt her fingers plucking at his sleeve. Her eyes caught his attention and directed it across to a polished mahogany shelf fixed to the wall close by her. A silver wreath of myrtle leaves lay upon it, the image of the one they had seen at Golver's in Andover's exhibition – its twin.

Neither of them spoke while he inspected it quickly. Like the vase, it lacked a price ticket. It had been cleaned recently but it looked no worse for the experience. Presumably it was for sale, although with the woman in her present unpredictable mood, she might take it in her head to refuse to part with it. Better to let Margaret open negotiations, he decided, and gave the slightest of nods in the direction of the enemy.

Margaret picked up the wreath. 'Isn't this a pretty thing?' she mused to him. The figure on the chaise-longue was no more responsive than the spaniel in the basket beside her. 'Do you mind if I try it on?'

No reply. Margaret found a convenient mirror, placed the wreath on her golden head and was transfigured, just as she had been at Golver's. However, she behaved as though the image in the mirror was entirely new to her – clasping her hands together with enthusiasm, the bubbling enthusiasm of a bride-to-be.

'I love it, I love it! Isn't it wonderful?' She swung round to face him. 'I tell you what, I could wear it with my veil on Saturday week. What do you think?' she improvised boldly.

Veil? The penny dropped. A *wedding* veil. He played up. 'Of course. Most becoming, my pipkin,' he replied, adding with the suspicion of an amateur, 'Is it hall-marked?'

That was a perceptive touch, he thought, and the owner rose to it.

He felt her response hit him in the back of the neck. 'It's foreign silver, I believe.'

'Oh.' Ramsay made an effort to sound disappointed.

'How much is it, darling?' Margaret demanded, and then in a stage whisper, 'Can we afford it?'

'Of course,' her newly-found bridegroom answered firmly. He loved the girl after all and it was going to be her big day. Lifting it with care off her head to avoid catching her hair in it, he had to place one edge of his hand on her smooth head and felt himself suddenly disturbed by the experience. Turning, he held the circlet out towards the proprietor of the shop, and said, 'We should like to buy it, please.'

'We really ought to ask the price first, darling,' remonstrated Margaret with concern.

He shook his head. Call him old-fashioned if you like, but nothing was too good for his pipkin. He fixed his gaze on the woman in the cardigan, delivering himself into her hands, which was exactly where he aimed to be. Before taking the plunge, she weighed him up again. 'Two hundred and seventy pounds,' she said.

SOME DARK ANTIQUITIES

That was outrageous – outrageous for what she thought it was. Which prompted him to test the ethics of the transaction with the touchstone he always carried with him – *Probitas*. Had the amateur sketch they had just played out been unfair to the woman? Of course not – she'd got much more for the wreath than she had expected. She was a dealer, for goodness' sake, a player in the game; he didn't owe her a living.

He reached into his pocket for his chequebook. One way and another it had been an intriguing afternoon.

'It's a victory wreath, as in a Roman triumph,' Margaret exulted back in his flat, holding it solemnly above her head so that the light flashed off it. Then it became a tambourine, and she was a blonde dancing gipsy whirling in a gleeful circle with it, the outburst of gaiety all the more startling because of the gloom of the past few days. When he called a warning she stopped, eyes gleaming, and obediently let him take it so that he could put it out of harm's way. The last thing either of them wanted was a dented wreath. Since Margaret had found it and he had paid for it, they ought to share the profit fifty-fifty, just as they were going to do with the Agra carpet.

'I wonder how much . . .' she asked herself, and he could tell from the look in her eyes that she was beginning to see the thing as a magic solution to her financial troubles – which was unwise. They had to get it verified by an expert first. There was to be no counting of chickens, he insisted, and poured her another glass of champagne to sweeten the pill.

'At least we can have a celebration dinner.'

'It will have to be a labour-saving one because I'm not in the mood for cooking,' she warned him, dragging him off to the delicatessen, the butcher and the wine shop to help her to choose the makings of the meal because she had no idea what sorts of things he liked.

After they had done it justice, she sat with her legs stretched out on his sofa and allowed herself to unburden. In a way, she said, the bankruptcy was a relief after the uncertain years she had spent working in that shop, cleaning it in the morning before opening, making herself pleasant to customers when she felt frozen with anxiety, checking the accounts the whole time, knowing how vulnerable she was, knowing that every time she banked the takings her husband might have gambled them away already.

'Why did I stay? Because I was married to him. Because in the early days when he promised that he would get us out of our financial straits I had believed him, and when it became clear that he couldn't, that our ship was sinking, I hadn't been tough enough to leave him to cope on the bridge by himself. He needed help,' she explained. 'Not like you at all. You are much more . . .'

Strong? Capable? Effective?

'. . . stable,' she said. That would have to do; it was better than nothing.

Chapter Nine

Ramsay picked up the sheaf of envelopes from the mat, tossing the junk mail into the waste-paper basket as he passed it. Glancing at the letter from his bank, he laid it aside on the desk along with a cheque from a client, setting the bronze Punchinello as a paperweight firmly on top.

Lastly he ripped open the manilla envelope his father had forwarded from Bressemer. A handwritten letter. He looked at the signature: *Becket*. Didn't remember him. Photocopies – what were they? Because they looked intriguing, he inspected them first. The style of the manuscript shook a faint chord in his memory, but it died into nothingness before he could pin down what it was. There was something about it which edged up to him like a ghost at his elbow, and when he looked round, there was nothing there.

The covering letter – he turned to that, and began to read. Immersed in it, he walked to the bathroom door and tried the handle absently.

'Won't be long,' Margaret called. She was taking a shower.

Waiting, he coasted through the first page. 'When we met last summer at Bressemer and you were kind enough to show me . . . the liberty of writing . . . your assistance in identifying a manuscript . . . I enclose photocopies of the first two pages . . .

If we could meet, I could provide more background . . . Help would be most appreciated . . . I can be contacted . . . Yours truly, Francis Becket.'

The telephone went. Dropping the letter on the desk, he answered it, and heard Sir Anthony Andover at his most magisterial at the other end.

'There's been a development about that casket of yours.'

'Yours', not 'ours' any longer, and the voice conveyed that, as far as he was concerned, the Burnill reliquary had become a loser since its proper sapphires had gone missing. Nevertheless, Sir Anthony's tone suggested as he went on, Glover's had its standards and it behoved him to bring the untidy episode to a decent conclusion if he could.

'We need to have a meeting. Could you come round here . . . to the office?'

'Certainly. When?'

'This morning, if that suits you. At ten?'

Sir Anthony was offhand. He seemed to be in a hell of a rush, thought Charles, but that didn't matter. It would be an opportunity to show him the wreath and get his opinion. Replacing the receiver Charles went and banged vigorously on the bathroom door.

'Could you find a box to put the wreath in while I shave?'

'I'm being as quick as I can.'

He should have brought her with him so that she could hear Andover's opinion for herself, Ramsay thought. Stupid though the baronet was, he could claim to be an expert on early jewellery and he wasn't too proud to go off and pick the brains of more knowledgeable colleagues, which was helpful.

The dark-haired secretary in her trouser suit of lime green

accompanied Charles to the door, murmured some sincere nothing, and slipped away.

Ramsay walked into the office. Into a surprise. To find himself staring down twin black tunnels. What . . .? The barrels of a shotgun threatening his face.

He pushed them aside.

'Oops! Sorry.' Knowing that he had broken the rules, Andover covered up with a boyish laugh. 'Just practising my swing. Five minutes every day, and well spent, let me tell you.' Apparently he had nothing better to do.

'I hardly thought you wanted to blow my head off!'

To make up for the mishap, Sir Anthony thrust the gun into Ramsay's outstretched hands, forcing him to jettison his parcel. 'Here, try that. Give yourself a treat,' he invited.

Ramsay gathered it up and had a feel, sighting along the barrel, swinging out towards the big windows and the sky. It was excellent.

'Umm,' he allowed, bringing it down to look over the breech.

'Holland and Holland,' prompted Sir Anthony at his elbow.

'That's right,' Ramsay agreed, non-committally handing it back. 'Nice gun.'

Looking cheated, the baronet took it from him, dismantled it and put its components, darkly gleaming stock and barrels, reverently back into the case lined in brown velvet on his desk. Bent over his task, he chose his words with equal care. 'As you know, this client whom we located for you has an agent.'

'Who is?'

He snapped the leather case shut. 'Can't tell you,' he answered. 'I thought we had been over all that before . . . Anyway, he's been in touch again.'

'He's aware that the sapphires are not . . .'

'Altogether pukka? Yes.'

Sir Anthony stood up and looked Ramsay in the eye. 'What he wants to know is this: would the trustees be willing to sell the reliquary just as it stands?'

'You mean synthetic stones and all?' Ramsay asked. What was the reason for this change of tack?

'Yes.' The monosyllable was sharp. Sir Anthony wasn't enjoying this conversation much.

'Have they given you any idea of a figure?'

'No. It would be up to your people to name their price.'

'What would *you* put on it?' Ramsay asked. Andover was supposed to be the expert.

The baronet screwed up his eyes and pretended to think a bit. 'It's not easy. Hellish narrow market, anyway. Don't know the client.'

Ramsay took note of that sliver of information. 'The ones I *do* know aren't playing – ' another sliver – 'I wouldn't like to . . .' As his voice trailed away, it was clear from his face that he wished the embarrassing reliquary would disappear and let him get on with his life, organising his exhibitions, practising his swing.

'Anyway, there it is – an opportunity for you.'

If all the other possible buyers had gone broody, why was this particular one still in the market? An unknown buyer. No idea of price.

'At any rate, ask your trustees to think about it, would you?'

Ramsay said he would, but it didn't sound like a starter to him. Perhaps they would get further with the other matter. He reached down and produced the parcel that Margaret, her blonde hair dark and damp from her shower, had packed for him

SOME DARK ANTIQUITIES

half an hour before. Tearing off the wrapping, he passed the wreath over to Sir Anthony, who warmed up when he saw what it was.

Extracting a jeweller's eyeglass from his desk drawer, he took the wreath over to the window where the light was better. 'Where did it come from?' The usual question.

'My affair.' Pause. 'Rather like the one in your exhibition, don't you think? Greek, fifth or fourth century?'

With one hand on either side of it, Sir Anthony placed it carefully at the centre of his desk and stood back.

'Maybe, maybe not. Don't get carried away. Can't say until it's been tested.' Although he was trying to sound indifferent, he couldn't manage it. As he picked up the wreath again to take another look at the modelling of the silver myrtle leaves, Ramsay could see his hands drawing it towards him, unconsciously taking possession of it. There was no doubt about it: he was lusting after it dreadfully.

'Could Golver's do the tests?' Ramsay asked.

The baronet havered; he would have to consult his technical people.

Why was he suddenly playing hard to get? There was one obvious answer – Sir Anthony wanted to keep the wreath to himself, didn't want Golver's to know anything about it. They probably had strict rules about conflicts of interest; they seemed to have rules for everything else.

'Very well, I'll take it to the National Museum of Antiquities.'

That didn't seem to be what Sir Anthony wanted, either. 'Wait a moment.' The cogs churning busily beneath his well-barbered scalp were almost visible. 'Wait a moment.'

The door opened and the dark-haired girl looked in. 'Almost time for the board, Sir Anthony.'

He glanced at his wristwatch.

'Just coming,' he replied, and started to get flustered, looking round his desk for his folder of papers for the meeting. Finding them on his side table, she handed them to him, giving his visitor an insider's smile.

'Thank you.' When Ramsay stood up and reached out his hand palm uppermost for the wreath, Sir Anthony's gaze locked on to it. If he didn't do something pronto, that curved silver fish was going to slip out of his grasp and away down the river. At the final second, an idea arrived and the words came rattling out of him. 'Tell you what. You know Lewis? Ethelred Lewis? He's an expert. He'll put you right. Ask him.'

Lewis? He couldn't mean that. Nothing had ever been proved against him after their last encounter, but . . .

'I know he's a bit of a rascal sometimes,' Sir Anthony hurried on, 'but where would we be if we refused to go along with the odd Artful Dodger once in a while? In the poorhouse, that's where we'd be. Angela, get Mr Lewis's address for Mr Ramsay, would you? In Brighton, somewhere. And give him a hand with repacking his parcel. It needs a woman's touch . . .'

'You're going to be late.' When the door was safely closed, she confided, 'I wish the chairman didn't bully him so.' It was not the thing to say to a stranger.

She returned with the address neatly printed on a half-sheet of paper, plus scissors and transparent tape. 'That's really nice,' she said, picking up the wreath and putting it back in its box. As, eyes on her task, she smoothed and folded the paper to rewrap the packet, she chatted busily. 'Wasn't it a pity about the reliquary? Could you just hold down that flap for me? That's great.' Her capable hands took the scissors and snipped just the right length of sticky tape, then pressed it into place.

SOME DARK ANTIQUITIES

'There.' She regarded her effort with pride as her tongue ran away with her again. 'Is that why you're going down to see Mr Lewis? About this new offer . . . for the reliquary?'

So Lewis . . . He didn't allow his face to betray what she had just told him. Instead, he replied carelessly, 'No, we need his opinion on the wreath.'

Innocently she handed him his tidily wrapped parcel.

'Thanks, Angela. You really have been most helpful.'

Before he went down to Brighton, he needed an objective opinion on its contents.

Earnest students in the forecourt were lounging about with clipboards in their hands, waiting to go in to some fine arts lecture. In the airy entrance hall, Ramsay completed an appointment card and had it signed and stamped. Then he was conducted by a blue uniformed officer along passages illuminated by a cold top light until at length they reached a small windowless room in the bowels of the building. It contained two chairs and a table and nothing else. He was left in this cell with his parcel to wait for Dr Baxter, who would be along directly, they said.

Eventually an apologetic young man in a beard entered the room and, after waiting for Ramsay to remove the neat wrapping, took the object into his professional hands.

'Ah,' he said on an eager note. It was a promising noise.

His father's voice seemed to come from a long distance. 'I'll talk to Stanfield and the others – I'm sure they'll take due note of what you say – and I'll come straight back to you.'

In the pause that followed, Ramsay waited for him to put down the receiver. Nothing happened.

'Are you still there?' he said into the void.

The old man spoke with a hesitant jauntiness. 'Just wondering. When are you coming up to Bressemer again?'

He'd only been away from there a week. His father was becoming as demanding as King Lear; Ramsay was no patient Cordelia.

'I'm busy – a couple of big sales to attend, new clients to be seen to... that expatriate Canadian banker... The diary's pretty full just now. Maybe in a couple of weeks. Can I bring Mrs Johnson?'

'As you wish.' The reply was abrupt. Perhaps it wasn't so much that he disapproved as that he wanted his son to himself.

All at once Charles had a mental picture of the figure standing in the study, alone in that grandiose house and belittled by it, with only the grizzled dog for company... He pulled himself up short – in a moment he'd be weeping into his beer.

'I'll be in touch,' he said. 'Take care.' He put the handset down.

Turning to Margaret, he realised he should have asked her first.

'You don't mind?'

'Anything you say.'

She actually smiled. That was an improvement.

It had been a draughty and disjointed journey, but now Frank Becket had almost reached his goal. Tired as he was, his step grew firmer and more urgent as he left the bus station and turned towards The Esplanade. There was a light breeze blowing towards him with all the scents of the sea carried on it, the scents he had smelt every day of that real life before he had been incarcerated in the Sayonara – salt, seaweed, a hint of fish, perhaps. They stirred up his memory vividly and painfully and he found that his eyes had started to water.

As he came to the corner, he had to set down the two small suitcases he was carrying, the leather one with the monogram and the other, and reach for his handkerchief. He hoped that the new tenant of the flat would be an accommodating person, willing to let him have a good look at the old place again. He had come a long way for it.

When he got there, he found that the door of the house was open and there was a hearse parked outside, old but highly polished. He went up the front path between neglected borders and looked into the wide well-remembered hall.

Beyond the reach of building societies, banks, and bailiffs in baggy suits, Frank's successor as occupant of 16a The Esplanade lay comfortably in his coffin as they steered him round that tricky bend in the stairs. There were certain advantages in being dead — very real ones. Computer-written letters demanding instant payment to bring his account into credit could not reach him now, nor urgent summonses to his bank to discuss the position. He had gone away — gone away to be protected by eternity. All at once Frank felt a fellow feeling for this interloper, the man who once upon a time had so profanely bought and occupied his precious flat. In times past there had been nothing but enmity, but now . . . if he had been wearing a hat, he would have taken it off. The economical casket gently scraped the front door, chipping a fragment off the paintwork on its way to the slab-sided hearse and the hereafter.

Before the undertaker's men could close the door, Frank, with a muttered 'Thank you' as though he still belonged there, slipped inside and stepped upstairs. The discreet letter-flap in his front door was still there. He bent down but found it stuffed with life insurance prospectuses, letters from banks offering holiday loans at insane rates of interest, bills from credit card companies. Impatiently he removed the wad, and from force of habit riffled through the mess. Among the envelopes there was an intimidating one marked on the flap THE TROJAN BUILDING SOCIETY, and on the front IMPORTANT—NOT A CIRCULAR. He looked behind him. There was nobody in the corridor except the ghost of himself. Decisively he ripped the envelope open and scanned the contents quickly. In the whole of his life he had never done such a thing before – wouldn't have dreamt of rifling anybody else's mail.

It was a notice of repossession.

'I'll tell Mr Lewis you're here,' said Julia in the expensive accent which went so readily with her clothes, moving away to seek him out behind the scenes. Margaret watched her slender shape depart with a glint of envy at her self-assurance, and retreated to a corner of the shop to study a showcase full of English porcelain while Ramsay began his customary survey of the contents of the showroom. Surely he had seen that Fabergé model of a tortoise before – yes, of course, it had been in Lewis's London shop ages ago – so had that worktable with the silk pouch in faded rose pink underneath it. He wondered just how rapidly the dealer was managing to turn over the rest of his stock because there were one or two things here that he could find a client for easily. Like that early walnut bureau . . . if it wasn't for its later feet.

Lewis came bustling in, too pudgy for his double-breasted suit, the buttons dragging creases across its front – an attempt at a smile on his face, and on his little finger his ring of many colours flashing busily. The same old Ethelred.

'How's business?' Ramsay asked.

'Brisk, despite this tedious slump. Very brisk indeed,' replied Lewis. 'It's heartening, isn't it, Julia?'

She, who had been brought up not to tell fibs except when absolutely necessary, gave him a glance of bewilderment before hunting for something truthful to say. She drawled, 'And we're close to the sea as well. It's fantastic.'

Except for the unfortunate people sleeping under the pier, she admitted to herself. She had a lively social conscience for someone born in silk as she had been.

Lewis spread his arms wide in a welcoming arc.

'Good to see you after so long, Mr Ramsay. What can I do for you? A silver wreath, you said. Wasn't that it?'

When it was shown to him, he didn't pick it up at first – instead he put on the pair of dark horn-rimmed spectacles which always hung from a black ribbon round his neck to give himself an air of dependability.

Keeping his knowing eyes on it, he asked, 'What was Sir Anthony's opinion?' The light gleamed from the lenses of his glasses as he turned his head a fraction to catch Ramsay's reply.

'He said that tests would be needed. He agrees that it's very like one of the things in that show of early jewellery he's put on at Golver's. You've seen it?'

'Their exhibition? The public relations thing. I did plod round it, certainly, but I don't remember . . .' Leaning across Julia with a muttered 'Excuse me dear', Lewis fingered through a pile of catalogues on his table, found the right one and flipped rapidly through it.

'Exhibit number forty-two,' prompted Ramsay.

'Here we are.' Helpfully he showed the photograph of the wreath to Julia standing beside him.

'It *is* like it, isn't it?' She bobbed her head with enthusiasm.

'Just a minute.' Lewis suddenly became active. Busily he made for a green leather screen stamped in faded gold at the back of the shop, and went behind it. They heard him having a good rummage among his reference books before returning an ample portfolio bound in what had once been vellum; now it was dusty and yellowed. Opening it, he took out a sheaf of grey photographs so elderly and washed out that they almost resembled steel engravings, all of them crumbled at the edges and captioned in spidery Greek; he riffled through them.

'There you are!' he exclaimed, picking one of them out. 'I knew I'd seen it before. Boy, what a memory!' Then the self-congratulation left his face. 'Of course it doesn't prove anything except that it wasn't made after. . .' He glanced back at the frontispiece of the portfolio, published in Athens, '. . . nineteen-oh-three. Still, that's progress, isn't it? All these tiny bits and pieces help with the puzzle. We'll get there in the end.' He dropped the big folder down on the table, and dust eddied upwards. 'I'm of the same mind as Sir Anthony. Well worth having tests done, I should think.'

He looked up and for the first time registered Margaret, and understood that somehow she belonged with Charles.

'Mr Ramsay, this is most remiss of you. You haven't introduced me to your friend,' he giggled a little self-consciously.

'Margaret Johnson. Her husband Ian has made us a splendid facsimile of the Burnill reliquary. The trustees commissioned it to replace the original.'

As he spoke, Charles watched the other man's extremities. He shifted his weight and one smart black moccasin moved behind the other, but the small white hands were motionless and his face was blank.

'Ian Johnson. You must know him . . .?'

Lewis made a non committal noise as he glanced at Margaret with an interest that flared up and then went out. About to confirm that he knew him, Julia opened her mouth to speak and was prevented.

'However, we've run into a problem. You may have . . .'

'I heard, yes. Something about the sapphires wasn't it? A bit iffy?'

Grinning, Lewis wrinkled his nose and put a horizontal finger underneath it, enjoying the discomfiture of all and sundry – Andover, the trustees . . .

His evident pleasure touched a nerve in Ramsay. Why should he get away with it?

'What you may not know is that the reliquary was to be sold for charity. To benefit the street children of Rio de Janeiro.' If he wasn't careful, his indignation would make him look a fool. Fighting to control it, he forced the details of their woeful lives on Lewis, the danger they were in, the hopelessness, deliberately patronising the other man in order to burrow under his skin, using his arrogant voice to bait him, implying that his values and way of life were tawdry, nothing to set beside the aspirations of the Brazilian priest whom they had so much wanted to support. Now, because the casket was halfway to being unsaleable, all those hopes would come to nothing. Emotion almost robbed Charles of words, and he faltered – he wasn't used to exposing his feelings. Certainly not to people like Lewis. Had he gone too far and only succeeded in being embarrassing all round? He waited for a mocking comment from him, but it didn't come.

Instead, the dealer had become uncharacteristically serious, all his drollery wilted.

It was Julia who spoke first. Tapping the dial of her slim gold wrist-watch with her forefinger, she admonished him, 'The time. Nearly half-past two.'

'So it is,' confirmed Lewis soberly. 'Excuse me for a moment. There's a call . . . I have to make a telephone call.' He went behind the screen again.

'Sir Anthony wanted him to get in touch. Such a stickler for punctuality,' Julia murmured, then turned her blue eyes on Ramsay. 'I do think you were a little hard on him.'

Hard on him? Lewis was as resilient as a rubber ball. What did she mean?

'You did go on a bit. All that about Brazil and the unwanted children. I know it's awfully sad, but that was a bit heavy, considering. I could see that it really got to him, and I'm not surprised.'

'Considering what?' They looked at each other, both puzzled.

'Oh. I thought you were an old friend of his.'

Friend? Charles had always kept Lewis at arm's length – where he could see him. She looked like a decent type, so he wasn't going to unskittle her illusions.

'I've known him for a year or two. We run into one another now and then.' He wanted to add '. . . when it's unavoidable', but didn't because all of a sudden he found himself anxious not to lose her good opinion.

'So you don't know his dark secret?'

Which of them? She threw a glance towards the back of the shop to make sure that Lewis was still tied up on the phone.

'Well, I think you ought to know for future reference . . .' She hesitated again in case she was saying too much, glanced at Margaret, and decided to hurry on. 'He was a foundling, brought up by a brace of fairly bloody foster parents, and when they found out he was gay they went right off the rails and threw him out. He went up to London, started with a stall in some market or other and made his own way. Alone in the world like that . . . at fifteen . . . you have to admire him.'

Julia was wiser than she might appear. She watched for his reaction, sizing him up, thinking that they probably had a lot in common. He was the kind of man she could relate to – a trifle overbearing perhaps but capable, and with his heart in the right place. Nobody could blame him for his outburst over the street kids – and he'd been prepared to make a fool of himself over the issue. She liked that. Charles Ramsay was value for money – she was interested, she admitted to herself – and that interest registered with him.

As if she felt left out of things, Margaret moved over and stood at his side, making him her ally against the girl. It would be too much to hope that she might be jealous. No, she just wanted to make sure that her own preoccupations hadn't been overlooked, because she began explaining in a vibrant undertone to Julia how she simply had to trace her husband and had reason to believe that Lewis might know where . . .

Back into the room he came, humming a snatch of *Rigoletto* to himself, quite jaunty again with his mask restored to its place. To nobody in particular he complained, 'The wreath. We seem to have quite got off the subject of the wreath . . .'

Unable to contain herself, Margaret broke in with her accusation. 'Wait. You *do* know my husband, don't you? And where he is?'

As though surprised at her small outburst, Lewis stared at her.

'The name is not unfamiliar, I have to confess, but, my dear, I know such lots of people. You should see my address book.'

His eyes looked to heaven seeking a witness to the monstrous size of it, while his hands suggested in the air a volume as big as a family bible. 'Mammoth – and absolutely confidential, I'm afraid.'

Turning his attention to the others, he resumed, 'The wreath, now . . .'

'My husband's whereabouts . . .' Now she found herself ignored, speaking to his back.

'Not to be revealed,' he repeated, 'even to you. Even if I knew, and I'm not sure that I do . . .' He screwed up his face as he spoke as if it was painful to consult his memory, then looked to Ramsay for his support, first as a reasonable man, next as a colleague in the trade. 'Have you considered disposing of the wreath?' he asked.

Was Andover employing him as a go-between, or was his question connected in some way with Margaret's need to find her husband? Ramsay wondered. When negotiating with Lewis, all such possibilities had to be brought into the equation. Perhaps a favourable answer would persuade him to break the seal on his huge address book. It was worth a try if it was going to help her – after that humiliation.

'Could be,' he said.

Lewis gave a weighty look at his assistant. 'Julia dear. Don't forget that you need to bank the takings before they close.' She looked blankly at him. What takings?

'Before the banks close,' he insisted more loudly. When the penny dropped, she left in a flurry of perfume.

More at his ease with her gone, the dealer got down to cases straight away.

'That piece would have to be verified beforehand by an expert nominated by me.'

Ramsay glanced at Margaret for guidance. It was her decision just as much as his. After a moment's hesitation, a small gesture said yes.

'Very well,' he agreed.

'No point in making a meal of it,' Lewis announced, adding rapidly, 'Two thousand pounds, plus the last known whereabouts of Mr Ian Johnson, for the wreath, if it's genuine. Is it a deal?' Like a gipsy selling a horse, he clapped his hands together and held out one of them towards Ramsay. The words, the sudden clap, the proffered hand were a little piece of theatre, and instinctively, as if he were playing a part in the comic turn which it conjured up, Ramsay took the hand and shook it.

He shouldn't have done that.

He'd lost her wreath for her – for pennies.

It had been done without thinking – just because it was expected of him. She made a small noise, little more than a whimper, as she realised what had happened.

Lewis's small dark eyes looked from one to the other. 'Good,' he said, and before they could protest, he picked up the wreath, dropped it back in its box and removed it from the scene.

'I'll take it to the Museum of Antiquities for testing,' he called victoriously over his shoulder. 'I'll let you know what they say, and then we'll settle up the score.'

There were no flies on Ethelred Lewis.

It was a bright and benign day. The sea shone like silver and the white onion-shaped domes of the Pavilion thrust upwards into a pale blue heaven; tourists wandered about in a satisfied way – and Ramsay felt like hell on a pair of feet.

'He caught me off balance,' he complained. Of course it was

his fault, but the whole thing had been so unexpected, had happened in a few seconds, almost as a joke – and it wasn't. More painful than being swindled by Lewis was having to admit it to her.

'It's simple. You go back in there now, tell him it was a mistake and get the wreath back.'

'But your husband's address? I thought you wanted it, and, besides . . .'

'Besides what?' she asked, standing there looking furious and less than her best in crumpled tunic and slacks. When he turned angrily on his heel, she pursued him, plucking at his sleeve, confronting him.

'Besides what?' she demanded again. She was standing across the pavement from him, half-blocking it. A passer-by pushed through, oblivious of the electric charge throbbing between them.

'I shook hands on it,' Ramsay said. 'It's as simple as that.'

Surely she understood that there had to be rules, and this was one of them. If you shook hands on a deal, that was it, whatever it cost. The girl Julia would have understood that.

'Don't be so bloody old-fashioned. He tricked you into it!'

'Arguably, but I'm not prepared to dispute the point.'

'You're not prepared? What about me? I'm going back to Lewis and that girl of his and demand that they give the wreath back to us.'

Two thousand pounds? What was the use of that? It was nowhere near enough. There had been a lot riding on it for her, and he'd blown it.

By the time she had prevailed upon him to go back to the shop it was closed, she was hungry and had been given time to reconsider. Was it likely, now that Lewis had it in his possession, that he would meekly surrender it? How would they get him to give it up? Threaten him? With what?

Although she had to accept the loss, she didn't take it gracefully at all. She sulked all the way back to London, and when they regained the security of his flat – as soon as she had closed the door behind her, leaning with her back against it as though held in place there by the force of her anger – she let fly at him again. Recriminations boiled out of her like lava.

'*Your* pride. *Your* principles. You used them as an excuse to run away from that podgy little man . . . You are weak, weak, weak.' She used the word like a whip to cut at his face, and waited, as if to see it raise weals on his cheek.

Again she attacked. 'It was feeble to let him get the better of you. Why didn't you go back on the deal then and there, when you had the chance?'

'He knows where your husband is.'

'If he does, you don't imagine he'll tell us the truth, do you?'

'We have to take that chance. He's been known to tell the truth.' Now and then.

Ramsay wondered why he had bothered to try. For her sake, and because of the sapphires, in that order. Did she really want to find her husband or not? At the moment he wasn't sure that he cared.

She hammered on. 'You are so *gullible*. What sort of a businessman are you?'

'At least I am solvent.' He shouldn't have said that, but she was getting to him. An inch further, and he would have picked up the phone, found her a room in the Royal York Hotel down the road and packed her off there. Or would he? He looked her up and down. Of course he wouldn't. There she was, at the end of her tether and determined absolutely not to give way to tears. She was vulnerable, that was her strength – her lack of any kind of defence.

Eventually the barrage diminished and a tacit ceasefire was put in place. After preparing a scratch meal together in an atmosphere of brittle politeness, they ate it with scarcely a word. Afterwards she avoided conversation by switching on the television and simulating an unswerving interest in a repeat of a fifteen-year-old sitcom about an unconventional bank manager, followed by a documentary on the social organisation of barbary apes. Once or twice Ramsay looked up from his auction catalogues to find that her gaze had wandered from the screen towards him, only to flick away again when their eyes met. Earlier than usual she announced that she was ready for a bath and bed.

That's that. There's to be no reconciliation today, he thought, and poured himself his third glass of whisky of the evening – third and last, he warned himself. Then, to his surprise, she came back fresh from her bath and sat down tentatively in the other armchair, with a rueful expression on her face.

It cut no ice with him. He turned a page of his catalogue and concentrated his attention on a photograph of an exceptional Regency table with a specimen marble top – the auctioneer's estimate was thirty to forty thousand pounds. These days? He wished them luck.

'Hi.' She wiggled her fingers at him. He took a sip from his glass and began to seethe again, looking for more excuses for that half-generous, half-mistaken . . . that cock-up over the wreath.

'Hey!' She waved a pink palm like a semaphore in front of his unseeing eyes. 'I'm speaking here.' That didn't seem to work, so she made a megaphone with her hands and pretended to shout, 'Hullo, there. Can you hear me? Is anybody there?'

If she could make an effort in the straits she was in – trying to find her sad sack of a husband while dependent on the next best thing to charity – so could he. He dragged his lips into something like a smile. 'Sure. Here, try this.'

As a peace-offering, he poured her a helping of his favourite and most precious malt. Taking the elegantly cut tumbler from him in both hands, she set it on the quartetto table beside her, then smoothed down the towelling dressing-gown with an almost sensual gesture and folded her legs underneath her, settling into the security of the chair as smoothly as a cat. Forgiven.

'Sorry,' she said. 'Sorry for behaving like a fishwife. I didn't mean any of it.'

Of course she had, but he wasn't going to contradict her. His wounds would heal soon enough, and some of them had been deserved.

She took a cushion and threw it at her feet. 'Come over here.'

Although it had become more and more difficult for him in the last day or two to stop himself from invading her territory, he had made the effort – given her state of mind it would have been unfair, unseemly, not to. Now that it looked as though she had changed the rules he wasn't sure that she was wise. Where would it take them both? Whatever he did, he had to avoid visiting any further sorrows on her by leading her into a cul-de-sac. He took a deep pull at his glass and the warmth of the alcohol expanded in his chest, changing his view of things a little. Her face betrayed no signs of doubt. Was he being too scrupulous?

She bent down to pat the cushion and, as she did so, her

dressing-gown fell open a little at the neck, revealing a private cave of curves and shadows. She didn't allow that to impede or bother her; there was no clutching at the collar. 'Come on.'

Because I couldn't refuse without snubbing her, he told himself as he sat down at her feet. Then it seemed the easiest thing in the world to lean back against her knees and relax – let it all go. A warm palm was pressed against his cheek, and he could detect on her skin the smell of his own bath essence which she had used with a generous hand. The emphatic scent somehow created a common bond between them and it dissolved the last of his inhibitions.

A little later she wriggled clear and stood up so that she could draw him to his feet and, chin in the air, trailing him behind her by one hand, she led him to the bedroom.

He had not expected her to be so candid. The next few moments were unreal, being composed of the same mixture of the strange and the everyday which one finds in dreams. This room was the same, the furniture, the pale Wilton carpet, and there, standing in the middle of it, was Margaret. Naked. It was a happy sort of dream.

Neither, if he was honest with himself, had he expected her to be so beautiful. Having shed her husk of everyday clothes, she no longer had reason to feel envious of women with more money to spend on dressing up than she had, women like that young one in Lewis's shop. She had nothing to fear. Her total lack of embarrassment made it no sin for him to watch her as she padded across the floor and pushed her glorious legs between the sheets. With her arms folded on her raised knees, she observed him too as he undressed, pulling off his shirt, unbuckling his belt, folding his trousers, just as unabashed as she had been.

Nor had he expected her to be so forthright in making love.

He had half-feared that she might be simply ready to yield and content to leave it at. Not so: she was inventive, ready to understand and improvise. It had been a long abstinence for both of them and she wanted a worthy celebration, she insisted gently. She wasn't going to allow any hasty coupling to spoil it – it was to be orchestrated, savoured like a meal at each wonderful stage.

When with triumph she received him for the first time, her hands pressed against the small of his back to steady herself, she murmured dreamily in his ear, 'This is not by way of thanks or apology, or anything of that kind.' By then she had no need to tell him that. This was a consummation. A necessity. Before long, with her body bowed upwards beneath him, she cried out hoarsely in the dark, calling out his name and half-sentences of love even when the delicious tension inside her collapsed, the last spasm of delight faded. When, eventually, they were both spent, lying in a damp and peaceful huddle of warm limbs, he could not even remember the doubts that had afflicted him earlier. He was conscious only as he felt her body entwined with his that he had made a willing commitment to her – one which he would not regret whatever vows she had made, kept or broken in that bed.

The next morning she was lively and domestic, taking charge of the breakfast, piling his washing into the machine and setting it grumbling away. It was only when the postman brought the day's handful of mail and she put it on his desk that she noticed Becket's letter of the day before, and, intrigued by the mysterious photocopies, brought it to him.

It was time he paid a duty visit to Bressemer, and it wouldn't involve much of a detour to visit Becket further down the coast on his way. He reached for the telephone. Her hand gripped his arm gently to get him to pause in dialling the number. It would be better, she murmured, if she stayed behind in London this time to give him time to sound out his father's views on the subject of her. She was, after all, a married woman, and Ernest Ramsay's generation often had a different view of things like that.

Chapter Ten

'I told you this so-called stratagem of yours would never work. I said that from the outset.'

Volet's words sang through the air like a knife across the shop – a knife flung at Chalon who was seated behind his desk, which afforded him a certain distance from his enemy's attack. In any case he was only half-listening to the diatribe as it sputtered on its predictable way. His gaze was distracted by the boulle clock – forty thousand was too much for it, alas. Should he send it to auction in Paris and cut his losses? No, their commission rate was exorbitant. Those robbers.

His ally Grimaud had made sure of the only other available seat, a Gothic Revival chair in the Cathedral style with something Puginesque about it, though that wasn't the sort of thing a philistine like him would know. He shifted his buttocks as if regretting he had chosen it – a masterpiece of carving, no doubt, but a torment for the backside.

This riven threesome was the kernel of energy, the driving force behind the Brotherhood. The others were merely providers of hands, materials, assent.

Volet stood in a challenging posture, one against two.

'To take only the sapphires . . .'

' . . . was a masterstroke,' Grimaud asserted vigorously. 'A misdemeanour wrapped in a nice little conundrum – impossible to prove.' He overrode Volet, who had leant forward to challenge him.

'To steal the casket itself? Too obvious a crime for even the English police to screw up on.' Grimaud had some experience of their capabilities and, as a casino-owner, he was well used to assessing risks and adept at keeping them well under control. The other thing his life in the gaming business had taught him was to make the best use of all his assets, even those which appeared to be next to valueless on the face of it – like the huge unpaid debt which the gambler Johnson had run up a year ago with his London operation. When Chalon had suggested it should be used as a lever to induce the Englishman to switch the gems on the Burnill reliquary, he had readily agreed.

Of course the idea might not work; they had both been well aware of that. To begin with Johnson was an unstable type, difficult to persuade and liable to let them down when it came to the push. And once he had done the job, it was always possible that the trustees would dig in their heels and refuse to sell their degraded casket. Indeed it looked now as though they had done just that – but what had been lost? Nothing, except a debt which he couldn't have collected on anyway. The Brotherhood would just have to think of a different approach, that was all. Chalon would come through with something – perhaps all they needed to do was to sit and wait – but that would involve keeping a grip on Volet, which was never easy.

Volet. Once, not many years ago, after celebrating the Fourteenth of July too freely, he had opened his heart to Grimaud – had confided how those few months of brutal action he had seen in Algeria had been a summit in his life, and his last

SOME DARK ANTIQUITIES

thirty years as a fair to middling notary in the town a long slide downhill. The heart hidden below the impeccable handkerchief in the breast pocket of his suit, behind that day's clean shirt, still hankered after another world far beyond his everyday round of legal obligations and circumspect clauses, of spider's nets constructed out of custom and precedent. Hankered after it more intensely as each day aged him and it grew less and less possible. In that world there were no moral shackles – the whole web of law and artifice to which he paid lip-service could be sheared through at one stroke as though with the clean edge of a sword in the hands of a Samurai. That was it exactly: a world of stern solutions, in which the chosen were free to achieve their aims – by which, of course, Volet meant his own – through their own masculine action.

Listening to this nonsense Grimaud had poured him another large glass of cognac – enough for a hero – and had filed the gist of it away in his memory. Later on he picked up here and there the odd word about the man, noted in the Café du Centre the types he associated with.

Grimaud did not like the smell of neo-fascism – it was a perversion which led nowhere in his view. Nor did he like having people like that in the Brotherhood. However, the notary and his boys would have their uses sooner or later, like that compromised Englishman Johnson. Nothing, and nobody, ought ever to be wasted.

'At least we have the sapphires. However you look at it, they are an asset,' he pointed out, hoping to head off another argument, another inefficient use of time. Anyway, whatever he said now, Volet had put his name to the decision when it was made; it was in the hidden records of the Brotherhood, kept by the son of the mayor.

'The stones? Do we have them?' Volet's question was deliberately offensive.

Chalon wasn't bothered. 'They're in my safe,' he said and, before Grimaud could dissuade him, he rose from his chair.

He returned with the familiar package. Taking a sheet of white paper, he laid it in the centre of his desk before peeling away the wrapping and spilling the two misshapen blue gemstones on to it.

Without a word, he handed a magnifier to Volet, who waved it away. 'I take your word for it.'

That wasn't good enough for Chalon. From his desk drawer he produced a set of photographs and held them stacked between fingers and thumb like a deck of cards.

'I had these enlargements made specially from my original photographs. To check that they were right.'

Selecting two from among them, he laid them down with precision at the head of the sheet of paper as though he were a poker player displaying the ultimate hand. Then he arranged the stones on the white background so that they had precisely the same orientation as in the photographs. Finally he adjusted the desk lamp to the best effect. Standing back with satisfaction, he pushed the magnifying glass at Volet once again.

'Come on. Your confirmation here and now, if you please. You owe it to me.' For support he looked to Grimaud, who stared at the notary with uncompromising eyes. No need to speak.

With a sigh, Volet stooped over the desk, the light from the lamp exposing the pink scalp beneath his carefully combed hair.

'I am not an expert, you understand . . .'

'Get on with it, Volet. Say it. Spit it out.'

The notary put down the magnifier, and admitted, 'As far as I can tell, these are the original sapphires from the reliquary. I presume that you will not be asking me for an affidavit.'

Ignoring him, Grimaud consulted his watch. 'You have just wasted nine and a half minutes of my time,' he said flatly. 'Now, I insist that we get on with our discussion.'

The sound of Raquin's footsteps on the granite setts of the *quai* precisely matched his own. That was how he wanted him, exactly in step. Volet halted at the parapet and looked down over the river, flowing slow and deep, its surface like a broad black mirror reflecting the pale stonework of the Pont Neuf with such clarity that it was impossible to tell where the real bridge ended and its image on the surface of the water began – reality and its reflection were joined together in one fantastic entity. One of the innovations in the town which Volet had not opposed was the council's decision to floodlight the bridge. Glancing at Raquin standing beside him, he sensed the young man's impatience to go back over the orders he had just been given. To show how effective he was, what a good memory he had inside that close-cropped head of his.

Very well.

'Repeat my instructions.'

First, Raquin looked round to check that they were alone on the grey *quai* – it was a frequent haunt for the commoner sort of lovers – then he did as he was told. Towards the end of his recital, he stumbled and looked furious with himself.

'Twenty-six Village Crescent. That is the address where you will join up with Smith,' prompted Volet. 'Here, I'll write it down for you.'

He groped in his pocket for a memorandum pad and pen and

then, realising that there wasn't enough light, he put them away again feeling irritated, as though that little mistake had washed away some of his authority. 'I'll do it later.'

'No need.' Raquin rehearsed the address fluently. 'And there I will find Smitt.'

'Smith,' said Volet impatiently. 'Th . . . th . . . the English th . . . Tongue between the teeth like this – th . . .'

Forget it. It didn't matter. What mattered was the money. Although not a rich man, Volet was a careful one who spent an hour or two on his finances every Friday evening. Over several months he had made certain economies – changed his car for something more modest, foregone his usual skiing holiday in Gstaad – and had collected together in a high-yielding bank account enough money to finance this project of his. Two days earlier he had drawn out the whole amount and converted it into sterling notes – anonymous and untraceable cash – the proceeds of his thrift and planning. Now he was about to lose control of it. Would Raquin use it wisely . . . honestly?

Reluctantly he opened his lawyer's briefcase, took out the fat manilla envelope and handed it over. Since he didn't have a choice, there was no point in losing sleep over it.

'There is sufficient in there to cover all your needs: the vehicle, equipment and expenses, together with seven hundred pounds sterling for contingencies. I shall need receipts for any large expenditures.'

Raquin took the envelope and stuffed it carelessly into his pocket – all those economies, that wad of cash was put away as though it were nothing more than folded newspaper, something negligible like that.

'Understood.'

The young man's unsatisfied hunger for action. Direct action.

SOME DARK ANTIQUITIES

That's the best hope, my surest safeguard, Volet thought, without complete conviction.

The traffic ahead of Raquin on the M25 was sluggish enough to blunt the edge of even his fancy style of driving, which wasn't helped either by the staid vehicle he had chosen for his trip to England – a square-sided camper van resprayed in pale blue. It was sound enough mechanically, he had made sure of that, and he had spent most of the previous Sunday servicing it, dealing with all the items like the exhaust pipe and tyres which might attract the attention of the English police and throw his schedule out. Finally he had given the vehicle a complete wash and polish to fit the character he had roughed out for himself – a young house-proud bachelor on his first visit to England whose occupation was his own, of course – a supermarket manager. A worthy one, but not adventurous enough for him. This project was going to be a test of his ability to survive outside the world of impertinent checkout girls, shoplifters and special offers '*A Saisir!!*' for one week only. It was an opportunity to make his name in the movement; to outstrip Volet, perhaps.

The pack of vehicles began to thin out a little, enabling him to steer into the outer lane and put his foot down. The workaday engine responded gamely, but its efforts to keep up with the fast stream fell short of what was needed. Before attracting attention to himself, Raquin drew back into the inconspicuous middle lane and congratulated himself; he was learning fast.

When he reached it, he didn't much care for the town, which was freezing cold and uncared-for. His first impression was of grime-soaked concrete; half the place seemed to be for sale.

He needed some supplies, enough for a week, so that he

didn't have to break cover unnecessarily when he got to the target.

Pushing his trolley through the empty aisles of the supermarket, he cast a professional eye over the shelves. A different range of vegetables; that English chocolate tasting of nothing – he could never sell that in his store – nor those sour brown sauces and the packeted bread resembling slices of plastic foam.

His purchases included a great many packets of fresh meat, which he stowed away in the little refrigerator in the kitchenette section of the van. After everything was shipshape, he made rapidly for the Post Office, hunched up in his white cotton jacket clammy with English rain. No doubt someone there would be delighted to direct a young foreign tourist with only a limited command of their language to 26 Village Crescent. Patiently he queued for an audience with the girl at the counter who was cashing giros for the line of unemployed ahead of him.

Number 26 Village Crescent was by no means as cosy as it sounded. Thirty years before, the estate might have been a model of all that public housing should be. Now the grass verges were worn and walls were adorned with antique graffiti; here a concrete lamp-standard exposed its steel entrails where a joyrider had assaulted it, perhaps; there a front garden was embellished with a used-up refrigerator, waiting to be collected by the council.

He didn't think much of the place. Like Volet, he believed that the movement would have to demonstrate its respectability if it were to conquer, and this house didn't go with that idea at all. It was timid. He pushed open the little wooden gate, which dragged on one hinge and had scratched a quadrant in the damp soil.

'Yes?' The man who came to the door was as large and reserved as a night club bouncer.

'Raquin.'

'Oh, yes?' The wide face looked unimpressed.

'I am come from Volet.'

'You are come? Oh.' Something dawned in the eyes, a stirring of recollection.

'Oh, yes. Come in. Come in.' In the little hall with its red carpet adorned with unconvincing flowers, he turned suddenly on his visitor. 'Identification?' he demanded, putting out his hand.

Raquin fumbled in his pocket for his identity card, and produced it. It seemed to be enough. The other man led the way into the back room, which was a grotto of trophies from yesterday's Germany, the Germany of fifty years before. Dress daggers, a recruiting poster with a helmeted soldier staring heroically into the middle distance – '*Der Sieg Wird Unser Sein.*' A Knight's Cross with oakleaves in a dusty little case. On one wall a Waffen SS helmet had been hung above a large flag – red field, white roundel, black swastika; both had been there a long time.

In a showcase was a collection of small moulded polystyrene figures arranged in a diorama, each one accurately painted with the uniforms of the Third Reich – apparently taken from some model kit designed for a very specialist market. Looking closely, he saw that the whole Nazi hierarchy was represented, with the Leader upfront on a cardboard dais, silently haranguing the rest of them.

'*Heil* Hitler!' exclaimed his host, thrusting out his right arm, his loose shirt-cuff flying. He had a pink butterfly tattooed on his right wrist.

Espèce de ... thought Raquin, then, deciding that he ought to humour this type, he responded in kind. Although it was a half-hearted apology of a salute, a mere flip from the elbow, it seemed to satisfy the other man.

'Feel free,' he said with a welcoming gesture. 'It's all round you in this room. Oh ...' He went to the sideboard and took out a flat volume. 'Here. You enjoy that while I go and fetch him. Smith.'

It was an album of autographs, not of the Nazi leaders, of course, but of their underlings; people whose names were now only footnotes in the histories, if they were mentioned at all: Goering's ADC, a gauleiter of Thuringia, a Standartenführer-SS, minor players like that. Raquin didn't object in principle to a bit of nostalgia, but all this seemed like a total waste of time and energy to him; it was the future that engaged his attention. The brute fact was that the Nazis had been comprehensively crushed. The Third Reich had been a total flop, a washout, and he didn't believe in celebrating failure. Adolf had managed to stay on top for only eleven years – before he had been cornered like a animal in the bunker and driven to blow out his addled brains. Raquin promised himself that the New Order which he, Volet and all the other comrades envisaged was going to last a hell of a lot longer than that.

He looked round him again, and caught sight of a framed photograph. A German officer with hands on hips, a shaven-headed orchestra ... victims with lowered heads digging. Inspecting it more closely, he grimaced. Is this collector of memorabilia altogether sane? he asked himself as he put the autograph album back in its place – a man who displayed that sort of picture in his living-room? The less he revealed of his plans and the sooner he moved on, the better.

It was then that Smith, his bodyguard to be, came into the room. He wasn't Raquin's type, either. At the time he had thought Volet's idea was sound enough, but now that he was face to face with the reality he wasn't so sure. Very well, he could see that here was a pugilist of the old school, battle hardened and street-wise, but could he be trusted? Could either of them be trusted? That was the question . . .

Chapter Eleven

The flat had been stripped by the auctioneers, stripped to the bone, so that there was nothing to sit on to give his legs a rest except the mahogany seat-cover of the Edwardian lavatory in the bathroom. Enthroned there like some bishop, Frank presently felt ridiculous – besides, it was the only corner of the place which had never boasted a *décor*, could evoke for him no memories of past elegancies. He stood up, feeling the ache in his calves return as he did so. His footsteps echoing on the bare boards, he went back to the living-room, where he lowered himself to the floor, squatting down with his back against the wall to peer into his attaché case yet again to check through its contents. He had arrived early to make sure that he did not miss his visitor – too early, and now in the flat that had once been his pride he was bored, uncertain what to do next.

This was his fourth visit. The girls at the estate agency were smart enough to tell a timewaster at a glance, but humoured him because he was elderly – old-fashioned and so polite. They didn't have to ask now which keys he wanted; they just handed him the usual set – a Yale for the front door of the building, the steel key for the mortice lock of the flat itself and a couple of others for cupboards, all held together on a twisted loop of wire with a brown tie-on label – 16a The Esplanade – IF FOUND

PLEASE RETURN TO . . . in bold black letters. All of a sudden he was overcome by an absurd fear that he had dropped them somewhere and had to run his thumb over their well-remembered metal profiles in his raincoat pocket to set his mind at rest. All present and correct. They had been his own keys once – no point in dwelling on the fact.

Since it was probably his last visit, he was irritated that on this wet afternoon he somehow couldn't recapture the glamour of the place, however hard he tried. Glancing at random in front of him, his eye was offended yet again by the patch of raw new boarding in the floor, exposed by the taking-up of the carpets. That was a pity.

He experienced another flood of anxiety: this time, about the visitor he was expecting now that he was about to arrive. Was he to be trusted or would he make a play for the manuscript? ask to take it away with him to be examined by an expert? demand a commission? even propose a profit-sharing deal? There was a forest of possibilities, and Frank found himself unable to cope methodically with them one by one. Perhaps he ought to take his treasure elsewhere and find someone else, some dealer in manuscripts, but who? Rare books and manuscripts had never been his line of country.

Could he scrape the energy together? He was so bloody tired, that was the problem – and he had cramp in the hinge of one knee. It was all very well squatting down; getting up was another matter altogether at his age. Glad that he was alone and unobserved, he leaned forward into a kneeling position and used the attaché case on its end to lever himself to his feet. A couple of steps took him into the embrasure of the bay window. The late autumn sun had come out now and was filling the room with a deep tawny light.

To get some air, he pulled up the sash, which still moved easily enough. That was better. The cries of one or two children playing on the beach came to him, like the sound of seagulls far off, he told himself, and then reproved himself instantly for that sentimental fancy... There were steps on the pavement outside. He glanced at his watch – three minutes past two.

Looking down obliquely through the window at his side, he could just see the top of the head of the young man who was standing at the front door. From that angle he couldn't see enough of him to tell whether it was Ramsay or not. He began counting. When he had reached fourteen, the harsh doorbell crashed out. With a certain reluctance he went downstairs to let him in.

His visitor was as he remembered him – an easy man to talk to who sounded like a gentleman – that is to say as though he had attended a public school for more than a term or two. So had his employer Burnill, he remembered, and he had been no model of virtue, so it didn't always signify. At the forefront of his mind the need to keep his visitor interested long enough to get an opinion from him was paramount; at a deeper level his doubts still kept him troubled, crawling to and fro down there like the worms which scavenge the sea bed.

On his side, Ramsay couldn't say that he remembered the elderly man who opened the door to him; he had met him only once for an hour or so and that had been months ago. As Becket led him slowly upstairs he kept apologising – for bringing his visitor out of his way to this odd rendezvous, for the lack of anything to sit on in the flat. He seemed unable to stop himself, and it was an unhelpful way to begin a business relationship. To break the flow of excuses, Ramsay made some token conversation about Bressemer, the garden, the Qianlong porcelain, but that didn't seem to catch the attention of the other man clinging so hard to his small attaché case – with initials on its lid which were not his own.

Eventually, almost rude in his haste, Becket snapped it open and handed his precious manuscript over.

'Is this the whole of it?'

'Yes.'

'Manuscripts are not my thing. I told you that, I think.'

Becket nodded. In the kingdom of the blind . . . Besides, it was advice he wanted as much as anything. Someone to consult.

Ramsay scrutinised the first six pages or so with care for a long-drawn-out minute or two while Becket fidgeted with anxiety. At length he felt impelled to ask, 'Have you noticed the back? There's part of a typewritten article.'

Ramsay reversed the sheet, studied it for a moment, and then read through a snatch of it aloud: 'If the Visigothic city of Carcassonne cannot be called concentric, it is only because there were never any concentric castles except here and there by accident. The aim in the mind of every architect of the smallest intelligence . . .' The untidy typescript was old-fashioned – Edwardian, even. His voice died away in the bare room, competing with the sparse and distant shrieks of the children on the beach.

'Does that mean anything to you?' Becket enquired.

It didn't. Turning back to the side of the sheet covered in small tight handwriting, Ramsay asked, 'Then what about this?' and spoke again. '"In the beginning we were innocent of evil but, on the other side, empty of good. Each of us as neutral as the winds which hurled over us by day, as indifferent as the black desert sky and its baldachin of silent stars by night . . ."'

Ramsay looked across, and raised a questioning eyebrow. 'A touch high-flown, isn't it? It could be a different writer altogether.'

Becket said nothing; perhaps he felt offended, as if somehow the gilt was being rubbed off this treasure of his which he had kept pristine in the dark for so long.

'How did you come by it?'

'My father gave it to me.'

'Where did he get it from?' Ramsay's repeated questions felt intrusive, but they had to be asked; both of them realised that.

'It goes back a long way.' Becket sounded apologetic again, as though unsure how the other man would receive his story.

He began slowly. 'It happened years ago,' he said, 'not long after the Great War. My father worked on the railways – he was an employee of the Great Western Railway all his working life, and proud of it. At the beginning of the 1920s he was assistant station master at Reading – and lucky to be so at his age.'

He paused, remembering his father's small triumph – coming home with the news.

'Then?' Ramsay prompted.

Becket continued, 'It was a summer day, mid-afternoon, he told me. A passenger waiting to catch the Oxford train – the through train from Paddington – was in the station buffet, in the corner near the door. My father was in there, too, passing the time by chatting to the lady attendant, since the place wasn't busy just then. This chap got up to go for his train and left his rucksack behind on the seat.'

'So?'

'As soon as my father saw it, he chased after the owner. Dad had been wounded in the knee at Cambrai, which slowed him down, and when he caught up with the man, he had already boarded the Oxford train. But the odd thing was . . .'

'Yes?'

'. . . when Dad offered him the rucksack, he denied at first that it was his.'

'Perhaps it wasn't?'

'No. He'd seen him bring it in and put it down on the chair beside him. There was no mistake.'

'What did he look like – the passenger?'

'An ordinary man, Dad said. Stocky with fairish hair, dressed in a sports jacket and flannels with no tie. Youngish and good-looking, but not young enough to be a student, even if he'd gone up to the university late because of the war. Could have been a junior fellow at one of the colleges, perhaps. Well-spoken.'

'Did he say anything else?'

'Only, "The coffee in your refreshment room is an atrocity. Your waiting woman should be made to journey to Jeddah on all fours to learn how to make it properly. As for the rucksack, you may keep it." Then he yanked up the window by its leather strap, slam, to cut off Dad's reply, and the train pulled out.'

'And your father was left holding it?'

'Yes. He thought he ought to try to contact the owner in case he wanted to change his mind – the railway company was very strict about lost property – but when he opened it up there wasn't a name or address on it anywhere.' Becket added hastily, 'And nothing inside except the manuscript with a thick red elastic band round it.'

A misty idea floated at the back of Ramsay's mind, almost taking a sensible shape, teasing him, then vanishing again – he couldn't catch hold of it. The short fair-haired man was . . . might have been . . . No. It was no good. He changed tack. 'Teviot,' he exclaimed suddenly. 'Teviot of Gloucester Street, near Russell Square. He's the best man to consult. He'll know what it is, if anybody does.'

Becket scribbled down the address on the back of the sheaf of paper, leaning against the wall to hold it steady. He breathed out, 'Do you think it's worth while to bother him?'

'Yes, I do. I can't say why, so don't ask me.'

Tentatively Becket broached the question of recompense. A fee? A commission? Perhaps he should have kept quiet.

Fee? Commission? Of course not. While Ramsay had done nothing much, he had to admit that he felt a bit let down. He had come some distance out of his way to this meeting, and the mystery was still unsolved; it still reminded him from time to time that it was there – like a sensitive tooth.

'Why did you suggest a meeting here?' he asked looking round at the empty flat.

Becket shrugged. 'I used to live here. It has an importance for me. Memories. Besides, it's private and sheltered from the weather, of course. I was worried about getting the manuscript wet.' As though to excuse his fussiness, an unexpected gust of rain slashed through the open window, and hastily he shut it.

His visitor had only been there a matter of minutes and politeness demanded that he make some kind of conversation, not just show him to the door; besides he wanted to talk. The trouble was that there was only one other topic in his mind apart from the manuscript.

'I was the victim of a bureaucratic nonsense. They sold the flat over my head when they had no right to – none at all. And all my beautiful furniture. The pictures. Everything I possessed.'

'Couldn't you have stopped them?' Ramsay demanded.

'I wasn't well,' Becket said quickly, unwilling to say what precisely had been wrong with him because he was one of the old school, 'and by the time I was myself again, it was too late. I gave the solicitor a roasting though, I promise you that.' He had needed someone to confide in for a long time and now there was this stranger. To give Ramsay the full flavour of his loss he ventured more detail. 'There.' He pointed to the floor of the bay window. 'I had an old Saruq rug – beautiful clear pattern . . . And over there a Regency work table – mahogany with claw feet. What would that be worth now, do you think?'

'Can't say without seeing it,' Ramsay responded. 'Seven hundred, a thousand.'

Whatever figure he offered, it wasn't going to satisfy Becket, who started again in an indignant tone. 'They ripped out the mantelpiece . . .'

To head him off, Ramsay said, 'How did you come to be so knowledgeable about antiques and so on?'

'I was secretary to Sir Simon Burnill for many years. I did all the buying for his collection. Burnill, the same man who donated that reliquary you're handling. I didn't buy that for him though. He bought that himself.'

For the first time Becket's face showed signs of animation, as if he wanted to be asked the obvious question.

'Why was that?'

The old man's eyes gleamed like those of a child with its lips closed tight, holding a secret in its mouth.

'Did he often take things out of your hands like that?' The answer couldn't be held back any longer.

'The reliquary was different – a very private purchase. It was brought to him by an ex-sergeant in the US Army who was staying on in England after the war was over, ready to dabble in anything lively and in need of funds to get started. There was money to be made in all sorts of stuff from the States.

Al Browning was the sergeant's name, or rather that's what he called himself. I didn't care for him, but I took him out to a pub for a drink once or twice to find out what Burnill was up to – I felt I'd been sidelined, that he didn't trust me. As it turned out, I could have saved my money because Burnill told me all about it himself not long afterwards. He had to boast about his acquisition to somebody, and I was the safest somebody he knew.'

Ramsay felt as if something had suddenly collapsed inside him and anger afflicted him, anger at all the effort he had wasted. It was obvious what Becket was going to tell him next; all that he didn't know was how he would wrap it up. He approached the question obliquely.

When the American Seventh Army landed on the Côte d'Azur in August 1944 the main body fought the Wehrmacht up the Rhône valley. Part of the force, however, was detached to push westwards to protect the American flank against a counter-attack. Under orders to cover as much ground as possible, its communications became stretched as it fanned out, units losing touch with each other as they drove hard through the countryside. As it turned out, there was little opposition from the withdrawing Germans in their sector so the GIs were relaxed and, when they stopped for a meal or to refuel, they often had a chance to do some exploring and now and then a little light looting on the side.

One day Browning found an empty church and, inside it, on display to the faithful in an old-fashioned iron showcase with thick glass sides, was a magnificent mediaeval reliquary. Presumably the priest had thought it reasonably safe where it was – that region of France had been quiet enough during the Occupation. What he hadn't allowed for was the Liberation.

Browning didn't have to be a connoisseur to know it was valuable. He shot the lock off the showcase, removed the casket, wrapped it in a spare shirt and had it in his haversack in twenty-two seconds flat. He could put a hustle in when he had to, he had boasted over his fourth gin and lime.

Burnill had paid him six hundred and fifty pounds sterling for it and had kept it in his strongroom for a long time to cool it off. Then he had donated it to the church of St Nicholas, as a joke as much as anything – on an impulse.

'He was an atheist,' Becket added. 'It tickled his sense of the absurd that the church was so grateful for his gift and displayed it with such pride when none of them, from the bishop downwards, knew that it was stolen property. What did they want with such a valuable and conspicuous object anyway, he used to ask me.'

'It's difficult to find suitable flowers at this time of year, but these dark rosehips look very well against the grey stonework of the chancel,' Mrs Alice Thornton explained to the black and white cat who had followed her into the church.

The animal ignored the remark and for some reason best known to itself began to retreat the way it had come, tail up like a flag, paws moving purposefully.

Cats are like that – unaccountable, she thought, primping the branches with fingers armed in stiff gardening gloves against the thorns. She stood back, humming a cosy tune, then looked behind for something to fill out her display.

'How many of the faithful will be at monthly service today,' she wondered aloud, and wished once again that the Reverend Oscar was not quite so uncompromising, so anxious to stamp on sin wherever he thought he saw it peeping out. If he wished to retain his flock in these days of unbelief, he would have to make an effort to be more congenial; a modern shepherd needed to come down from his pulpit and shake a few hands.

There was the sound of a cough. It reverberated under the clerestory like the blow of a hammer.

What?

In a flurry she looked behind her. What was that?

A young crop-headed man in sharply pressed jeans and a T-shirt which advertised a well-known brand of designer perfume was standing in the aisle. Must be a foreigner.

He was standing beside the small square cavern in the wall of the nave where the Burnill reliquary stood lit up behind a sheet of armoured glass and four stout steel bars; bars whose ends were buried deep in the stone. The arrangement looked impregnable enough, but had it been wise to put their treasure on display again after all that unwanted publicity, she wondered? No, it hadn't.

He came towards her and explained in halting English that he was a tourist taking a late holiday in the East Anglian countryside.

'Oh yes. Lovely. Full marks,' cried Mrs Thornton, for she felt it was something to be encouraged in foreigners these days. Nation speaking peace unto nation, and everything. She tried to recall some of the French she had learnt at school more than – well, admit it, fifty years ago – sought for words, clutched mentally at random scraps of conjugations here and there. How did one say, 'I do hope you are enjoying yourself?'

'*Je souhaite que vous vous . . .*' Clever Alice Thornton to remember the reflexive bit, she thought – but then the verb evaded her; what was it? It was quite an easy one, she knew that.

'*vous am . . .* have a good time,' she concluded briskly with a smile and what she hoped was a Gallic shrug. To cover up, *vous savez*. The French were a bit of a touchy nation, weren't they? – had such a down on you for any little damage you did to their language. They'd got it from that petulant bean-pole De Gaulle – what an ungrateful man he had been.

'I must be getting on,' she added. 'I'll be here if you want anything explained. The Burnill reliquary or those carvings on the pew ends. Rather lovely. Mattins is at ten-thirty.' Of course he was RC probably. Picking up a sheaf of cotoneaster branches rich with scarlet berries, she made towards the other side of the nave.

The French boy continued to inspect the reliquary. Not like a tourist, somehow, she thought, more like a technician of some kind, sizing it up. A practical person – perhaps he was a silversmith like Mr Johnson had been . . . was . . . wherever he had got to now.

As she snipped the sparse branches and twisted thin wire to hold them in place, she reflected that it might be as well to mention this Continental visitor to the Reverend Oscar when he arrived to put his robes on, so that this fellow member of the European Community could be given a proper welcome even if his beliefs wouldn't permit him to stay on for their modest morning service. She was thoroughly ecumenical herself.

She looked round again to find the young man had vanished. Now where had he got to?

'Hallo,' she cried in a decorous voice. 'Hallo! *Où êtes-vous?*'

The vestry door was open, and behind it she heard a shuffling noise. She strode down the aisle with high purpose in her step. The Entente Cordiale was all very well. However . . .

Fortunately when she put her head round the door, a holiday memory came to her aid.

'*Passage interdit, vous comprenez,*' she said firmly, shooing him back into the public part of the church. '*Passage interdit.*'

The little monkey! The Reverend Oscar would certainly have to be told.

Smith had been waiting for some time in the back and was getting restless when his companion emerged from the church of St Nicholas at ten thirteen. Their lack of a common language made it difficult for them to get on terms. They were both still edgy and distrustful, unsure exactly what the other meant. This time, however, Smith was querulous and had no difficulty in making himself understood. Ignoring his grumbling, Raquin consulted his map for a few minutes as the incoming worshippers hurried past his van, one or two of them dropping a curious, half-apologetic glance into it. Where would he find what he needed? His gaze strayed over the map. Norwich? No. Ipswich? No. Somewhere further away than that. Birmingham, to make sure. That was where he would go.

Luckily the wall was sandstone. The question was – how deeply were those steel bars buried in it? Four centimetres? Five? How long would he have? Not more than three minutes, because the presbytère was so close to the church and the priest was living there; he had done his homework. Just enough time if he was really fast.

But before that he was going to spend a good chunk of Volet's money. He was looking forward to that.

Towards eight o'clock in the evening the following day, they got back from the Midlands, edgy from the journey and hungry; before they could eat, Raquin had to find a suitable camp-site, which wasn't so difficult at that time of year. He would need a day or two to finalise his plans and test his equipment.

After the meal, as a joke, he showed Smith what he had bought, tearing the packaging off the disc, twenty centimetres in diameter, which had cost him the equivalent of eleven thousand francs from a man in Smethwick with a knowing look in his eye. He had given away as little information as possible and had judged it safer not to bargain, especially as Volet was footing the bill. He'd kept a receipt. The purchase had left him perilously short of money. Why, he demanded of his companion, couldn't Volet do his homework properly? Smith didn't vouchsafe a reply – just looked blank as usual, with that stare which was getting on his nerves.

A wide grey cloud hung low above Bressemer, extending over the sea, and it was pouring with rain. Ramsay pushed open the front door and found that it was already dark in the hall, although it was only three in the afternoon. Not much of a welcome – why wasn't there a light? Was the old man economising or was he in trouble? Heart trouble or stroke trouble. It was a thought which bothered him more often these days.

He walked down the passage to the kitchen, past the scullery, where there was still so much detritus surviving from the early years of the century – a patent knife-polishing machine left over from the days before stainless steel blades, an ice-chest, a copper electric kettle, the remains of the old kitchen range. None of it had been moved since he had played there as a child. His father hadn't got rid of it all to a museum because he had a strange affection for the stuff. It was a sort of security blanket for him. Where on earth was he, though?

Under the kitchen door he saw a thread of light. Ramsay

opened it, and there was his father, of course, on a backless kitchen chair expertly plucking a cock pheasant. Its severed claws, wings and head were laid out forlornly on the draining board. Open in front of him, between his knees, he had a black polythene bin-bag, and he was stuffing the feathers right down into it as he worked methodically over the breast, taking particular care not to tear the skin. Erratic in so much else, he was a stickler when it came to plucking a bird – the way he had been made to do it by his father's gamekeeper as a boy.

'The moment your hands get wet, the bloody feathers stick to your fingers,' he grumbled as he always did. 'Sorry I didn't come to the door. If you don't keep still, they fly all over the place.' The cock's deceased mate was hanging, head askew, from a noose of baler twine from a knob on the door of one of the kitchen units.

She was destined for the freezer, Ernest Ramsay said, unless his son had brought his girlfriend with him. No? As he turned his attention to the back of the bird, he looked not so much pleased as relieved. These days when it came to meeting women he wasn't a great conversationalist – not much small talk left in him; he'd lost the knack.

Raquin pushed experimentally against the leaded window of the vestry with the nose of his bolt-cutter, and felt it give a little. The spot of light from the masked torch which he held uncomfortably in his mouth wavered all over the place as he did so. Grunting, he trained it again on the crucial area and applied a little more weight against it. A small square pane of ruby glass gave inwards – he heard it chink and clatter as it hit the floor – and give him the opening he needed.

Inserting the cutters in the hole, he began to snip the lead frames one by one in a rough circle, pausing after a while to test with delicacy how loose the ragged fragment of the structure was. Eventually it collapsed and swung down towards him before he caught it. Reaching in with his hand, he bore down on the handle of the window. It screeched for a moment. He stopped, held his breath, then pulled it open in one quick movement.

Bravo! Not bad, for a supermarket manager, to enter an English church in the middle of the night with such efficiency. He wished that when he returned he could confide in Denise, the brightest and cheekiest of his checkout girls, who was not easy to impress. He gestured quickly to Smith to go in over the window ledge first – going first came with the job.

Inside, the spot of light from the torch skated about at random over the contents of the vestry. A cupboard, the ghost of a smell of incense that Raquin found almost reassuring, a framed sepia photograph of an Italian cathedral, benches and coathooks. The door. He hefted his heavy bag and followed Smith into the church on quiet shoes.

Dreaming that he was going downhill on a bicycle, ringing the bell in a double beat to warn a pedestrian who was wandering uncertainly out into the road in front of him, Ramsay awoke just before he made contact, the insistent ring of the telephone in the study below an irritating pulse in his head. He'd better answer it before it woke his father. He drew in a sharp breath as he got out of bed – the house was damn cold. He had brought no dressing-gown, so he put on his rainproof jacket and descended the staircase.

After three in the morning, and it was Stanfield of all people on the other end of the line.

'Ramsay? I'm sorry for calling you at this hour, but somebody has got into the church.' He made no attempt to sound apologetic.

'Are you certain?' Crying wolf wasn't usually one of Stanfield's many faults.

'I was given warning. I have been keeping an eye open. Something's going on over there. A light, noises.'

'Call the police.'

'They'll never be here in time.'

'I'll come over.'

He went back to his bedroom, dressed haphazardly and came downstairs again, pulling on his coat. Then on an impulse he went into the study and tried the gun cupboard, finding, as he expected, that his father had left it open – yes, he was getting more forgetful. Taking out the second-best shotgun, he rummaged about in the box at the bottom for a handful of cartridges and transferred them to the big side pocket of his coat.

He wouldn't take the car; quicker to walk.

Raquin had told Smith to keep watch in the porch. Now he plugged the reel of flex into the socket in the vestry, trailed it past the electric kettle flanked by the upside-down coffee mugs and pulled it into the church in virtual darkness. The small disc of light from his torch enabled him to negotiate the doorway and avoid colliding with the last row of pews as he threaded it up the aisle to the place where the reliquary was kept. He plugged the other end of the lead into the brand-new stone saw with its disc armed with industrial diamonds which he had bought in Smethwick.

He could not allow himself to switch it on until he was ready to make the first cut in the stone. Carefully he lowered his battery-powered lamp to the floor, and put it on. The image of the reliquary sprang gleaming out of the darkness, and the glare lit up the stone arches of the nave like a stage set with dense theatrical shadows behind them. He pulled the trigger on the saw.

A flash in the vestry, and the snap of a sharp little explosion. The fuse on the plug had blown in there. Inadequate. *Merde de merde.*

Reproaching himself, he switched off the lamp and groped in the bag for a spare fuse. By the light of his little torch he verified the amperage and strode back to the vestry door with two screwdrivers in his pocket. There were no curtains in there, but perhaps the open cupboard door would give a shield to keep his light hidden more or less. He laid the torch on a shelf, propped it in place with a couple of hymnbooks, and breathing heavily he replaced the fuse as quickly as he could. Smith presumably was still in the porch; no time to check.

Following the heavy flex as a guide in the dark, he worked his way hand over hand back to the stone saw and turned on the light. Now he was doubly short of time to make the cuts in the stone above and below the steel bars. Pulling the plastic goggles over his eyes, he took a deep breath and switched on the saw.

The noise, magnified by the great space which surrounded him, was deafening. He felt the flush of adrenalin in his back as he pressed the saw against the stone and it screeched and screamed as though in pain. Now he must have woken up the priest. The sharp blade sliced into the stone as though it was cheese, smoke and stone dust pouring back in a stream under the saw, stinging the backs of his hands clamping it as they moved it forward steadily through the stone. The noise was colossal. The first cut was complete, and now the priest would be pulling on his trousers. Raquin grinned as he shifted the blade at right angles to make the transverse cuts between the bars up to his original line. Hurry! By this time, the priest would be coming downstairs.

Raquin moved the saw to a point about six centimetres from the bottom edge of the reliquary's resting-place and went through the whole procedure again. Where would the priest be now? He had finished the second cut and only a brittle transverse plug of stone held each bar in place. He put down the stone saw and picked up a broad-bladed cold chisel and a short hammer. The chisel was quickly inserted in the slot he had cut. Then he banged the head of the chisel with too much force and caught his hand. *Merde* again.

The first bar was free, leaning drunkenly outwards. The next. He chopped at the head of the chisel again with the hammer. Then slammed the hammer at the glass, which crazed into a loose jigsaw of fragments.

The door of the church opened with a clatter. Raquin glanced at the dark figure and grimly went on hammering. The second bar was clear. He began to hammer desperately at the third, seeking to dislodge it by blind force alone. Nearly there. He was relying on Smith to keep the intruder occupied for long enough.

Smith had been taken on for this job because he was a professional bodyguard, street-wise and battle hardened. His task was to stay with Raquin and protect him just as conscientiously as if he were a pop star or a footballer. Not being a snob, the fact that his current employer was neither didn't bother him. Stepping out of the shadows, he faced Ramsay squarely in silence.

Quite a bundle of mischief, Ramsay thought. He noticed that the vicar hadn't put in an appearance yet. For him, presumably, fighting the good fight was just a spiritual thing. Groping in his pocket for a couple of cartridges, he slipped them into the breech of the shotgun and closed it as unobtrusively as he could, watching Smith as he did so.

The small eyes set wide apart in his head gave nothing away, no clue to his feelings, which meant that he had to be watched the whole time. He was a machine which was empty of instructions waiting to be programmed. Once the necessary information had been lodged somewhere in his flat skull, Smith would oblige.

By now Raquin almost had the third bar free, and the gap was large enough for him to extract the casket. The cold chisel clanged on the tiled floor. 'Go,' he shouted, as he got his right hand on it. 'Go!'

Giving a roar like a whirlwind, the bodyguard came for Ramsay who, with the gun waist high, the muzzle no more than six inches from Smith's ear, jerked at the first trigger and blew half his head away.

Chapter Twelve

Ethelred Lewis's voice came flouncing down the wire.

'I took the celebrated wreath to the Oxonian Museum; I know the man there. Quite well, as a matter of fact.'

'And what did you ask him to say?'

'I didn't. It's plate. Electroplate.' The last word was spoken with relish.

'Nonsense!'

'You don't think an expert can't tell plate from the real thing? Come on!'

'It wasn't heavy enough,' said Ramsay, playing one of the pair of cards in his hand.

Lewis assumed a tone of patience greatly tried. 'Look, cocky, there were two craftsmen in Rome around 1888, one called Castellani and the other Guilano. They produced Revivalist jewellery after Greek and Roman models. Egyptian, too, I dare say. Not exactly like the originals, but inspired by them. My buddy at the Oxonian thinks they made the wreath as a kind of apprentice piece to convince themselves that they could copy authentic stuff when they tried and give it the exact feel of silver. You know, the weight.'

Ramsay played his other card. 'What about the one in Andover's exhibition from the Museum of Antiquities? Their man swore that ours was right.'

'He would say that, wouldn't he? Theirs is as dud as a cockmetal half-crown too. I've spoken to him, and it's being reassessed. It hurt.' He chuckled – then the significance of what had just been said got as far as his brain. 'You don't mean to say that when you shook hands on our little deal you really thought your wreath was genuine? Well, blow me down for a sailor! All I can say, Ramsay me old tosher, is the more fool you.'

That was one way of looking at it.

'You shook on it.'

'I don't remember doing so,' Lewis shot back without thinking.

'You said so just now.'

Lewis gave this stark fact his attention for a hairsbreadth of a second. 'OK, suppose I did. My word isn't my bond, and never was. Stap me, what a very outré idea!' He gurgled at the thought. 'Anyway, the deal was only on if it was verified by an expert, and it hasn't been, has it?'

Ramsay surveyed the strengths of his own position; the keep and curtain walls, the barbican. Strengths? They all had a seriously crumbled look about them. Lewis had the wreath in his possession, and anyway it was a doubtful asset now. There was no leverage at all there to help them discover where Margaret's husband had gone off to.

'Since you aren't going to buy it, I want it back, of course.'

'No problem,' answered Lewis. 'I'll bring it when I come up to see you. I'm on my way. I just made the decision, *voilà, tout à coup*, just like that. I'll have the object with me.'

The object which had set Sir Anthony lusting after it a few days ago and now was merely a bit of *fin de siècle* electroplate put together by a pair of Roman jewellers to test their skills, or so this friend of his believed. What about that washed-out photograph of a similar wreath that Lewis had shown them himself in Brighton – the picture in the Greek portfolio? How did he explain that? At least the configuration of the thing must be right.

Later on, when Ramsay phoned the flat and told Margaret, she only reinforced the distrust he himself felt.

To begin with she was flatly dismissive. 'That fat little man is simply talking it down.'

But on second thoughts that didn't make sense to Ramsay. 'Why should he want to do that?'

'There must be a reason. He's up to something,' came the frustrated reply.

'As long as we have got the wreath back, what have we lost?' he demanded.

There was silence on the line as that sunk in, as she waited for him to revive those extravagant hopes of hers, and he couldn't.

At her end the receiver went down with a click.

Nothing to be done about them.

Stanfield was on his hands and knees washing the floor of the church beside the wall where the reliquary was no longer kept. Too shocked to argue, he had agreed to its removal to the vault of a local bank. As, humbly, he wrung out his dishcloth, the water ran a dirty pink through his fingers into the bucket, a touch of the boxing ring that seemed to be an apt reminder of a bruiser like Smith. A man was coming tomorrow to tidy everything up – the mess of glass and stone in the dark hole above his head where the steel bars leaned out drunkenly, and loose, too, if one touched them.

There were plenty of old blankets in the vicarage – in fact there wasn't any other kind – every one of them worn thin and smelling of mothballs. He had looked one out and wrapped Smith's stiffened body in it. When he had finished his chore, he carried his bucket to the vestry, his left arm counterbalancing its weight, and made a cascade as he emptied it into the sink. After the accumulated strain on his nerves of dealing with the corpse, he couldn't bring himself to fold it in his arms and hold it against his chest. So, conscious that he had chickened out, he took hold of the four corners of the blanket, half-dragging, half-carrying the awkward burden, and crossed the misty road to his home. Going down the path towards the big house of grey brick, he didn't enter through the navy-blue front door but went round into the garden behind, with his load bumping against his black-skirted legs. First he laid it down beside a straggly St John's Wort. Next he fetched a spade from the outhouse, and after hitching up his cassock and tucking it into the broad leather belt he always wore, he began to dig a deep oblong hole. He didn't have to sacrifice many plants, since the garden wasn't far from being a wasteland in any case. Most of its Victorian glories had been allowed to die off years ago except for the odd loosely growing shrub and the monkey puzzle tree which stole the daylight from the drawing-room.

The spade clanged on the occasional stone. Was it deep enough? Should he bury the corpse with the blanket, or just as it came? Something caught his eye, a pale shape. He looked up from his labour and saw Ramsay coming towards him.

'Giving him a Christian burial?'

Stanfield merely grunted at the cliché; he had lost some of his moral certainty, knowing as well as the man who stood next to him that he hadn't come well out of the emergency the previous night. What was the good of arriving after the fireworks, offering merely to telephone the police? He was a man of peace, he told himself, and so he had held back. At least the reliquary was safe enough: that was a comfort. Jabbing with his spade at the edges of his hole to tidy it up he made a decision. He could still get some use out of that blanket – it would be a waste. With little reverence he pulled it from beneath the corpse and they both gazed down.

Smith, a pit-bull terrier – the dog who had been the thief's bodyguard – who hadn't understood much of what was going on around him or of what was said to him, whether in French or English, just enough to obey orders when it mattered. An old sweat who had grumbled, done what he was told, and met his death like any other mercenary. Black as pitch everywhere, but rather dusty now with his forepaws stretched out stark in front of him, the great wound in his skull mostly hidden because it lay against the wet earth. One eye still staring.

Inspecting the animal, he had been lucky enough to kill with his first shot, Ramsay admitted, 'It was a clever idea to make use of a dog like that.'

Whoever had tried to burgle the church the previous night had been familiar enough with the law to know that if he were caught he would face much lighter penalties for employing a dog to do his killing for him than for doing it himself. Smith was cheap, expendable, and wouldn't demand a share of the proceeds of the robbery. A slice or two of sirloin would keep him quiet. Moreover, Smith had served his purpose since the thief had escaped – out of the vestry window.

Into his grave they tumbled the corpse of the pit-bull; it was followed by a trickle of earth.

'Lewis is threatening to come up and visit us,' warned Ramsay as he helped to cover it with soil. 'Whether he does or not remains to be seen.'

But four hours later he was on the phone cadging a lift from the station. There wasn't a taxi to be found anywhere, he said.

'Where is the wreath? Produce it.'

'I forgot it. I truly did.' Lewis's hands fanned out helplessly; he was locked into his most theatrical mode. 'I went to the station in such a rush. Julia's stubborn little car wouldn't start, so one got flustered as one does . . .' For a moment he tried to think of another more compelling excuse, and couldn't . . . 'So it was left behind, along with my tuna and cucumber sandwiches,' he concluded, eyeing Ramsay with circumspection as he paused.

'It really wasn't the genuine thing, you know.' Pause again. 'As soon as I get back to the shop, I'll pack it up in a good stout parcel and send it back to you. You'll realise as soon as you see it again.'

He'd made another of those promises of his. To argue with him was impossible; it was like trying to split a feather down the middle with a pickaxe. While the others were thinking out what came next, his eyes did a quick look-see round the vicarage drawing-room in case there was anything nice – and since there wasn't, he made a little face.

'Why have you come such a distance? Why have you come at all? What are you after?' the vicar asked sharply.

'It's you I've come to see, Stanfield, as a matter of fact,' he replied, and proceeded to give him a grilling about his Brazilian scheme. Then he switched over to Ramsay to ask some pertinent questions about the reliquary.

'Where is all this getting us?'

Stanfield was growing impatient because he'd been under strain and he still had his routine duties facing him – a talk for the Institute to write, parishioners to tackle about the damage to the church before they started to blame him for it. There was a list on his desk of troublesome things to be done, and after the dislocation of the last twenty-four hours he wanted to get on with it.

It was then that Lewis steered off on an unexpected bearing. 'Where were you born?' he asked.

Colchester, Stanfield told him, not that it was any business of his.

'What sort of background? How would you describe it?'

'White collar, just, since you ask. My father was an accounts clerk.'

'Was it a secure background, would you say?'

'Yes, I would,' Stanfield shot back with irritation. 'Mine was a solid family.'

He opened his mouth again to deliver a formula of dismissal, but was pre-empted by Lewis, who cut in with a kind of pride in his voice, 'I was born on the floor of a compartment in a disused third-class railway coach, and there's nothing you can teach me about deprivation. I'll tell you something else. I know where Johnson is, so you'd better listen. Don't you want to know, either of you? Say yes.'

They did. Lewis's moment had arrived, and he took it like a surfer catching the crest of the incoming wave he has been waiting for.

'Care of the Overseas and Colonial Bank. Monte Carlo branch. Just off the square in front of the casino,' he said, and found that this announcement wasn't giving him nearly the thrill he had thought it would. 'At least, that was when he rang me this morning. I think he's staying at the Hôtel de Rome, but I can't be sure.'

Stanfield was scribbling on a wad of paper he had dragged from the pocket of his cassock – it looked like the *Diocesan News*.

Soberly the plump dealer answered the question he saw in their faces. 'I was a street boy myself, once upon a time. You know what I mean, one of those boys. One has to survive,' he murmured, remembering. 'So I said to myself: Ethelred Lewis, you grievous sinner, you ought to make some sort of effort for those poor little sods in Brazil.'

Cocksure, he waited for a pat on the back, something, but it didn't come. The other two seemed to think it was the most natural thing in the world that he should disclose these facts which were his personal property, these valuable facts, without any kind of compensation being as much as hinted at. Someone, he felt, had let him down badly here. Not being given much to displaying virtue, he had yet to learn that, as a general rule, it was its own reward.

Margaret Johnson couldn't understand why they had to travel by road, but Charles had insisted on it, having managed against all the odds to book the car at short notice on to a ferry. The journey would have been much quicker by air, but perhaps he was trying to do it on the cheap, and that thought made her feel embarrassed. It wasn't pleasant to have to sponge on him continually, and even worse having to live in a kind of limbo while the bankruptcy proceeded silently on its way, out of sight like some fatal and expensive illness; only on good days was she able to put it out of her mind, existing in a protected state as though in a hospital ward with nothing much to call her own. No money. It would be three months before the Agra carpet was sold, and that together with her income support – no, call it by its real name, the dole – was the only source of cash she could count on now that the wreath was as good as worthless. So Charles had told her, though there were things in his story that she didn't follow. A speciously pretty circlet, a mirage of silver. She would have liked to be able to see it again for herself before leaving London; it had given her style, she thought. Whether it was nineteenth-century plate or not, the workmanship had an integrity of its own.

Her feeling of uneasiness at being a charge on him came back to bother her again. He was paying for the whole of this excursion to find her errant husband, everything – meals, hotels, petrol, even down to the tolls on the motorways. He had assumed responsibility for her for the time being, but there was no clear sign that he was minded to embark on what they called, in the magazines she sometimes read in the evening, a long-term relationship. Whatever he cried out when he was arched above her in the vivid excitement of their bed, whatever thanks he offered, vows he made, he showed no desire to speak the handful of words she really wanted to hear. She was like a swimmer out of her depth, anxiously pausing every so often to probe underneath her for firm clean sand and finding nothing beneath her outstretched foot except uncertainty.

But for the need to trace Ian, she would have gone out and fought to get herself a job, recession or no recession – a job of any kind as long as it put some distance between them and gave her time to think. Much better that than this feeling of vulnerability, of being exposed to view the whole time.

She had no idea how Charles's own finances stood. What

was he using for money – his working capital, his savings or an overdraft? – because, as far as she could tell, he hadn't made a sale of any kind since the day she had arrived in his flat – not a penny of profit. Perhaps it was simply that he didn't want to bother her with his affairs when she had so many trials of her own to face. They couldn't live on air, however – she was sick and tired of that for a diet.

They. The fact that she had bracketed herself with him brought her up short because she still knew so little about him, only what he allowed her to learn. He had proved to her that she was still young enough for an explosion of what had been known as romance when she had been a sixteen-year-old – admittedly in that area he was better than anybody who had come her way before – but it wasn't enough, was it? At sixteen she wouldn't have hesitated, would have leapt; today she was more circumspect.

Years of wrestling with her husband's shortcomings had made her suspicious, and so far Charles's promises had yielded nothing tangible. Suppose this probity of his was merely a front which he had put in place to pull her towards him and he wasn't such a plaster saint after all. The last thing she wanted was another mistake like Ian, she thought, only to find herself amending that phrase to 'another man like Ian' in a burst of loyalty which took her by surprise. Surely a taste for gambling could be cured, just like any other addiction, couldn't it? There were treatments.

One thing was certain, if her life with him had been a mistake, she couldn't afford another like it. You were given only one or two bites at the cherry, then they put the bag away for good.

As the large estate car hummed down the autoroute, she

placed the little red air-cushion in the corner of the headrest, set her head against it and feeling the warmth seep over her, composed herself for sleep. Before letting go, she summed up her thoughts like a judge on the bench and found that she had sentenced herself to a term of dissatisfaction. Glancing down the notes she had taken, she regretted that there was so much about money there ... and trust. Money and the lack of it, trust and the lack of it. It was nothing to be proud of, allowing those anxieties to overlay a much more wholesome preoccupation, a secret which a few months before would have had her light-headed with joy but now merely added another battalion to her army of insecurities. She was pregnant – there was no doubt about that.

A minute or two later, when Charles Ramsay glanced across at her sleeping face, he felt an emotion of transcendental depth and purity. What used to be called love. It was, he believed, one of those moments which would be photographed, frozen in his memory for life; the journey had been well worth the sacrifice, however great a distance he had still to travel.

Margaret reconnoitred their room on the fourth floor with disbelief. The Hôtel de Rome was luxurious in a relaxed way; it didn't have to try, because it was. Noting the marble floor in the bathroom, the bath big enough for two, the spotless washbasins set in matching marble, one for each of them, she found herself wondering what it had all cost – there was no corner-cutting here. Had it been done only to reassure her? If so, it had not succeeded. No, she decided, it was the kind of act of bravado that Ian might have indulged in before the end of the world arrived.

Then it occurred to her that he was staying here, too. How did he think he was going to pay his bill? The wifely concern in that thought for Ian this time made her feel awkward for a moment, surveying this bathroom which she shared with a different man, standing there wondering where she belonged.

She went to join Charles at the window, her bare arm warm against his on the sill and looked out at the palm-fringed square in front of the casino with its Second Empire front moulded in what looked like icing sugar. An architectural wedding-cake. At least it was a lot warmer than East Anglia. As daylight faded, the lights were beginning to shine through the green leaves of the trees below. A dark taxi drew up outside the casino, discharged its occupants and left. Having been tipped, apparently with generosity, the driver called out, 'Good luck, monsieur,' his gruff voice softened by the evening air.

She was determined that before they went down to seek out Ian she would bath and change into the very best outfit she had with her – something Charles had bought her, just to show her erring husband what he was missing these days.

Charles had insisted that she should be first to take a bath, and she had insisted with just as much emphasis that he should join her. Unpacking his own bag, he had produced a large and expensive cake of soap he had bought in London, anticipating this moment. Now she was rubbing this very same soap slowly up and down his spine. To this agreeable sensation were added others even more delightful; gentle and capricious movements along his side, soft contacts which came and went with ravishing uncertainty.

Emerging, they lay on the bed, and in five minutes they were dry. Spreadeagled there with his eyes closed, he could hear Margaret cooling herself with duty-free cologne. Each tiny sound was distinct: the bottle being shaken, the gentle hiss of the spray, her hand patting her skin. Then the equipment was put on the bedside table.

Darkness had closed in by now. He was lying on his back, staring at the shadows on the ceiling created by the motion of the trees against the lights in the square outside. Movement at random, never twice the same.

'Charles.' There was a touch of urgency.

He looked up at the ghostly white face. 'What's up?'

She hesitated, unable to find the words, and decided to say nothing after all.

He said nothing either. That was the problem.

Far below the plate glass window in the spacious dusk, a figure in a striped sleeveless shirt and white slacks was untying his cruiser, getting ready to put out into the darkening sea. Who is he? Ramsay asked himself. Perhaps he was a criminal. A drug smuggler starting the evening's smuggling or an incompetent Lloyds underwriter getting away from it all – the investigation by the Sunday press, the hue and cry, the ruined members of the syndicate baying for his blood? No, he decided, he was more likely to be a shopkeeper going for an evening's fishing after a blameless day.

'Absent again,' Margaret complained, exploring the strange interior of her lobster. 'You haven't been listening to a single word!'

That was because he had been putting together a form of words of his own. Creating it was easy, uttering it was another matter altogether. She had still to meet her husband again; nothing was fixed or decided. Charles was a scrupulous man and, above all, he had to be easy on her. Wasn't it rather too early to force the issue? He vacillated, feeling the decision ebbing and flowing inside him.

He had almost brought himself to speak the words that would commit him – they had all but reached his lips – when the hovering waiter interrupted them, coming forward to replenish the wine glass of each of his diners, deftly twirling the bottle to avoid spilling a drop and sliding it back into its bed of ice in a single continuous movement as smooth as a dancer. Pleased with himself, he smiled at each of them in turn, 'M'dame, m'sieur', and then withdrew, having done his duty as he saw it, what he was paid for.

Now the little cruiser was put-putting past the virgin white vessels of the billionaires at their moorings, making towards the dim horizon and any minor hazards it might hold in store. Ramsay could just make out the striped shirt of the one-man crew, whoever he was, the guy who had accepted that limited challenge. While he envied him, he didn't feel like rushing his own fences.

Margaret pushed her ravaged plate aside, sipped some wine, wiped her lips with the crisp thick napkin in her hand and looked at him over it, half-expectant. Now, having rejected the formula, he couldn't think of anything else to say, so, leaning forward, he attacked the congealing Sole Niçoise laid out defencelessly in front of him. After a minute or two of one-sided combat, he laid down his knife and fork and, glancing across the table, found that she was still watching him, seeing in her eyes and an almost imperceptible and loving movement of her lips the memory of the luxuries they had shared only an hour or so earlier.

Remembering her rising naked and unconcerned by her nakedness from that magnificent bath, he felt himself overwhelmed with a fresh longing for her. Pushing away his plate, he observed with unconcern, 'We don't have to start searching for him tonight. Surely it'll keep until morning?'

And still the right words were held back while she waited for them, the words he hoped would clinch the matter. There was no hurry, he told himself.

The night porter was already on duty at reception downstairs when Ian Johnson handed him a large manilla envelope containing his chequebooks, travellers' cheques, credit cards, and all his cash except for a hundred and twenty thousand francs.

'Put this in the hotel safe for me, would you? Whatever the circumstances, it is not to be removed from there until eight o'clock tomorrow morning. I shall collect it then.' These days, his manner was more relaxed and at the same time more compelling.

Like a newly-hired nanny taking charge of a first-born infant, the porter accepted the package that, he guessed, contained everything of consequence this guest had in the world. It wasn't an unusual responsibility for a man in his position, sitting behind his counter only a couple of hundred yards from the doors of the casino.

'Understood, monsieur,' he said, marking it with the name in a clear Continental hand, together with the room number and the number of the pink receipt which methodically he handed over to Johnson, who was itching to get to the gaming-rooms. Congratulating himself on his prudence, the gambler patted his inside pocket. He had made sure now that he could lose no more at the tables than he had in his wallet.

The underling was unsurprised. Fortyish and plump, he

looked like the domestic sort. He was beginning to go bald, although his hair was cut very short in the hope of disguising it. *En brosse*, it used to be called.

'May I ask if you are married?'

'Oh yes, m'sieur.'

The porter spoke with the kind of man-to-man self-confidence that one meets in properly managed hotels; there was no servility here. Taking the room key, he hung it on an old-fashioned numbered board behind him.

Being childless himself, Johnson suddenly wanted to ask as well if the man had any children, but knew that would have been going too far. A rather dull character, perhaps, but certainly reliable – a good father . . . if that was what he was.

Johnson's hunger for action tugged at his elbow. He was ready to go.

The entrance hall of the casino boasted some framed caricatures of the action at the tables in the Nineties. Porcine men in full evening dress, their heavy lips sucking at cigars ridding themselves of the profits from the daily labour of mill-hands in Manchester or steel workers in the armaments factories of Essen. Money lost in the thousandth part of the time it had taken to make it. Sipping champagne behind them stood the demimondaines, frizzy hair dyed red or black, displaying their stockinged legs under frilled petticoats, their pale breasts uncorseted. Gamblers and women were well matched. The women were the dupes of the industrialists, who, in their turn, were beguiled by the casino into throwing away those crisp finely printed banknotes by the handful – leaves in the wind.

After his arrival in Monte Carlo, Johnson had spent two days watching a particular table and had then made the key decision, to continue to stake on black, the colour that had been so generous to him in London. Black as a raven's wing. The colour of his true love's hair – except that Margaret's was blonde, more or less.

He had to get to work. Now that he had the resources to absorb the impact of long runs against it, his wealth had continued to grow irresistibly. For several days the random walk of the colours had gone on moving in his favour and he was still able every now and then to squirrel away another oblong chip in the side pocket of his jacket.

Then, at exactly eight thirteen, black lost its ascendancy and his luck began to slump. He didn't know it until later, of course – at the time he took it for just a normal setback from the rising trend – a wave drawing back from the oncoming tide before throwing itself forward again. Two hours later his confidence had begun to slither away. Had black turned or not? By two in the morning he had lost every franc he had set aside for that night's play on trying to answer that straightforward little question.

It was the moment when his perspective abruptly altered and he ceased to be the cautious type who earlier on had handed over everything to the porter in order to save himself from himself. Damn that for a game of soldiers; it wasn't his style anyway. He became manic and impatient with himself. He wasn't going meekly back to his hotel bedroom with a bloody great failure like that hung round his neck. It had to be made good, and the only way was to go for broke – to set his resources against the bank's and slug it out toe to toe in a battle of attrition, and for that kind of strategy he needed reinforcements.

A minute or two later he found himself walking past those disturbing caricatures again, out of the casino, and on under the lights of the square shining under the dark green canopy of the trees, towards the hotel.

The night porter was asleep in his cubbyhole behind the reception desk.

'M'sieur,' Johnson whispered urgently, but the porter did not stir, so he tapped with a coin on the counter in a regular rhythm like a dripping tap. There was movement on the other side of the counter. 'Wake up, if you please.' He banged the coin down hard on the polished wood.

The porter jumped as he awoke, his mouth moving as though he was chewing on something that wasn't there. Grabbing his spectacles, he put them on, making himself look older, less self-assured. 'Oui, m'sieur,' he said automatically.

Hurry up, thought Johnson. This delay was driving a juggernaut through his calculations.

He produced a pink receipt. 'Would you be kind enough to give me back the envelope which you placed for me in the safe last night?'

The porter picked up the flimsy scrap of paper and studied it with interest as though he hadn't seen it before.

'Impossible, m'sieur, I very much regret.' It was handed back with a little bow as he swallowed a yawn which made his eyes water. 'Impossible.'

He stood with his hands on the counter, waiting politely for Johnson to say something else. Perhaps *au revoir*?

'But that envelope belongs to me. It is my property, is it not? I want it back, please. Now.'

'Of course it is yours, sir, but it is not available at the moment.'

'Not available? What do you mean?'

'There is a time lock on the safe. It prevents it from being opened until later on this morning, eight o'clock in fact, as you specified.' He looked at his watch, a good Swiss affair. 'That is to say in about five and three-quarter hours' time.' He shook his head sympathetically. 'There is nothing I can do, sir. Nothing anyone can do except wait.'

The porter pretended to check his keys, his receipts, to indicate without undue brutality that their interview was over and that, as it were, was that.

Johnson's hands clenched with frustration at this man playing silly-buggers with him. He swayed forward as though to launch into one of those impossible arguments and stopped himself at the last moment, inhibited by the silence of the hotel in that dead hour, so very early in the morning. His anger would shatter it; there would be trouble.

'Good night.' Although he managed to speak quietly, his voice carried the insolence his sudden wealth had brought him.

'Good night, sir, and good luck.'

Margaret and Charles descended the staircase into the fresh morning, turning through the carved mahogany doors glazed with heavy bevelled panes into the airy breakfast-room smelling of fresh coffee and smoked ham from the Ardennes – a whole leg, waiting to be carved, rested on the sideboard. The waiter led them to a table beside the window that looked out on to the square. In the early light the casino looked white and innocuous; the night staff were just leaving, all with the same gait, each one making the same gestures, taking his keys from his pocket, selecting one before getting into his little car and taking off in a burst of exhaust fumes.

Johnson was sitting with his back to them, tearing the soft heart out of a crisp roll and spreading it with fresh butter bedewed with moisture. He looked at his watch with the impatience of a general waiting for his artillery to lift the opening barrage it had taken him so long to plan.

Finally he got up and marched up to the office of the night porter, who, his shift over, was about to leave, collecting his possessions and putting them into a well-used attaché case. He had not yet had time to shave.

'Perhaps I could have my envelope now?'

Ignoring the last truculent word, the man collected the receipt from him and went into the inner sanctum, leaving the door ajar so that everything mundane that lay behind the scenes was exposed – his electric jug, last night's newspaper, the used breakfast tray they always brought him from the kitchen first thing – and the famous safe.

Built to last, it was a shabby dark green affair with ornate brass fittings and must have been about as old as the hotel itself – vintage Napoleon III. The porter bent down, found the key in his bunch, and unlocked it. Surely he needn't have bothered; a well-placed kick would have sprung its antique bars and levers.

'M'sieur.'

He handed the thick package to Johnson, who jerked his head impatiently towards the iron safe.

'No time lock, I see.' There was no point in making a fuss now.

'Oh yes, there is, m'sieur.' The contradiction was made with a touch of self-esteem beneath the professional civility.

'On that safe?'

'Yes, indeed.' Drawing a quick breath, the man launched himself into his explanation. 'It is I who am the lock . . .'

His customer's gaze said that he must be mad; the screws of

SOME DARK ANTIQUITIES

his mind loosened by years of solitary night duty.

'You gave precise instructions that the envelope was not to be handed over until eight o'clock this morning, did you not? Under any circumstances. Those were your orders?' The look on his face dared Johnson to pretend otherwise, and forced him to nod as he continued, 'I was merely the machine that carried them out. To the letter. That is my function. A human time lock.'

He spoke with a kind of pride in this mechanical job of his, and regarded the safe ruefully.

'A real time lock? Computerised, no doubt?' He shook his head. 'Not with that make of safe there, I think. I have spoken to the manager more than once about it, but,' he shrugged, 'he says he likes its personality. I feel that, considering our clientele, it is inadequate.' Having delivered this hint at a schism behind the scenes, he resumed politely, 'Nevertheless, that was what you wanted, m'sieur, was it not? You are satisfied?'

He watched while Johnson ripped open the envelope and disposed each item, travellers' cheques, cash, into the appropriate pocket, then he looked him up and down – the unshaven night porter at the end of his shift who had saved his fortune for him. They both knew that.

Johnson still had not replied to the question. 'Absolutely,' he said, not bothering to make the four syllables sound grateful. Keen to get the conversation over, he handed the man his tip – a barely defensible one.

'Thank you.' Showing no sign of resentment, the porter folded the small note neatly into four and tucked it into the breast pocket of his dark jacket. Johnson was just another punter – one of those who came and went, exultant or suffering, whereas he was a man with a position. Not only that, he was a rich one by most people's standards. A comfortable flat in the town and a Mercedes. These minor ennuis were a small price to pay for such security.

Turning away, Johnson found himself face to face with his wife.

'Where did you get that money?' she demanded, and immediately looked ashamed of the crude question which told him too much.

'Margaret! What a surprise! And the chivalrous Ramsay squiring you?' The same Charles Ramsay who had saved his life, although the episode on the church roof was comfortably forgotten now – it didn't fit his new persona. This was a self-satisfied Johnson, even aggressive. Neither of the other two spoke while the fact sank in.

'We'd better get it over.' Johnson led them to a table which had just been cleared by an attentive waiter.

The breakfast-room was filling up now, and Margaret was forced to keep her voice down. Although she spoke surgically, sparing him nothing, there was no bitterness in her voice.

'Let me tell you what has happened since you left me.' She ticked off the items one by one on her fingers. '*One*, the business has been put into liquidation. *Two*, I had to cope with all that entirely on my own – handing everything over, the accounts, explaining to the bank what was happening – dealing with that man the creditors sent round. *Three*, I am penniless. *Four* – how long do you think I have spent looking for you? Even if you couldn't face the problems you created for us, you might have told me where you could be found.'

Conscious that he was being left on the sidelines, Ramsay decided to let her get it off her chest. His own concerns could wait.

Johnson said, 'All that was *then*. Things have changed now.'

'Look,' his wife replied, 'you can't simply shrug all this off. At some time in your life you must take responsibility for . . .'

Johnson broke in with a brisk question, 'How much to pay our creditors and put the business back on its feet?'

It took her no time at all to produce the figure; she must have been working it over for days in her mind. 'One hundred and thirty-six thousand.'

Johnson fished in his inside pocket for the same chequebook that he had just rescued from the night porter, took out an expensive-looking fountain pen and began to write out a cheque. The date? After an overnight session at the tables, he needed reminding. Tearing it out of the crisp new book, he handed it to her. That problem was solved.

'Ian, don't play games!'

He looked at his watch. 'The Overseas and Colonial Bank will be opening its doors in twenty-five minutes. They will be glad to cash it for you and transfer the money in whatever currency you like to wherever you wish. I won't desert you meanwhile. I'll even stay here as a hostage and have coffee with you and your friend.' He put up a hand to summon the waiter.

'There are other matters . . .' Ramsay began, but the man had arrived and was already running over the choice of hot drinks available.

When he had been sent on his way, Ramsay resumed, 'The sapphires. Where are they? You are aware, I suppose, of the dangers of your own position?'

'That's a brilliant way to go about finding them,' observed Johnson, 'rushing to judge me like that. On top of that you've been sleeping with my wife, which doesn't make me feel any more amiable.' Not that he sounded as though he cared much.

He continued, 'You'll have a considerable job trying to

prove that I removed them. Besides, whose are they? Whom do they belong to? Tell me that.'

He had a point.

'We need to know . . .'

'Look,' said Johnson, 'I think we should leave it there. I've been up all night. I need to be allowed a bath and a modest amount of sleep.'

Margaret had forgotten how he looked. In the few minutes that had elapsed since her husband had entered the sunlit breakfast-room, the picture had changed like a newly shaken kaleidoscope. How far had he altered, and in what ways? What new and exciting veins of ore had been exposed by this shift in his circumstances? The decision which had arrived at last was not one she had looked forward to making, but now it seemed easy enough. She leaned across the table to touch him just above the heart with her forefinger. It was a wifely gesture; not the kind of liberty he would have allowed a stranger, these days.

'All right, you've made the point – you need looking after. Tell Charles what he needs to know. Your contact in France.'

After so many years of marriage, she didn't need to elaborate on the proposition she was putting to him – they understood one another.

Weighing it up, well aware that he had won the unseen battle Johnson gazed back at her. Then, taking out his pen and a scrap of paper – a purchase note for some francs he had bought at a bureau de change on the way there – he jotted down a name and address, and pushed it across the table.

Ramsay picked it up quickly to look at it, and as he did so, she rose beside him from the table.

He glanced up with a proprietorial air, and asked her, 'Where are you going?'

SOME DARK ANTIQUITIES

'To the bank. I'll be back. Don't worry.' She gave him a big smile to avoid a scene. There were so many people sitting around them, taking the first coffee of the day and indulging in polyglot chat now and then in secretive voices. One or two interested pairs of eyes glanced at Margaret Johnson and her husband as they left the breakfast-room together, arm in arm. A couple in their late thirties, rather handsome, one of the onlookers thought.

Chapter Thirteen

After starting his journey in the direction of the Massif Central, Ramsay drove automatically for a while, as though most of his mind had been left behind in the breakfast-room of the hotel. It wasn't until he found himself driving north too fast along the curve towards a tunnel, its rough entrance blasted out of the rock, that he pulled himself back to the present, the here and now. On his left was a dry slope covered with scrub leaning steeply into the sea; not a sheer drop, but almost as bad. He had to stop and take hold of himself. Bringing the car to a halt on the hard shoulder – it was probably forbidden – he got out. Something else was bothering him.

For a long while he stood facing outwards to the Mediterranean, feeling the sharp breeze on his face, trying to decide what he should do next. The occasional vehicle swept past him; a local car hooted cheekily at this Englishman standing there, the sound of its horn shifting down the scale as it passed him at well above the speed limit. Should he go back to the Hôtel de Rome and make a scene, force a showdown, face another rejection? The odds were that this time it would be a much harder one to take because everything would have crystallised. He imagined Johnson alongside her, wrapped in his new self-confidence, taking her back into his possession and ready with his own reasons in her support. Man and wife standing together instinctively.

No. Grabbing at the decision at last as though it were a nettle he had avoided for too long, he realised what else was getting to him – one of those sore spots which are almost invisible but which smart and itch and will not heal whatever soothing ointment is applied to them. He went back to the car, jerkily like a doll being walked by a novice puppeteer – as another driver went past on the other side, whirling up the dust which blew inland, away from him, from the opposite edge of the road.

As he opened the door on the passenger's side, the inflatable red cushion of hers that had been trapped by it against the seat sprang out and fell on to the stony verge beside the car. Suspiciously, he bent down to sniff at it – yes, it stank of the perfume he had given her. Picking it up by the very corner like something small and dead that had to be shut out of the mind until it had been disposed of, he flung it down the slope, where it bounced a couple of times, was caught for a moment by the wind and ended up resentfully against a rock. Very well, he was a litter lout, if you like; he would allow himself that luxury for once. The memory of that blonde head of hers encircled by the silver wreath slipped back into his mind. He tried to send it bowling down the slope after her cushion, but it persisted. He needed something to blank it off, some mantra, empty of any significance, which he could repeat to deaden his mind to it.

Returning to the car, he studied his autoroute map inside its plastic cover, forcing his eyes to focus on the small pale print, estimating distances and times. Then, slapping it together, he put it firmly into the side pocket and steered back on to the road. The engine roared suddenly as he pushed unnecessary gas into it and accelerated towards this last meeting of his.

SOME DARK ANTIQUITIES

* * *

A cold day halfway through, with the river flowing along the side of the empty *quai* and nobody looking over the edge of the parapet to watch it; no tourists admiring the Pont Neuf; no children dropping empty cartons experimentally to float in the slow water. Chalon was sitting in his shop, casting up his accounts and beginning to sense a void in his stomach where his lunch was going to be in a minute.

The doorbell tinkled. He stopped tapping at his calculator and looked up – a young dark-haired man was pushing against the door with his shoulder; then he had it half-open and was sliding a squat holdall through it in front of him. With care.

No, not a customer, Chalon decided, but somebody who was hard-up bringing an article in to sell – probably stolen, he thought realistically, and tried to recall where he had put the last list of missing goods circulated by the police.

What was in that bag? To amuse himself, he tried to guess. A box of some kind, perhaps – it looked the right shape for that. Made of what? He focused his eyes on it to assess its outline. It could be a wooden box in there, but somehow it looked too heavy for that; some sort of metal then, copper or brass? A far-fetched thought flashed into his mind. It wasn't a bomb, was it? A present from one of Volet's crazy bunch? No, it couldn't be, because the owner came in after it and he didn't seem like the type to want to blow himself up, being English by the look of him.

Picking up the bag and holding it in front of him, he walked down the aisle towards the desk in an almost ritualistic way – the English always had been prone to ceremonial, marching about in slow time with large military flags hanging ahead of them for reasons of their own. What was inside that bag? As it drew nearer to him, Chalon felt the small muscles round his eyes clench with curiosity.

Ramsay put it down in front of the desk and gestured to indicate that he needed some room on top of it. 'May I?'

He helped Chalon take away the clutter – the ledger and the calculator, a half-used ballpoint and his coffee cup. Then, dragging up the bag with a weary pair of arms as though he had brought it on foot like some mediaeval penitent every inch of the way from England, he dumped it in the space they had just cleared.

With a sort of finality he tore open the zip and allowed its floppy sides to collapse around whatever it was that lay inside. Lastly, without looking down, with his gaze fixed on the other man's face, he delved inside, feeling for the shape of the Burnill reliquary. Lifting it out, its gilded sides, its gems gleaming dully in the subdued light, he slowly presented it to Chalon.

'I think you know where this belongs,' he said, sensing an alleviation within him, as though he had surrendered a burden.

In the Palais that night, it lay on the big table scented with beeswax with Chalon and Grimaud standing beside it as self-appointed guardians, glasses in hand, while the members of the Brotherhood filed past it as though it was a respected corpse at a rural laying-out.

'Don't touch, if you please,' said Chalon, as someone stretched out a tentative forefinger. The words were spoken quietly because he didn't want to appear to be capitalising on this triumph of his. He took another sip of his champagne.

Behind him, Volet asserted with false candour, 'Chalon has certainly pulled it off.'

Someone else replied, 'He's always been lucky. That's all it is. Luck.' The other voice sounded cheated.

Soon there would be no more of these privileged meetings conferring a feeling of importance on the unimportant, giving them an excuse to take an aperitif or two on the way home. Now that the reliquary had been recovered, the occupation of the Brotherhood was gone, and soon the bond that had united their society over so many years would be dissolved and they would go their several ways.

Then Volet was facing him, erect even in defeat. One had to admire the man. 'My congratulations. We are all in your debt. I regret that I cannot stay for the discussions.' He received an understanding nod from Chalon. But naturally – that would have been too much to expect from anyone.

When he got outside, Volet's pace quickened as he turned in the direction of the Café du Centre. Ten days ago he had foreseen this moment, and he and Raquin had made their preparations. As he had realised when he had received the invitation to this jamboree of theirs, it would be much too late for Chalon to lodge the reliquary and its sapphires in the vaults of a local bank by the time it was over. Tonight they would have to be kept in his shop. It was their only opportunity – the hour had arrived.

They had tied Chalon to his chair and gagged and blindfolded him with pieces ripped from one of his curtains. The colours clashed with the orange nylon climber's rope they had brought, which was pulled tightly round his chest and upper arms, clamping them close to his sides. Because they had wanted to avoid wasting it, they hadn't cut it at all; instead they had simply wound the rest of its length round his forearms, lashing them to the arms of the chair. His right hand was spreadeagled on the desk by one of Volet's short-haired toughs who, for reasons of his own, was dressed in the English fashion in a dark blue blazer complete with regimental buttons. He leaned down on the hand with all his considerable weight.

Volet was too slight for that job, and anyway it was beneath him. Control and direction were his proper role – the iron functions of the leader. The butcher's work could be left to younger members of his team. He had put everything on the line – his reputation, security, his family and position, but every precaution he could think of had been taken. Their voices were disguised with electronic gadgets devised by Raquin; their heads covered with Balaclava helmets – the usual thing. Volet found his intolerably hot and itchy, the hole roughly cut for the mouth wet now with sweat and spittle. He wanted to get back to his spacious bathroom at home for a shower and change of clothes.

Still, it wasn't too much of a price to pay for anonymity, or at least the creation of enough confusion in Chalon's mind to muddy his evidence completely if it ever came to court. It would be the word of the dealer against that of the respected notary, and provided his team stood together, any case brought against them would be impossible to prove, leaving merely a bad smell for the canaille on the Left to sniff over.

The bonus was that Chalon was suffering pain – had done and would again. Raquin had a hammer in his hand – one of those expensive ones with the head and handle machined from a single piece of steel, the haft covered with rubber to protect the palm from the shock of the blows in use.

'The number. What is it?' Raquin spat in a whisper distorted by the gadget at his lips.

Instinctively he kept his voice down, although it was pointless – the gag they had rammed into Chalon's mouth was not enough to muffle his screams completely. Somebody must have heard him. Another of Raquin's instincts was that it was time to leave, but he was kept in his place by what was left of the oaths he had sworn and an inner need to complete a task which wasn't finished yet.

Two paces away, Volet forced himself to look down at Chalon's hand, and found himself with a thread of vomit in the back of the throat, which was made more bitter by his own failure. The hour had arrived, and he was only just managing to prove equal to it. This was not how he remembered things happening in the harsh judicial sunlight of Algeria, but he had been younger then and there had been more at stake.

He saw it – despite the weight clamping it to the table – Chalon's maimed and bloody hand jerk and flinch like an animal; he watched it as Raquin repeated his question.

'What is it?' On the word 'is' he brought the hammer down again with all the strength he had in him. The antique dealer's body bucked as though a strong electric current had jolted through it.

Uncannily, it reminded Volet of something he had seen before. The magneto in use on one of its victims in the bleak barracks at Oran. That was it, of course.

'Watch it, *espèce de cochon*, you nearly hit me that time,' gabbled the regimental one as he struggled to keep Chalon's hand pinioned to the table.

There was time for only one more blow. Any further delay, and they must surely hear the boots of the police on the cobbles outside. Yes, they had to make their escape, but were trapped against just as hard an imperative on the other side. They had to get hold of the reliquary and the original stones; the complete prize.

Chalon's muffled scream had changed into an urgent noise, a kind of regular sobbing, coming and going fast.

'Take the gag off,' gargled Volet through his mouthpiece.

Raquin hesitated.

'Take it off.' It was removed.

'Four nine three four,' groaned Chalon, and began to yell again.

Clumsily they tried to ram the gag back between his teeth, and found it was askew, letting the gouts of noise spill out around it. Pressing both hands over the victim's face, they crammed the bunch of cloth back somehow, anyhow, while Raquin wrenched his mask off, up over the back of his head, throwing it down gadget and all so that he could call out clearly to the last of the team waiting in the inner room. 'Four nine three four. For God's sake get on with it!'

Now that they had got what they wanted and saw what a tipsy cake they had made of the dealer's hand, they felt shaken. The man by the safe fumbled as he sought the combination; although he had not seen what they were doing, the sound of it had been enough to put him off his stroke. When he turned to verify the third digit over his shoulder, Raquin pushed him aside and clicked the flat steel knob of the lock himself.

'We must leave now,' Volet rapped out, already at the door.

'Not yet,' Raquin shouted back, hyped up, rummaging in the safe. He dragged the bag out, looked inside it. The casket. Yes, yes, on to the table. Where the hell were the sapphires? Papers flung out, boxes and jewel cases emptied and thrown rejected to the floor. What was this? A pre-war Dutch cigar box. There they were inside, wrapped in tissue paper.

'Give them to me and get mobile,' snapped Volet, determined to reassert himself; he still had just enough authority left to make the other man do what he was told. To even the score, Raquin grabbed the bag with the reliquary in it.

Go, go. The roar of a car engine outside, running footsteps on the cobbles, a hammering on the door, and voices. One was shouting instructions while another was at the front, rattling the handle of the door and calling out, 'Monsieur Chalon, are you there?'

The policeman kicked at the door, the noise resounding in the shop.

Raquin was already at the side door, but his chief was elbowed aside by the blazered tough with the blood-smeared hammer in his hand; there was no arguing with him. Fiercely they jostled each other as Raquin put down the bag and wrestled with the key – as the door opened, the two men behind him bundled him out into the street, like a cork from a bottle. Bastards! He recovered and turned back to get the bag. He had to. The bag. *Merde* – the police had reached it.

Letting loose a high yell of frustration, he went after the others, outside in the cold air where a light was flashing ahead of them – the parked police car. They stopped.

It was then that the floodlit image of the ancient Pont Neuf lying beyond it caught Volet by the throat, his chest heaving. Its stone arches and parapets seemed to float serenely on the black waters of the slow-moving river, the reflection so clear and smooth that it merged without an obvious break into the reality of the bridge itself. Coming to it after the stress and carnage inside Chalon's shop, it was as though he were seeing the familiar picture for the first time.

'This way!' Raquin shouted, leading the rest of them to the

left up an alley past the Au Petit Canard restaurant and through the wooden door in the high fence beside it, stumbling in the dark to safety along the escape route he had worked out the previous Sunday.

Their leader wasn't with them. Mesmerised by the sight of the bridge, Volet made for it, wanting to reach the mass of shadow behind the police car. Had he been three seconds earlier, he would have been through with a clear run beyond the bridge to where he had left his car – but he wasn't. A white hand came out of the darkness, as though disembodied, and grabbed at him.

'Stop!'

He dragged himself free and ran towards the bridge, which now seemed to him to be a kind of haven. After too many years behind a desk, he was not as fit as he had imagined. The beams of torches were swinging in the shadows behind him as he stumbled into the overspill of light from around that marvellous bridge.

'Stop!'

He swerved indecisively, uncertain whether to expect a shot from behind. His heart thudding, he tried to remember. Rules, police rules on the use of firearms? He ought to know: what were they? It was like being caught out in the open on patrol in Algeria – the feeling that there was a paper target in the small of one's back, expecting the sledgehammer blow of a bullet just there, on that spot, at any moment. He dared not turn either way along the *quai*, and now he had come up against the waist-high parapet beside the river, which carried on its black surface the perfect reflection of the bridge.

Cover, he had to find cover – that was what his instinct said. Volet scrambled up on to the stone coping and looked back at the gendarmes approaching him at the double. Not one of them had a gun in his hand, but that fact reached his mind too late – by that time he had committed himself, had leant outwards, too far out to catch his balance back. He was already falling with his arms pushed out stiffly above his head and his legs flailing, to find his hiding-place at last in the river, splashing its peaceful image of the Pont Neuf into shining fragments.

Halfway through his fall, another thought came into his mind, or rather an afterthought. As a child, he had never quite learnt how to swim.

Chapter Fourteen

Frank Becket had the sensation that he was a patient awaiting a medical verdict, but this was Bloomsbury, not Harley Street, and Teviot was not some specialist but a dealer in rare and valuable books and manuscripts – and too cocksure by half, in his view. What was left of his future was in the hands of the casually dressed youngster with sandy hair who was lounging opposite him, there in his imposing swivel chair against a backdrop of books from floor to ceiling. Ramsay had said he was the top man, but he looked too young, no older than what, thirty, and full of himself – you could see that. Why was he so set on going step by step through his diagnosis? So that there could be no misunderstanding? Possibly, although it was more likely he just wanted to show how clever he was, that was all. He was human.

On the table beside him lay, not the manuscript Frank had left with him a fortnight before, but a single sheet of paper. Picking it up, he handed it over.

'Exhibit A.'

It was a photocopy of the *back* of the first page of the manuscript, the same as the one the girl in the Queen's Street shop had taken by mistake the day he had broken out of the Sayonara, the one he had sent on to Ramsay.

Glancing through the uneven typescript, the occasional phrase came back to him. 'There were never any concentric castles except here and there by accident . . . The Roman, and of course the Visigothic towers . . . whose narrowness made hollow towers almost as secure as solid . . . to be closed with heavy hinged louvre-boards . . .'

'I shouldn't think that gives you much of a clue about the author,' commented Teviot, too pleased with himself.

No, it didn't, and what was the point of the remark? For God's sake, that was why he was sitting there – to find out who the author was. He had the feeling that Teviot wanted to provoke him into asking the predictable question, and he was damned if he would. Damned if he would!

Without mercy, the young man smiled, reached over for a book which he had ready at his elbow and offered it to his visitor, forcing him to rise awkwardly half out of his chair to receive it.

'Exhibit B. I've marked the place,' he said.

Removing the slip of paper, Frank held the pages of the book open with his right hand, away from him so that he could focus his eyes on the text: '. . . whose narrowness made hollow towers almost as secure as solid . . .' Those were the same words. He looked further down the page, then glanced across at the photocopy to verify another sentence – yes, those words were identical as well. Sensing that he was being watched for his reaction, he turned to the front of the book. Carefully, so as not to risk damaging it, because he knew from the way Teviot had handled it that it was valuable. He searched through . . . the date . . . 1936 . . . that was the year his parents had taken him away from school . . . What did that matter now? . . . Here . . . published by the Golden Cockerel Press. No, it was the frontispiece he wanted, the title page. It wasn't easy to turn it over, as the paper seemed to be stuck. Don't tear it and put yourself at a disadvantage, Becket, whatever you do.

Looking down, he saw, *Crusader Castles* by T.E. Lawrence.

Because he had the sluggish memory of an old man, it took a moment for the name to register. When it did, he felt giddy for a moment, as if the blood was draining from his head, although he was too elated to allow that to cause him a moment's disquiet.

'Lawrence of Arabia,' he exclaimed, finding himself suddenly hoarse, and receiving a nod from the brisk young man by way of reward for his astonishment. The author of the manuscript was Lawrence of Arabia – one of the idols of Frank's generation, the only authentic hero to emerge from the bungle and carnage of the Great War. That was before the debunkers had started to scratch away at his reputation. The film that had been made about him had not been unfair, though – some of the scenes from it rushed into his mind, the scene where . . .

'Exactly.' Teviot's hard little voice brought him back to earth. 'While he was up at Oxford reading history before the Great War, Lawrence wrote a thesis on Crusader Castles after extensive research on the ground in France and the Near East. It was brought out by the Golden Cockerel Press in a limited edition the year after he died, with a companion volume of his letters. Now,' Teviot's tone grew more didactic, 'there are known to have been two copies of the thesis, a typewritten draft and the final version which the examiners returned to Lawrence because they thought he would want to have his drawings back. This was another draft which nobody knew about.'

'Are you sure it isn't just a copy somebody typed up

afterwards?' Frank asked reluctantly. There was no way of evading the point.

'It doesn't matter. All the notes are in Lawrence's hand. That is certain.' Was there mockery in Teviot's eye, or was it excitement?

Frank had to goad himself to put his next question. 'And on the back of it? The writing on the back . . .'

'That is undoubtedly Lawrence's handwriting too. It appears, Mr Becket, that on the back of this extra copy of his thesis he wrote the first, the original, version of *The Seven Pillars of Wisdom*, which some would call his masterpiece although others have been less enthusiastic.'

Teviot looked too satisfied with his performance as a literary detective.

'For many years there have been stories that he lost or deliberately mislaid it, because he wasn't satisfied with it. Now, from what you say, it is clear that in fact he gave it to your father on Reading station and that your father passed it on to you – which makes you a fortunate man. Have you any idea of its value?'

Another of those rhetorical . . . Of course he hadn't, and now that the question he had asked himself so often was about to be answered, he wasn't sure that he wanted to know. At this, the last moment, he had the idea that Teviot was playing a game with him. Get it over.

The book dealer's lips were set in a sober line. Literary detection was all very well and loads of fun, but money was serious.

'Provided that it is marketed properly this manuscript ought to make close to nine hundred thousand pounds.' After he had spoken it, the figure seemed to hum in the air between the two o them like a musical note, a harmonic singing out from one of the upper strings of a guitar which died away to leave silence behind.

It was Teviot who broke the enchanted moment.

'If you have it in mind to sell it,' he offered, 'we should be delighted to look after the transaction for you.'

'Please do,' said Frank. 'Yes. If you would be so kind.'

'That American was back,' said Julia.

'Which American?' Ethelred Lewis asked, only half-listening.

'I told you about him. The first time I thought he was just another tourist, but he was in the shop again yesterday afternoon – being most persistent.'

Ethelred smiled. 'Oh yes,' he said, moving a Minton vase to a different position and considering it judiciously. Did it have more of an impact there, saleswise?

'I didn't show it, but he made me feel quite unsure of myself. Next time you go out, it would be nice to know where I can get hold of you if I need to,' she complained. 'He kept on asking all sorts of difficult questions about the stock. As soon as I answered one, he fired off another. I can't take another inquisition like that, not without support. After all, I'm supposed to be a trainee – not the manager or anything.'

'What kind of questions?' he asked idly. Yes, he decided, the vase did look more interesting there.

'Where things came from mainly . . . How long we'd had them in the shop . . .'

Reaching out to make a slight adjustment Ethelred's hand stopped in mid-air.

'Did he ask you what anything was?'

She shook her head. 'No, I don't think so.'

'How old it was, or what it was made of?'

She thought for a moment. 'No, not really. I suppose he must have known all that.'

Ethelred's back stiffened. 'Did he say his name?'

'Jim Burns. He gave me his card, too. Here.' She found it and handed it over. 'Oh, and he did ask one other thing. If I knew of a reliable firm of packers and shippers in the locality.'

Looking at the card, Ethelred felt warm excitement rising inside him.

'Why didn't you tell me?' he demanded.

'That's what I've just done,' Julia retorted.

He didn't argue. He gave her his calculator, the latest print-out of the stocksheet, and her instructions. He wanted the overall cost of the stock uplifted by twenty per cent by lunchtime, he told her; how she spread the extra around was up to her. Then she could bring the results to him for checking and help him to put new price tickets on everything. Lewis wasn't going to sell himself short when this Burns person made him the offer for his stock which he could smell coming in on the wind. It would be a clean sweep; like another rebirth. From time to time, he thought philosophically, he had a need to slough off his old skin – like a snake.

No, not quite that . . . He frowned. Still, there was something to celebrate. In his inner sanctum he poured them both a glass from the bottle of stately oloroso he had bought in anticipation – he had a tendency to count his chickens before they were hatched, he was aware of that, but there you were.

Next, he had a small job to do. Something his self-respect demanded and which he had postponed for much too long. First he fetched the silver wreath still wrapped in its white paper, then he went to the box of tools kept at the back of the shop and selected a pair of pliers – the kind which cut wire.

He peeked round the screen at Julia who, the glass of sherry beside her, seemed to be fully absorbed in the figures on the concertina of computer printout laid in front of her. In fact they weren't monopolising her attention: she was also working on a deeper and more interesting problem of her own – the nature of the relationship between Charles Ramsay and Johnson's wife. Were they lovers? That was the simple question she asked herself as she wondered how much she could add on credibly to the value of that walnut Victorian prie-dieu in the corner. She tried to recall in detail how Margaret Johnson had behaved towards him and how he had reacted to her – his gestures, the sound of his voice. A man who was far more attractive than he realised. Remembering him, Julia knew what she would have done in the other woman's place.

No, thought Ethelred Lewis as he watched her covertly, there was no danger of Julia noticing what he was going to do next. Heaven forbid that she should. It was something that gave him a guilty thrill and made him feel fulfilled at the same time – something which would demonstrate conclusively, to those who had to be told, that Ramsay didn't have a monopoly of honesty and fair dealing.

He took the wreath and pliers behind the screen and seated himself at his desk as though preparing for a personal ritual. Moving objects aside to give himself plenty of elbow room, he finally settled forward in his chair and located the cutting edge of the pliers on the thin metal. As he did so he took in a half-breath and held it, grimacing as though he expected the bringing of the jaws together to cause him a jab of pain. Snip. It didn't – t was easier to do than he had thought it would be. Snip again. There, it was all over, and it hadn't been so bad. The last bright strand of wire had been severed and the wreath lay in halves in front of him. As quietly as he could, he wrapped each of them up in its own piece of crumpled tissue paper and reached in the drawer below for a couple of padded envelopes. Drawing a sheet of his smartest notepaper towards him, he began to write the message he had dreamt up to go with the first of them.

Chalon pushed away his demolished *pintade au porto* and allowed the waitress who had so helpfully cut it up for him to replenish his glass. Having raised it courteously to Ramsay, he cast his eye over the menu gastronomique in search of an interesting dessert. His hand was throbbing heavily in its plaster cast which was hung in a black silk sling. It had not been permanently damaged, or so they said, and it would be almost as good as new when the fractures had mended. A bit stiff at first, but a couple of weeks of physiotherapy would work wonders, his doctor assured him. As always when listening to doctors, Chalon was sceptical.

Nevertheless it wasn't all bad – there were good fat items on the other side of the balance sheet. All that publicity had given the business a real shot in the arm. He'd been featured on the front page of a national newspaper as the 'heroic antique dealer tortured by assassins of the Right'. His appearance on TV had been a triumph. The story of the reliquary and its sapphires a godsend in a thin week for news. The shop had been thronged for several days by sightseers who had bought a hell of a lot of things – and hadn't been able to steal much, thanks to his new state-of-the-art security system. The Charles X (possibly) table had gone in a flash, followed not long afterwards by the boulle clock that had been a source of frustration for so long. Sold to an importunate journalist, of all people – down from Paris in leather jacket and ponytail – a collector, or that's what he said he was.

The small items, the engraved drinking glasses, Cantonese plates, the odd pieces of early faience – all that stuff had been cleaned out in short order and in the end he had been forced out into the highways and byways to find more stock. He had no complaints about that.

And Volet had drowned, which was something else to be thankful for. Although he wasn't the vindictive sort, the removal of the notary from the scene gave Chalon a comfortable feeling in his well-filled gut. Not only was there one less hazard in his life but Madame Volet and her family had been spared a lot of distress. It was *tidy*.

The little supermarket manager had been caught without difficulty. Once the examining magistrate had established that he was one of Volet's associates, the police forensic laboratory took no time at all to match his saliva with that on the knitted black mask he had left behind on the floor of the showroom. The arrest had been a fierce topic of conversation for a day or two between the checkout girls – until a replacement manager had arrived and got a grip on things. He needed to, because after the initial excitement its turnover had taken a knock, the locals being an old-fashioned lot who didn't like the idea of Chalon, one of their own, being savaged like that . . . But he was neglecting his guest.

Handing the menu over to Ramsay, he murmured, 'What would you prefer for dessert? Or cheese, perhaps? We have some intriguing local cheeses.'

At the back of his mind he felt a much less trivial question bothering him, like something caught between the teeth. He couldn't resist a probing of his own.

'The plan then was that the reliquary was to be sold and the proceeds given for charity in Brazil?'

'That was the general idea.'

'Then why did you not make an effort to recover the true sapphires, restore the reliquary to its original state and sell it elsewhere? There were other buyers, surely?' Chalon's free hand sought an answer, palm uppermost. 'Why not?'

As he spoke, he was seized with the unwelcome suspicion that the Englishman on the other side of the table was a more honest man than he was himself. Unwilling to allow it, he waited expectantly. Could the reason really be as simple as that? Just then the waitress arrived with their desserts and, busy with their plates, delayed Ramsay's reply . . .

When it came, it was matter of fact. 'The casket wasn't ours to sell. It had been stolen from you, and it belonged over here.'

He looked embarrassed. So apparently it was indeed as simple as that.

'Now, having answered your question, I have one for you,' Ramsay went on. 'Why didn't you reclaim the reliquary as the property of the village through the English courts? Why all that business with the sapphires?'

Chalon shrugged. 'You should not forget that the reliquary was stolen from us almost fifty years ago. What documents could we produce? None. What witnesses? Two or three old women in the village with uncertain memories and who spoke not a word of English . . . Cécile, Emilie Durand . . . One of your barristers would have torn them into confetti in a few minutes of polite cross examination. We wouldn't have had a chance. And the cost!' Chalon inflated his cheeks and blew the impossible idea away as though it were a feather, with a little puff of air. Then, at a loss for anything else to say, he inspected the *gâteau aux marrons* the waitress had brought and reached for his little fork with enthusiasm. At another level he felt melancholy, though, experiencing a kind of regret for his lost virginity. Once he had been honest himself – and it had been too long ago. They were a strange lot, the English. Of course they weren't all like that, not by any means.

The path up to the village was clay of a pale beige colour dried into a thin dust. Their feet slipped on it, and Ramsay had to put out a hand to help his companion, who was disadvantaged by his arm and the after-effects of his serious lunch. Somehow they reached the top of the slope, where it led on to the village street, and found it empty.

Chalon explained that as the native inhabitants had died off or their children had left this village on the hill, fortified since the Roman Empire, their houses had been taken over by incomers. Although it was much better than letting the place go to rack and ruin, it meant that during the week it was more or less deserted.

An old girl dressed chiefly in black tottered towards them.

'*Bonjour*, Cécile!' Chalon cried in an optimistic baritone, and received a solemn stare in reply.

'One moment.' He strode off towards the church and banged peremptorily on the door of the narrow stone house, bathed in thin sunlight, which leant against its southern wall.

After a terse conversation with the occupant, he returned with the key to the great door of the church, an ancient many-slotted affair which was a tribute to the skill of the locksmith who had made it. Dramatically he pushed it into the keyhole and with a gesture invited Ramsay to turn it for him. As the door swung open, a warm smell of incense hit them. The nave was square, with broad Romanesque arches along each side, lit only by a few votive candles set firmly in a mountain range of sacred wax in front of a darkly varnished portrait of a Madonna.

Chalon gestured at an iron-clad glass case beside the stoup of holy water. 'This is where the reliquary will be displayed,' he explained. 'This case was constructed for it in the 1840s. We had it repaired.'

Ramsay looked down at it and wondered how many sightseers would take the trouble to borrow the key from the sacristan and come into the cool dark church to view it. A handful every summer. And what about the winter, when there was nobody in the village but Cécile and her neighbours? They didn't think it was going to be secure in that showcase, did they?

'Are you sure it will be safe?'

'No, certainly not,' Chalon admitted. 'However it was not my decision. I was against the idea, of course, but the rest of the Brotherhood overruled me.'

'Why? What possessed them to do that?' demanded Ramsay.

'I suppose they were so overcome with delight when the reliquary was returned that their brains were affected and they lost all sense of caution,' the other man shrugged. 'The church was where it belonged, and *le bon Dieu* would keep an eye on it. That's what they said to me.'

As he knew very well, that hadn't prevented half the churches in Italy from being plundered, and Italy wasn't so very far away.

Together the two dealers wandered round the church, their desultory footsteps echoing on the flagstones. Finally they came to the church's other treasure, which hung beside the altar, and stood underneath it in silence: the huge primitive painting of the Expulsion of Adam and Eve from the Garden of Eden by a stern-looking God with a grey beard. It resurrected a memory in Ramsay's mind, a memory he stifled before asking himself how

SOME DARK ANTIQUITIES

long it would be before it was sliced out of its frame and sold to some corrupt collector in Milan or Zurich.

The reliquary wouldn't stay for long in this resting place, either: he had done what he could – they both had – and now it was out of their hands.

'Hullo,' said Julia. 'If you're looking for Ethelred, he isn't here. He's off buying some more new stock in Wales or somewhere, so I'm in charge.' Feeling good, she preened herself a little. 'What can I show you?' It was a bonus to see Ramsay again.

He looked round the shop for an item to be interested in. The Fabergé tortoise? It had disappeared. The worktable with the pink silk pouch – that had gone, too.

'Go on,' prompted Julia airily. 'Ask me about something. Anything.' After coping with the sale of the stock to the forceful American, she was brimming over with confidence.

Although it was Lewis he had come to see, Ramsay decided at that moment that he wasn't going to say so. Instead, he pointed at a cup and saucer.

'Worcester,' she pronounced with authority. 'Barr Flight and Barr.'

He checked the mark underneath it.

They had both got it right. And *that*?

'Early English Delft.' And so it was.

From his pocket he produced the item Lewis had sent him and handed it to her. 'What about this?'

She took the half-wreath from him, a lock of her hair falling over her eyes as she bent over it.

'The wreath! What a pity. Who did this?' With a single gentle finger she stroked the wound where the plated wire had been severed.

'Guess.'

'Ethelred! I'll strangle him when he gets back. Why?' Her candour got to him as he watched her, which delayed his reply.

'He only wanted to prove a point, and he succeeded, in my view.'

Very much my sort of girl, he thought.

The interval that followed seemed to expect something from her, and she did her best. 'Where's Mrs Johnson? Your friend?'

There was no harm in revealing that as perhaps a concern of hers.

'We found her husband in Monaco. I've just come back.'

Although he said it lightly enough, he didn't try to pretend that the experience had been enjoyable.

'Oh.' Not caring if it sounded foolish, she left the word out there on its own. In her experience, his kind of wound was better kept properly covered up until it had healed more or less. Besides, she had no wish to appear inquisitive or pushy. Being a wise girl, she knew that since she had no clue to his feelings she had to stand back and leave everything to him, whatever hers were. Yet she still had to give him back this spindly piece of silver plate. At least she could allow herself that small liberty.

'It's nice. Was, rather. Here.' She slanted her hand until it slid back under its own weight into his outstretched palm so that, with a particular delicacy, she had avoided touching his skin; there had to be no false step. Looking down, she watched his hand close firmly over the fragment and waited with head bent for whatever might or might not happen next.

'Does Ethelred let you go out to eat at midday? May I offer you lunch?'

Although the words were plainly nothing special, they

shivered through her as though they had developed an electrical charge of their own. It was a trifle unnerving, and exhilarating.

'Are you propositioning me?' Looking up, she took care to sound no more concerned than he had allowed himself to be; both of them were feeling their way after all.

'No, I'm not. I'm inviting you out to lunch.'

'How do you know that I don't already have a chap?' The truth was that following the ending of an episode some months before, which she preferred not to recollect in detail, she hadn't. Not only was she a discriminating person but she'd been living in Brighton for only a few weeks and there wasn't much of a social whirl with half the young men out of work. What was this one like, who seemed to be expecting her to catch him on the rebound? That last thought didn't altogether please her, but there was only one way to find out.

'OK. I'll get my coat and lock this place up.'

As she spoke the casual sentence and saw first the surprise and then the gratitude for it in his face, the idea came to her that perhaps a frontier had been crossed.

In the days of the Emperor William I the citizens of Bad Immerich faced a tricky ethical problem which came about like this. One of the town councillors, more adventurous than the rest, decided to take his wife on holiday to the south of France. At the first meeting of the council after his return, when he had finished telling the others what they had missed, he put forward the astounding proposal that the town should build a casino to be owned by the municipality.

His three weeks in the sun must have unbalanced him, they thought, glancing at one another with gravity and concern. Puritanism had deep roots in Bad Immerich, which had been

Protestant since before the Thirty Years' War, and the idea had a rough passage until the proposer of the motion handed out copies of a note of certain figures he had been given by an entrepreneur whom he had encountered in Nice. This man was willing, for a suitable share of the profits, to set up and run a house for them. He had excellent references from a high and unexpected source.

An arduous silence had fallen over the bowed heads of the councillors as they studied the figures in their baroque meeting chamber. Undoubtedly the wages of sin were death: on the other hand, the profits of sin were most enticing. At that rate they could have the lowest local taxes in the whole of the principality. So they came upon a compromise. Yes, there would be a casino, they decided, but it would cater only for foreign tourists. It would be forbidden ground for their fellow townspeople who, thus protected from temptation, sin and heavy municipal taxes, would prosper. And so indeed they did.

Today one of those foreign tourists was Ian Johnson. Having shown his passport to the doorman to establish his credentials, he was already inside the casino – at ten in the morning and well away.

His wife had stayed behind at the Bismarck Inn. It was comfortable, and situated far from the traffic in the centre of the park where Edward VII had once strolled incognito with Alice Keppel on his arm before weightily taking the waters.

Margaret hadn't been able to face the full-blooded breakfast the hotel put on every morning sharp at eight in its restaurant crowded with businessmen smelling of cigar smoke and aftershave, so she had ordered a cup of tea and a roll and butter to be brought to their room. Even though she had only picked at the roll, she had been overcome by nausea. It was time she broke her news to Ian, but today, because he was so impatient to get to the tables, she hadn't had a chance. A solid night's sleep had restored his confidence, and this bright morning he was certain that luck was on his side now – that was what he had shouted out to her as he shaved, vouchsafing not much more than that. These days he didn't waste much time talking to her. She had no idea which way his fortunes were moving – up, down, or sideways – nor did it matter, really.

She had dreamed last night that she was trapped with him on a giant switchback which had no beginning and no end. Clinging to him as he mouthed assurances at her which were drowned by the noise, she had prayed that when she told him she was expecting a child all this impatient mania of his would subside, that the onset of fatherhood would persuade him to behave responsibly – at least for a while. A child was what they both had always needed, wasn't it? As the switchback car had plunged sickeningly again and she had felt herself overwhelmed by the screams of the other occupants, she had corrected herself dismally – a child was what *she* needed.

When she awoke, the acrid taste from her sleep at the back of her mouth, she had experienced that moment of relief which comes when one emerges from a dream into reality – only to realise straight away that reality was false to her as well, that there wasn't a chance that he would change. Not a chance. In a couple of weeks, with the habit still sitting on his shoulder, he would be watching the wheel intently in another town. The coming of the child wouldn't stop him. Nothing would stop him.

On the tray beside the used teacup, its inside stained orange-brown, was a padded envelope decorated with an expensive array of British stamps. It was tucked against the saucer. When she had seen it first, she had ignored it, unready somehow to believe that it could be for her. Now she was about to open it when a wave of sickness summoned her urgently to the bathroom. The last thing she wanted was to have to apologise to the chambermaid in a rush of useless English for the mess she had made.

Feeling the cold sweat standing on her forehead, she rinsed her mouth in the functional bathroom with its chrome pipes and dead white porcelain, leaning forward over the basin to swallow a drop or two of water, uncertain for a moment whether another paroxysm of nausea was going to crumple her up. No, not just then. She had been spared for an hour or two.

She sat in the tub chair beside the bed, concentrated on the packet, and tried to stop herself trembling. Taking the knife from the tray, she wiped it clean of butter with her used paper napkin and slit the envelope open where Lewis had so carefully stuck the flap down with transparent tape. She extracted his letter, and with it half the wreath, looking forlorn. She examined the edge where it had been clipped, and pursed her lips, then turned her attention to what he had written:

Dear Mrs Johnson,
The silver wreath, so-called silver, is a fake, you know, just as I said it was when we last met. I sensed then that you were more than a little sceptical, that you couldn't credit that a shop-soiled old gay like me might be telling the truth for once. Ever since then I have spent hours, literally hours, dear Mrs Johnson, casting about for a way to persuade you and your friend (such a prig, don't you think?) that he is not the only honest pebble on the beach.

I think I have hit on the answer, don't you? Here it is – an elegant and economical proof.

Salutations,
Ethelred Lewis

PS I have sent the other half to the aforesaid prig.
PPS Remind your husband that he owes me fourteen hundred pounds, give or take a pound or two. It would be nice to be paid the bulk of it before the well runs dry, as it will, most assuredly.

EL

What had she done to him to deserve that last flash of bitchery? She examined the half-crescent in front of her with care, poking it with the knife to bring it into the zone of the bedside light. There could be no doubt. He was right. It was plate, of course. Anyone could tell it was.

Hurriedly, before the maid came to clean the room and set the bed to rights, she picked up the telephone and asked in a different voice to be given an outside line. Consulting the telephone directory which she found in the bedside cupboard beneath a wad of tourist literature detailing the delights of Bad Immerich, she hastily dialled the code for London and then the number she remembered. If she didn't call him now, she never would be equal to the task again.

The double beat of the calling tone was close to her ear – it could have been coming from the next room – four times and then there was a pause and a click. It was not his voice, but that of a woman, slightly unsure of what she was saying. 'I am afraid we are not available at the moment. If you would leave your name and number, one of us will get back to you as soon as we

'... that is one of us ... can. Please speak after the tone.'

The line was clear enough for Margaret to recognise the voice of the girl in the shop in Brighton. That was who it was – what was her name? Somehow, the fact that she couldn't remember it made the thing worse. Her name, for goodness' sake, whatever had it been?

There was a short whistle followed by a long tone, then an expectant silence. Caught out in the open with nothing to say, she could only listen to the emptiness for a moment before replacing the receiver.

After a perfunctory knock on the door, the chambermaid came into the room.

'*Bitte*,' she said, as she padded over and leaned across, smelling of bleach and fresh bread, to retrieve the scanty breakfast tray without so much as a glance at her guest.

Margaret Johnson looked at the grey park outside, then at the very expensive watch her husband had bought her on the way there. This morning and this evening would be the fifteenth day.

Repent at leisure, the tedious proverb said – she had all the time in the world to put it to the proof.

Bag in hand, Julia was making a last approving survey of his flat when her moving gaze was caught by the bronze figure of Punchinello on the desk and she stopped, intrigued, stock still.

Ramsay was standing by the open door, glad enough just to watch her as time went leisurely past them. But – he glanced at his watch – they had to get on.

'I promised the old man we'd be at Bressemer in time for lunch, and on the way I want to show you the church tower where I saved Johnson's life,' he said mock-modestly.

There, she thought, another good sign. It had been an

SOME DARK ANTIQUITIES

enchanted slow-motion morning, which wasn't making it easy for either of them to get fully to grips with the day ahead.

At that moment the telephone began to ring with a quiet but intrusive voice, and it startled her. Instinctively she put out her hand towards it, when it rang the second time.

'Let the answerphone take care of it,' he counselled calmly. A third time – she hesitated. A fourth, and she was about to go and answer it when the recorder took over. Its tiny red light flashed for a moment and then subsided as the tape stopped turning.

'I wonder who it was? They didn't bother to leave a message, so it can't have been so very important can it?'

Smiling as she passed him through the doorway, she stood waiting with contentment while he double-locked the door behind them. She was looking forward to today.

Frank Becket took out his spectacles and read the letter again. It was from Teviot, reporting that it was going to be possible to improve on his first estimate of the price the manuscript would make. A fortunate rivalry had developed between the library curators of three particularly well-endowed American universities, a rivalry which he had been at some pains to nurture, he said. The bidding was going nicely.

Frank put it away and gave his attention to the sitting-room again. This time, taking up his steel tape, he considered the space between the fireplace and the window. Not too close to the fire or the piece would suffer from the heat; the top might even warp. He glanced back at the splendid coloured photograph in Crowther's catalogue.

'A fine George III giltwood side table in the manner of Robert Adam . . .'

The sun came out, and its light regilded the picture in front of him as he put his head on one side and deliberated. What a delightful agony it was to have to choose. Was it too ornate for his little flat? He turned back a page or two. What about this other one? Perhaps that was more the thing.

'A George II mahogany side table, *circa* 1755, the rectangular top . . . chinoiserie fretwork . . . See *Chippendale's Director*, Plate LIV.'

Discontentedly he tossed the catalogue back on to the pile of brochures at his feet. It was too easy, simply going up to the West End and outbidding the dealers. It took all the fun out of it. It would be much more amusing to do some auctions in the provinces.

He bent down again and retrieved the weekly *Antiques News* from the heap and felt his nose itching as he turned the crumpled pages. This was more like it – a sale in Chesterfield, another in Ripon. It would be like old times going from country hotel to country hotel; waking early for the viewing with a tang of anticipation in the air, giving him relish for his breakfast. Bacon, fried bread, mushrooms, marmalade.

In the bay window stood a simple glass vase holding a bunch of flowers. A present from the girls in the estate agency when he had, against all their expectations and with the backing of a sensible bank manager, made a successful offer for the flat. One of them had given him a hug when she handed over the keys. Such emotion was unusual, surely, in estate agents? The flowers were looking a trifle dried-out because he hadn't taken care of them as he should – the last few days had been too busy. He took the vase and went into the kitchen to change their water.

Now, what about his social life? He needed to make some contacts. That nice woman with the dog was still living upstairs.

When the flat was refurnished, he would ask her down for sherry. Sherry? No, he wouldn't. He would ask her in for a glass or two of champagne . . . a decent dry champagne gently effervescing in elegant flute glasses . . .

Another item on his list was an early visit to his solicitor to draw up a will – he had no relatives left, not that he knew of, and it was certain that he wasn't immortal. If he didn't do something soon, he might die intestate, and he had a suspicion that such a lapse would mean that everything would go to the Treasury or the Duchy of Lancaster or some equally undeserving section of the Establishment. He wasn't having that.

Whom could he leave his estate to? Who was worthy of it? He ought to leave some of it to charity, he supposed, though you could never be sure that they would make the best use of your money. Ramsay had mentioned a project to help the children in Rio when they had last met, but Brazil was a long way away. It was simple. Why not leave it all to Ramsay himself? True, the service he had done him hadn't been much – no more than giving him an address – but look at the outcome. What a difference it had made to him . . . and there was more to it than that. In a bewildering and treacherous world, Ramsay had not made the slightest attempt to take advantage of him over the manuscript. His integrity, that was his new friend's real contribution, and the thought of it made him feel warmer.

Leave everything to Charles Ramsay. Yes, he rather liked that idea. It was well worth thinking about.

More Thrilling Fiction from Headline:

DEAN KOONTZ

FROM THE No 1 BESTSELLING AUTHOR OF *DRAGON TEARS*

THE HOUSE OF THUNDER

In a cavern called The House of Thunder, Susan Thorton watched in terror as her lover died a brutal death in a college hazing. And in the following four years, the four young men who participated in that grim fraternity rite likewise died violently. Or did they?

Twelve years later Susan wakes in a hospital bed. Apparently involved in a fatal accident, she is suffering from amnesia. She doesn't remember who she is or why she is there. All she knows is that her convalescence is unfolding into a fearful nightmare – and that the faces that surround her, pretending loving care, are those of the four men involved in that murder years before.

Have the dead come back to life? Or has Susan plunged into the abyss of madness? With the help of her neurosurgeon, Susan desperately clings to her sanity while fighting to uncover who or what could be stalking her...

Also by Dean Koontz from Headline Feature
HIDEAWAY   COLD FIRE   THE BAD PLACE   MIDNIGHT
SHADOWFIRES   THE SERVANTS OF TWILIGHT
THE DOOR TO DECEMBER   THE EYES OF DARKNESS
THE KEY TO MIDNIGHT   LIGHTNING   WATCHERS
THE MASK   THE FACE OF FEAR   STRANGERS   WHISPERS
NIGHT CHILLS   DARKNESS COMES   CHASE   THE VISION
THE VOICE OF THE NIGHT   PHANTOMS   TWILIGHT EYES
SHATTERED   DRAGON TEARS

FICTION/GENERAL   0 7472 3661 5

More Compelling Fiction from Headline:

DAN SIMMONS

LOVEDEATH

PASSION AND HORROR
from the award-winning author of *Children of the Night*

Love and death are almost obsessive themes in Dan Simmons's fiction.

ENTROPY'S BED AT MIDNIGHT – winner of a Locus Award for Best Novella – explores the role that accident plays in death, love, pain and laughter.

DYING IN BANGKOK may be Dan Simmons's most shocking and provocative comment on the horror of AIDS, that pairing of love and death that has transformed our world.

SLEEPING WITH TEETH WOMEN, a celebration of the richness of Native American lore, narrates the epic tale of Hoka Ushte, a seventeen-year-old Sioux warrior given the awesome responsibility of becoming the saviour of his people.

FLASHBACK explores the point where the ability to recapture the past – and those lost to us in the past – becomes a sickness rather than a source of solace. If a simple drug would allow you to re-live segments of your life, would you take it?

THE GREAT LOVER takes us into the terrible crucible of the First World War in an attempt to understand how the mind and heart of a sensitive poet could have survived such horrors.

With searing vision, award-winning Dan Simmons examines the dark, exquisite conjunction of love and death in five novellas of intense power and imagination.

"First-rate storytelling" *Publishers Weekly*

"Simmons has never been more stylish than here...'The Great Lover' is a relentless tour de force that may well become a classic (along with 'Dying in Bangkok')" *Kirkus*

Also by Dan Simmons from Headline Feature: SONG OF KALI (Winner of the World Fantasy Award); CARRION COMFORT (Winner of the British Fantasy Society Award, the Bram Stoker Award and the Locus Award for Best Horror Novel); HYPERION (Winner of the Hugo Award, the Locus Award for Best Science Fiction Novel and the Prix Cosmos 2000); THE FALL OF HYPERION (Winner of the 1991 British Science Fiction Award for Best Novel); PHASES OF GRAVITY; PRAYERS TO BROKEN STONES (Winner of the Bram Stoker Award); SUMMER OF NIGHT (Winner of the Locus Award for Best Horror Novel); CHILDREN OF THE NIGHT (Winner of the Locus Award for Best Horror Novel); THE HOLLOW MAN

FICTION/GENERAL 0 7472 4345 X

A selection of bestsellers from Headline

ELEPHANTASM	Tanith Lee	£4.99 ☐
NIGHTSHADES	Tanith Lee	£4.99 ☐
DIVINE ENDURANCE	Gwyneth Jones	£4.99 ☐
DRAGON TEARS	Dean Koontz	£5.99 ☐
THE HOUSE OF THUNDER	Dean Koontz	£5.99 ☐
ALARUMS	Richard Laymon	£4.99 ☐
HOUSE OF LOST DREAMS	Graham Joyce	£4.99 ☐
THE EMPEROR OF EARTH ABOVE	Sheila Gillully	£4.99 ☐
THE LONG LOST	Ramsay Campbell	£5.99 ☐
GOLDEN EYES	John Gideon	£5.99 ☐

All Headline books are available at your local bookshop or newsagent, or can be ordered direct from the publisher. Just tick the titles you want and fill in the form below. Prices and availability subject to change without notice.

Headline Book Publishing, Cash Sales Department, Bookpoint, 39 Milton Park, Abingdon, OXON, OX14 4TD, UK. If you have a credit card you may order by telephone – 0235 400400.

Please enclose a cheque or postal order made payable to Bookpoint Ltd to the value of the cover price and allow the following for postage and packing:
UK & BFPO: £1.00 for the first book, 50p for the second book and 30p for each additional book ordered up to a maximum charge of £3.00.
OVERSEAS & EIRE: £2.00 for the first book, £1.00 for the second book and 50p for each additional book.

Name ....

Address ....

....

....

If you would prefer to pay by credit card, please complete:
Please debit my Visa/Access/Diner's Card/American Express (delete as applicable) card no:

Signature .... Expiry Date ....